PRIMER AND PUNISHMENT

OTHER ST. MARTIN'S PAPERBACKS
TITLES BY DIANE KELLY

THE HOUSE FLIPPER NOVELS
Dead As a Door Knocker
Dead in the Doorway
Murder With a View
Batten Down the Belfry

THE MOUNTAIN LODGE SERIES
Getaway With Murder
A Trip with Trouble

THE PAW ENFORCEMENT NOVELS
Paw Enforcement
Paw and Order
Upholding the Paw
(an e-original novella)
Laying Down the Paw
Against the Paw
Above the Paw
Enforcing the Paw
The Long Paw of the Law
Paw of the Jungle
Bending the Paw

THE TARA HOLLOWAY NOVELS
Death, Taxes, and a French Manicure
Death, Taxes, and a Skinny No-Whip Latte
Death, Taxes, and Extra-Hold Hairspray
Death, Taxes, and a Sequined Clutch
(an e-original novella)
Death, Taxes, and Peach Sangria
Death, Taxes, and Hot-Pink Leg Warmers
Death, Taxes, and Green Tea Ice Cream
Death, Taxes, and Mistletoe Mayhem
(an e-original novella)
Death, Taxes, and Silver Spurs
Death, Taxes, and Cheap Sunglasses
Death, Taxes, and a Chocolate Cannoli
Death, Taxes, and a Satin Garter
Death, Taxes, and Sweet Potato Fries
Death, Taxes, and Pecan Pie
(an e-original novella)
Death, Taxes, and a Shotgun Wedding

PRIMER AND PUNISHMENT

DIANE
KELLY

St. Martin's Paperbacks

This is a work of fiction. All of the characters, organizations, and events portrayed in this novel are either products of the author's imagination or are used fictitiously.

First published in the United States by St. Martin's Paperbacks, an imprint of St. Martin's Publishing Group.

PRIMER AND PUNISHMENT

For information, address St. Martin's Publishing Group, 120 Broadway, New York, NY 10271.

www.stmartins.com

ISBN: 978-1-250-81606-1

Printed in the United States of America

St. Martin's Paperbacks edition / March 2023

10 9 8 7 6 5 4 3 2 1

To my father, Paul R. O'Brien Jr., a pilot and captain.
See you on the other side of the horizon.

ACKNOWLEDGMENTS

I am fortunate to work with such a talented and tireless team at St. Martin's Press. I appreciate you all! Thanks to my editor, Nettie Finn, for your insightful suggestions on my stories. Thanks to Executive Managing Editor John Rounds for leading the charge. Much appreciation to Sara Beth Haring, Sarah Haeckel, and Allison Ziegler for all your hard work on marketing and publicity. Thanks, also, to artists Danielle Christopher and Mary Anne Lasher for the adorable cover for this book.

Thanks to my agent, Helen Breitwieser, for keeping me under contract and doing what I love.

An ongoing debt of gratitude goes to my fabulous friend Paula Highfill, who suggested the concept for this series, and to my author friend Melissa Bourbon who suggested a houseboat for Whitney and Buck's next flip project. Thanks also to Kathy Elsie, for suggesting the engagement ring description, as well as my sister,

Donna Parsons, R.N., for the information on hospital supply management. It takes a village!

Finally, thanks to all of you wonderful readers who chose to spend your precious reading time with this story. I'm honored you picked my book, and I hope you enjoy every second of your time with Whitney, Sawdust, and the gang. Ahoy!

CHAPTER 1
ALL DECKED OUT

WHITNEY WHITAKER

On a Saturday morning in mid-April, I sat at the breakfast bar in the kitchen of the cottage my cousin Buck and I had rehabbed a while back, the place I now called home. We'd originally planned to flip the cottage but, due to some unforeseeable circumstances (a body in the flower bed), we'd been unable to sell the property for a reasonable price and decided to hang on to it for the time being. I'd happily moved out of the cramped converted pool house behind my parents' home and into the much roomier cottage, which allowed me to stretch both my legs and my wings.

My blonde hair was pulled up in a sloppy ponytail to keep it out of my face while I drank my coffee and scrolled through the local real estate listings on my laptop, looking for our next potential flip project. With the Nashville real estate market booming, bidding wars were common and many houses sold for over the asking price. Even fixer-uppers commanded a high price these days. I sighed as I scrolled past yet another overpriced dwelling. *Maybe the heyday of house flipping has come to an end.*

My sweet buff-colored cat, Sawdust, sat on the kitchen counter watching Colette, who was both my best friend and my roommate, prepare cranberry scones. Colette was a professional chef and had recently launched her first restaurant, the Collection Plate Café. The café was housed in a repurposed parsonage that sat on the same grounds as the Joyful Noise Playhouse, a former country church Buck and I had turned into an entertainment venue. The Collection Plate was the perfect pre-show eatery, as well as a great place for the audience to have dessert and coffee after seeing a performance. Colette also served a wonderful Sunday brunch. She'd hired our other roommate, Emmalee, to serve as her assistant manager. Having worked the late shift at the restaurant last night, Emmalee still dozed in her bedroom down the hall.

The morning sun shined through the kitchen window and glinted off Colette's engagement ring. The ring featured a traditional round stone, around 1 carat, in a simple yet sophisticated 14k gold setting. Tastefully elegant and not gaudy, much like Colette herself.

A quick, soft knock came at the front door—*rap-rap-rap*—but it was merely a courtesy gesture. A second later, we heard a key in the lock and in came my cousin Buck, who also happened to be the guy who'd put that ring on Colette's finger. Like me, Buck was tall, blond-haired, and blue-eyed, though he sported a full beard, broad shoulders, and strong muscles developed from years working in carpentry.

A grin on his face, he proceeded into the kitchen.

"Hey, babe." He wrapped his arms around Colette from behind and she turned her head up with a doe-eyed smile to accept his kiss on her cheek.

"Ewww!" I teased. "Don't let him kiss you again, Colette. He's got cooties!"

Having greeted the love of his life, Buck turned to me, "Hey, Cuz."

I raised my coffee cup in response and took a gulp of the warm brew.

Buck poured himself a cup and dropped into a seat at the table across from me. "You can put your laptop away. I found the perfect property for our next project."

"Oh, yeah?" I closed the computer, glad he'd discovered a prospect since I'd found squat online. "Tell me more."

"It's a three-bedroom, two bath."

That number of bedrooms and bathrooms would appeal to a variety of buyers. Growing families; older couples downsizing from larger family homes as their nests emptied; single people who'd use one of the bedrooms for guests and the other for an office, or who might share the home with a roommate. "What about the outdoor spaces?"

A grin played about his lips. "It's got a two-story deck."

"Nice." The buyers would have two levels on which to relax and enjoy themselves outside. "Square footage?"

He looked up, as if performing math in his head. "Around six hundred."

Colette looked over from rolling out the scone dough. "Did you say six-hundred square feet? How in the world can three bedrooms and two baths fit into that small a space?"

I wondered the same thing. I looked from her to Buck and took a guess. "It's a tiny house, right?"

"Not exactly. You'll see. I'll take you there." He continued to grin but would say no more.

While the scones baked, Colette and I hurriedly cleaned up and dressed, curious about this potential new project. Colette packed up a basket of scones for us to eat in the car, and we headed out to my red Honda SUV. Buck slid into the passenger seat, while Colette climbed into the back.

I shoved one of the pastry triangles into my mouth and held it between my teeth, speaking around it as I buckled my seatbelt. "Where to?" I asked my cousin.

He directed me to head north on Interstate 65. I started my engine and off we went. We ate the delicious scones, sipped our coffee, and cruised up the freeway.

After about ten miles, he pointed to the sign for Exit 95. "Take this exit."

I exited and took a right turn onto State Route 386. After another three miles, he instructed me to take the exit for Hendersonville. Soon, we rode up on Old Hickory Lake, catching glimpses of the sparkling water through the trees. The lake had been formed decades ago, when dams had been placed along the Cumberland River. I unrolled my window an inch or two. The wind blew in, bringing the smell of lake water with it and opening a floodgate of happy memories. When I was young, my parents often took fancy European trips in the summer. Not the type of thing a young girl would enjoy. They'd leave me in the care of my aunt Nancy and uncle Roger, Buck's parents. Uncle Roger would round up some inner tubes for all of us, Aunt Nancy would pack the cooler with orange soda and peanut butter and jelly sandwiches, and we'd drive down here to Old Hickory Lake. Buck, his brother Owen, and I would spend the day floating and playing around on the water, while Uncle Roger fished and Aunt Nancy lounged in the shade with a romance novel. Those days at the lake were some of the happiest from my childhood.

I cast a glance at my cousin. "Is the property a lake house?" A vacation home would explain the relatively small square footage. Secondary homes were often much smaller than primary homes, especially in areas where people would be spending most of their time outside, such as in the mountains or near a lake.

"Exactly." His eyes glittered with mischief, telling me there was more to the story but that he wasn't going to share it yet.

I suppose I'll find out soon enough.

We passed an old convenience store called the Get-N-Git. Hand-lettered signs in the windows of the aged building advertised its wares. BAIT & TACKLE. FLOATS. SWIMSUITS. SNACKS. DRINKS. BEER. SOUVINEERS. Whoever made that last sign could've used some help from a dictionary or spell check, although the misspelling did give the place some folksy charm. Racks in front of the store held fishing rods, foam pool noodles, inflatable toys, and colorful beach towels. A locked freezer for bagged ice stood outside next to the entrance. With summer having yet to arrive, business was slow and only a single car sat in front of the shop.

We continued on for another half mile before Buck pointed to a sign for a private marina. "Pull in there."

Colette and I exchanged a glance in the rearview mirror. *Buck is up to something.* We both knew it. We just didn't know what, exactly.

My cousin instructed me to pull into a gravel parking area. I parked next to a flashy bright blue Chevy Camaro. *Nice car.* We climbed out of my SUV and I scanned the area, looking for a lakefront home with a FOR SALE sign on it. Though I saw no vacation homes nearby, my eyes spotted a sixtyish Black man with graying hair sitting on a portable canvas lawn chair near the edge of the nearby woods. He wore a nylon sun hat, a vest with a lot of pockets, and cargo pants, all in colors made to blend into his surroundings. He consulted a small guidebook, then raised the binoculars to his eyes and scanned the treetops. A bird-watcher, apparently.

"This way." Buck motioned for us to follow him, drawing my attention back to the matter at hand.

Colette and I trailed after my cousin—who was her fiancé—as he descended a few steps that led from the parking lot to a floating wooden dock. All sorts of boats were moored to the dock, separated by narrow walkways that formed numbered slips. Nearly all had been backed into their spots, which allowed us to read their funny, punny names as we passed. A fishing boat named *Kiss My Bass*; a pontoon boat called *Out of Toon*; a ski boat named the *Nauti Boy*.

The air was filled with the fresh smell of lake water and the sounds of cawing birds, the metallic *clang* of halyards banging against the masts of sailboats, sputtering boat engines, and muted *clunks* as the rippling waves caused boats to surge and sway against their bumpers.

Buck stopped when he reached a houseboat dubbed the *Skinny Dipper.* The outside of the houseboat had once been white, but the paint had oxidized to a dull, ugly gray. The lower level comprised the living quarters, behind which was an open deck. The upper level included an enclosed helm and another partially covered deck. The upper and lower decks were connected by two corkscrew-shaped structures—a spiral staircase on the left and an enclosed plastic spiral slide on the right. A circle of still shiny white paint beside the rear door on the lower deck indicated where a life preserver had once hung, though the safety device was now AWOL. An inflatable rubber duck big enough to ride on also sat on the deck, though it had long since lost all its air. The deflated ducky looked up at us with big eyes, as if pleading for us to give it breath. The boat floated at a slight tilt. A FOR SALE sign had been taped in the back window.

I pointed to the boat. "*This* is the project you're proposing?" Maybe my cousin had become unbalanced, too, like this aged party barge. "The *Skinny Dipper*?"

"It sure is." Buck grinned. "People live in all kinds of unconventional homes these days. Some hipster would snap this up in a heartbeat. Or maybe a retired couple looking for a vacation home."

I glanced at the boat again. We'd never rehabbed any type of pre-fab dwelling, let alone one that sat on water. A special type of paint and primer would probably be required to paint the metal. "We don't know anything about refurbishing a houseboat."

He shrugged. "We never let ignorance stop us before."

He had a point. In the past, if we didn't know how to do something, we learned how by watching YouTube videos, reading books on the subject, or cornering the staff at building supply stores and asking for advice. Even so, a boat was a very different project than a permanent structure on land.

Seeming to sense that I was wavering, he stepped off

the dock and onto the deck, holding out a hand. "Come aboard, mateys. The owner took me on a tour of the boat yesterday. I told him I'd need to get you two on board if we were going to do this project. He gave me the code to the lockbox so I could show it to you."

Colette took Buck's hand and stepped gingerly onto the deck.

I followed. The tilt was even more evident now that we were standing on the boat. I had to spread my legs and hold my arms out to my sides to steady myself. "This boat feels like a carnival funhouse."

"That's an easy fix," Buck said. "One of the pontoons has a leak, but we can patch it or replace it."

A fiftyish woman with a platinum blonde bob strode up the dock, her shiny black pumps *clunk-clunk-clunking* against the wooden boards. She stopped behind the *Skinny Dipper*. She wore a pair of gray dress pants paired with a silky white blouse and a black blazer, looking very businesslike. She frowned on seeing the empty slip next to ours. She turned our way, pointing to the empty slip. "Is this where Grant Hardisty docks his boat?"

"Sorry," I said. "We don't know who docks there. We're just here to look at this houseboat for sale."

Her frown deepened. "Damn." She heaved a frustrated huff, turned, and stalked off.

I wonder what that's about. Realizing it was none of my business, I turned back to the matter at hand, glancing around. "What else does the boat need?"

"New motor," Buck said. "New generator. A fresh coat of paint, obviously. But everything else is cosmetic."

"What would a motor and generator cost?"

"Twenty grand tops, combined, and that's if we go

with higher-end models. We're looking at around fifteen thousand if we go mid-range."

He'd already done his homework. I wasn't surprised. Buck might be a risk-taker, but he wasn't impulsive. The risks he took were calculated ones. The same went for me.

Buck continued. "The owner said he and his wife used to take their kids and grandkids out on the boat, but they're all grown up now and most have moved out of the area. They considered fixing it up themselves and renting it out as an Airbnb."

"Air?" I said. "Wouldn't it be a *water*bnb?"

Buck groaned. "Hardy har har. Besides, there's air in the pontoons."

He opened the lockbox, removed the key, and used it to unlock the back door. He opened the door and held out a hand, inviting Colette and me to enter first. We stepped into a small living area. While I'd expected the space to be filled with all built-in furniture like an RV, the living room was actually a mix of built-in shelving and cabinetry, with a traditional sofa, love seat, and armchair forming a semicircle around a square coffee table. The couches and chair were wood-framed with removable cushions. Some of the cushions had torn and were patched with duct tape. But while the cushions would need to be replaced, the wood frames could easily be sanded to remove the scratches and restained or painted to look as good as new. A tingle of excitement began in my toes.

We continued through the living room to the kitchen. The kitchen space was a bit more pre-fab, with a table bolted to the floor and benches on either side to form a booth. But the table and benches were a nice, heavy wood rather than cheap aluminum and, like the living room furniture, could be rehabbed without much effort or cost. Ditto for the cabinets. The stove and oven appeared to be working, as did the refrigerator, freezer, and microwave. The kitchen faucet had a small leak, but that would be an easy fix, too. It probably only needed a new washer. The vinyl flooring in the kitchen was scuffed and grungy, but the total square footage was small. It would be cheap to replace it with new flooring. *Gray vinyl plank would look nice.*

The "three bedrooms" Buck had promised were three small berths with built-in platforms on which mattresses were situated. The beds took up nearly the entire bedroom space, with only a narrow walkway inside the door of each berth that led to a small closet. Drawers were built into the platforms to serve as dressers. On inspection, I discovered that most of the runners on the drawers were broken but, again, they'd be a simple fix, especially for a couple of trained carpenters like my cousin and me. Two of the beds were doubles, while the third was a king size. Windows along the side of the rooms provided wide views to the outdoors. A tiny bathroom with a triangle-shaped shower tucked into a corner was situated between the two double bedrooms. The master bedroom featured its own en suite bath with a slightly larger square shower stall. Though the spaces were small, they were functional, economizing on room but still allowing for comfort.

The excited tingle that had started in my toes spread throughout my body, and my mind began to buzz with ideas for decorating the place. Navy-blue-and-white striped all-weather fabric would be cute for the living room furniture. Accent pillows with anchors on them would add a nice touch. The light fixtures could be replaced with bright red sconces to look like old ship lanterns. *Maybe Buck is onto something after all.*

Buck led us back out onto the rear deck and up the spiral staircase. The upstairs deck was furnished with cheap plastic mismatched lawn furniture, most of it weathered and looking like it might break if anyone sat on it. We'd replace the chairs and table for sure.

Colette stared out from the deck across the lake. "This would be a perfect place to watch a sunset over dinner or drinks."

A grin tugged at Buck's lips. "Colette's sold." He turned to me. "What about you, Whitney?"

I'd certainly be interested—for the right price. "How much is the seller asking?"

"Forty-five thousand," Buck said. "He claims the price is firm, but I'd bet I could talk him down to forty-two, maybe even less. I asked around. It's an old boat, a 'seventy-eight model, and it's been for sale for months. Not many people want to tackle a project like this. Plus, people can buy a part interest in a houseboat and share the maintenance costs. That sounds like a better deal to a lot of folks."

"Part interest?" Colette asked. "Like a timeshare, you mean?"

"Yup," Buck said. "Except they like to call it *interval ownership* now. The term *timeshare* has negative connotations after so many people got stuck with timeshares they couldn't afford and rarely used." He turned to me again and cocked a brow in question.

I mulled things over. This could be a fun project, but we weren't in the house flipping business simply for the fun. We were in it to make a living. "How much do you think we could sell the *Skinny Dipper* for once we fixed it up?"

"With brand-new equipment?" he said. "Hundred K. Maybe one-ten."

My enthusiasm waned slightly. "That's not a big profit margin compared to the other houses we've flipped."

"No, it's not," he conceded, "but we'd make a decent profit for the amount of work and time we'll put in. It will only take a couple of weeks to fix this boat up. Maybe three."

Colette looked up at him. "You sure you want to start a new project this close to our wedding date?"

"Why not?" he said. "It'll help me burn off some of my nervous energy."

Her eyes narrowed. "What do you mean 'nervous energy'? You're not getting cold feet, are you?"

"How could I have cold feet when I'm marrying a gorgeous woman like you?" He chuckled, grabbed her hand, and held it to his lips. When he released it, he said, "The only thing I'm nervous about is standing up in a monkey suit in front of a hundred and fifty people and saying all that mushy stuff about how I'll love and cherish you to the day I die. I'll sound like a hopeless sap."

I couldn't help but snort. "It's not exactly a secret how you feel about Colette. You've been making puppy dog eyes at her for years."

Colette rolled her eyes before returning her gaze to Buck. "Would you feel more tough and manly if you wore your tool belt with your tux?"

His cocked his head and raised his brows. "Is that an option?"

Colette and I answered in unison, "No!"

She added, "You're just going to have to deal with feeling emotionally exposed and vulnerable."

He gave her a grin. "You're worth it." Turning back to me, he asked, "What do you say, Whitney? Should we buy this boat?"

The breeze blew past, bringing that fresh lake water scent and pleasant memories with it again. *What the heck. Why not give it a go?* I raised my hand to my forehead and gave my cousin a salute. "I say, aye-aye, Captain."

CHAPTER 2

SLIPS AND SLIDES

WHITNEY

Buck called the owner of the houseboat and told him we'd take the vessel off his hands for forty grand. While they negotiated, I examined the rubber ducky. Seeing no obvious holes, I figured I'd try inflating the adorable big-eyed bird. I wasn't about to put my mouth on the air valve, though. Who knew whose mouth had touched that valve, or how many mouths for that matter? The last thing I wanted was to end up with a herpes sore on my lip from a rubber ducky.

I was nothing if not resourceful. Colette watched with interest as I rounded up a plastic funnel from the toolbox in the cargo back of my SUV. I retrieved the hair dryer I'd seen in the boat's master bath, stuck the small end of the funnel into the air valve on the flaccid rubber ducky, and plugged the hair dryer into an outlet on the deck. When the hair dryer roared to life, Buck cut me an irritated look, put a finger in his ear, and stepped away from the boat to continue dickering over the boat price. Lest I melt the vinyl, I turned the dryer to the cool setting and stuck the end into the funnel. *Whirrrrrr!*

The ducky rapidly came to life, rising like a phoenix from the ashes, until he was as full as I dared to make him. One more air molecule and the little guy was likely to pop. I turned off the hair dryer.

Colette poked a finger in the ducky's round chest. "He's cute."

"Before we sell this boat, we need to have a party on it. We can take turns riding the duck. Maybe we can get a rope and tow it behind the boat." I wanted to try the spiral slide, too. Maybe I'd even go down the twisted chute headfirst. Another idea popped into my mind. "You know, the *Skinny Dipper* would be the perfect place for me to host your bachelorette party."

"Yes!" Colette squealed and clapped her hands. "It'll be so fun!"

I returned the hair dryer to the bathroom. I walked back to the deck to find that Buck and the seller had agreed to forty-two thousand for the boat. *Not bad.* The price gave us even more potential for profit. I raised my hand to give my cousin a high five. "Good job, Cuz."

He slapped my hand and cut a glance at Colette, grinning. "I know how to get what I want."

She narrowed her eyes and wagged a finger at him. "Don't you go getting cocky on me."

He feigned innocence. "I wouldn't dream of it."

Between our other carpentry gigs the following week, Buck and I completed the paperwork to have the boat's title transferred to us and signed paperwork to assume the slip rental. We also bought the materials we'd need to rehab the boat. Vinyl plank flooring.

Sandpaper. Aluminum patch and epoxy to repair the leaky pontoon. Primer and paint. We'd even run by a boat store and bought a new lifesaving ring. We'd also looked into getting boating licenses. While older folks weren't required to have a license, Tennessee law stipulated that any adult born in 1989 or later was required to have one. Fortunately, there were free study materials online, though we'd have to take the test in person and pay a ten-dollar fee to sit for the exam.

By Friday afternoon, we were ready to get started. I bubbled with excitement. The boat promised to be a fun flip. It would be nice to try something new, expand our skills, find out what we were capable of.

Buck and I met up in the marina parking lot. To speed the work along, we planned to live on the boat while we fixed it up. Lake life would be a new experience for me, and I was looking forward to a kind of working vacation. To that end, I'd brought a small suitcase filled with spare coveralls and essentials, as well as my cat, Sawdust, in his plastic travel carrier. Like the man we'd seen the other day, Sawdust would enjoy watching the birds around the lake. Besides, I'd miss my sweet furry boy if I was gone for two weeks and didn't get to see him.

Luggage in hand, Buck and I headed down the dock to the *Skinny Dipper.* The slip next to ours that had been empty before now contained a shiny cabin cruiser dubbed the *Sexy Sheila*. The boat bobbed in the water. A beach towel hung from an improvised clothesline. A large cooler sat on the deck, and a small charcoal kettle grill was attached to the boat near the back, its arm designed to be secured in one of the holes intended to hold a fishing rod. Although a black Lab mix stuck his snout out of an open window on the cabin, there was no human to be seen. Either the boat's owner was below deck, too, or he'd left the vessel. I wondered if the real-life sexy Sheila was the blonde who'd come by when we'd been looking at the boat a few days earlier. The dog wiggled as we approached, telling me that his unseen tail was wagging away. He greeted us with a *woof.*

"Hey, boy!" I called.

The dog woofed again. *Woof-woof!*

Sawdust stood in his carrier and returned the greeting. *Meow!*

I took Sawdust inside and claimed one of the smaller berths, leaving Buck to take the king-sized bed in the master. I set the carrier on top of the bed and opened it. Sawdust poked his head out tentatively, sniffed the air, and ventured forth, curious about this new place. Lest the furry little love of my life inadvertently go overboard, I slipped him into a bright red kitty life jacket. He had no idea why I'd outfitted him with the vest. He tried to back out of the thing but couldn't. He rolled over, hoping that would get the jacket off him. No luck with the roll, either. He looked up at me, his eyes imploring me to remove this torture device.

I scratched his ears. "Sorry, Sawdust. You'll just have to get used to it. Mommy loves you and wants you to be safe."

He resigned himself to the fact that the life jacket wasn't going anywhere. He shifted focus and jumped down from the berth, setting off to explore the boat.

I turned my attention from my cat to our rehab project. Step one of any remodeling job was to empty the structure of unnecessary items. To that end, Buck pulled out the ancient kitchen flooring, while I carried the furniture cushions out to my SUV and crammed them into the cargo bay. Next, I removed the bedding. The mattresses had been protected with waterproof covers and were in good condition, but I'd buy new sheets, pillows, and nautical-themed bedspreads to spruce things up.

Sawdust followed Buck and me as we ventured up the spiral staircase to the top deck to remove the cheap plastic patio furniture. From that higher vantage point, I could see past the marina to the open part of the lake. The sun glinted off the water as a man puttered by in a small johnboat. He resembled the man who'd been bird-watching the last time we were here, but he'd been too far away for me to get a good look at him then, just as he was too far away now. He wore a fishing hat, a short-sleeved shirt with a life jacket over it, and a pair of shorts. A fishing rod stuck up out of the boat. Farther out, another fishing boat bobbed in the water, three men aboard. They sat on the deck, rods in hand, a retractable canvas Bimini top shielding them from the sun. The water was calm. Only a gentle, cooling breeze blew across the lake. *What a beautiful day to be out on the water.*

I carried the patio furniture down the spiral staircase, carefully watching my step. I loaded it onto a flatbed trailer hitched to Buck's van and tied it down to ensure it wouldn't fall off in the road when he drove it to the dump later.

Now that we'd cleared things out, Buck and I donned safety goggles and dust masks, and set to work with various grades of sandpaper. While he tackled the kitchen table and cabinets, I buffed the bathroom cabinets and the living room furniture frames. We kept the windows open and enjoyed a nice cross breeze. Sawdust lounged in a bright spot on the deck, soaking up the sunshine and watching as ospreys circled above. Once things had been sanded to our satisfaction, we used a vacuum cleaner to suck up the mess we'd created.

Five o'clock rolled around, and Buck and I decided to call it a day. Colette was working at her café tonight, and Buck planned to take advantage of his free night to watch a basketball game with some of his buddies. I had a date with my boyfriend, Collin Flynn, a homicide detective for the Metro Nashville Police Department. I'd convinced him to go see the latest rom-com at a theater tonight, promising to balance things out with an action flick next time. Relationships were all about compromise, right?

Buck and I were tossing the used sandpaper into a trash bin on the back deck of the *Skinny Dipper* when the fishing boat with the three men in it trolled up, its engine softly puttering. Sawdust padded over to the side of the boat to see what was going on. The boat appeared to be a relatively simple one, functional not flashy. I'd need my tape measure to get a precise length, but by my best estimate the boat extended a modest fifteen or sixteen feet. The captain was a sixtyish guy with shaggy gray hair sticking out from under a faded fishing hat adorned with bright-colored lures. He sported a gray beard a few days overdue for a trim, a middle-aged paunch under a lightweight pocketed beach shirt, and a relaxed smile that said the casual lake life agreed with him. The man in the front passenger seat looked to be in his sixties, too. He sported similar attire and a fishing hat, too, though his face was cleanshaven.

The third man had been sitting on a bench seat in the

back. When the captain reversed the motors and the boat came to a stop next to the dock, the man eased off the vessel, using a cane with four prongs on the bottom to steady himself as he stepped onto the dock. The black dog inside the *Sexy Sheila* returned to the window, sticking his head outside and wiggling and woofing again in excitement to see his shipmate returning home. *Woof! Woof-woof!*

Once the man had found his footing, the passenger handed him a string of fish. The guy with the cane said, "Thanks, guys."

The captain dipped his head in humble acknowledgment. "Let's do it again soon. Later, gator." The other man raised his hand in a silent goodbye. The boat swung around in a slow semicircle to leave the marina. As it puttered off, I could see the name emblazoned across the back: CAUDAL OTTA FISH. *Huh?* The pun was lost on me.

Once he passed out of the no-wake zone, the captain revved his engine, the bow lifted a little, and off they went. The guy who owned the cabin cruiser ambled up the walkway with his fish in one hand and his quad cane in the other. He wore a faded blue T-shirt and a pair of bright yellow swim trunks in a pink flamingo print. To my surprise, he appeared to be only in his early forties. The cane had thrown me off, made me assume he'd be older, closer to his buddy's age. His skin was sun-kissed and shimmery with suntan oil, and his blue eyes sparkled like the water in the lake behind him. Natural blond streaks highlighted his light brown hair, sunshine acting as a hairdresser. He looked like a casually dressed, slightly aged Disney prince.

Buck cast a glance at the man. "Looks like the fish were biting today."

"They sure were." The guy raised his hand to show off his catch. "Jojo and I will be eating good all week." He stopped at the window and momentarily lifted his hand from the cane to stroke the dog's neck. "Won't we, Jojo?"

The dog wiggled in the window, the tail wagging the dog, as the guy took his cane and circled around to the back platform of the *Sexy Sheila*. Once aboard, he hobbled over to the door that led down to the quarters. Bracing himself against the fiberglass, he unlocked the door. The dog bounded out, nearly knocking the guy over. He'd have fallen if he hadn't grabbed the top of the door. "Careful, boy!"

The dog danced around on the deck, enjoying his freedom. The man disappeared below, probably putting his fish in his freezer. He returned with two bottles of beer dangling from his fingers, another beer tucked into the pocket of his swimsuit. He called over to Buck and me. "Looks like you two are calling it quits for the day," he called. "Care to join me in happy hour, lake style?"

Buck said, "Don't mind if I do." He looked my way. "You in, Whitney?"

"Sure." I'd have preferred a frozen margarita to a beer, but beggars can't be choosers. I'd also have preferred to go inside and stand under a hot shower to ease my aching muscles, but I didn't want to come off as unfriendly. We'd be making a lot of noise over the next couple of weeks while we rehabbed the *Skinny Dipper*. It couldn't hurt to get on good terms with the owner of the boat next door, especially since it appeared he lived on the vessel.

I removed Sawdust's life jacket, put him inside the boat, and followed Buck as he climbed off our boat and circled around to the back deck of the *Sexy Sheila*. As we boarded, the enticing coconut scent of the man's suntan oil smelled good enough to eat. Or drink. It gave me a hankering for a creamy, slushy piña colada. *Mm-mmm*. To heck with the margarita I'd been thinking about a moment earlier.

My cousin must have noticed the oil, too. He gestured to the guy's arms. "Boy howdy, you're as slicked up as a male stripper."

Our neighbor laughed and handed the bottles of beer to Buck and me. "I'm Grant Hardisty."

Buck pointed the longneck at himself. "Buck Whitaker." He turned the bottle on me. "My cousin, Whitney. Same last name. Our dads were brothers."

It was true that our fathers were brothers, though the men were as different as night and day. While Buck's father enjoyed working with his hands and had gone into carpentry, my father had been much more interested in science and pursued a career as a doctor. In many ways, I was more like my uncle Roger than I was my own father. I, too, enjoyed physical labor. Not that it didn't require quite a bit of brainpower, too. A lot of calculations were involved in remodeling homes.

Grant gave us a smile as warm as his tan. "Nice to meet y'all." Now that his left hand was free, he pulled his phone from his pocket. "We need some happy-hour tunes." He jabbed the screen with his thumb and the music started up. I recognized the first few bars in an instant. It was the old Kiss hit "Rock and Roll All Nite."

Buck and I took seats on the built-in benches. The

dog came over to me, looking for affection. I gladly provided him with ear rubs. He thanked me with a continuous tail wag.

As I petted the dog, I angled my head toward the rear of the boat. "Who's Sheila? Your wife? Girlfriend?"

"No. Sheila's married to a buddy of mine."

Buck's brows shot up. "Your friend doesn't mind that you named your boat after his wife?"

Grant chuckled, released his cane, and held up his palm. "It's not like it sounds. This boat used to belong to him. I took it off his hands. You know what they say. The two happiest days in a man's life are the day he buys himself a boat and the day he sells that boat."

"Is that so?" Buck angled his head to indicate the *Skinny Dipper*. "I hope we'll be happy the day we sell our boat. That's the whole reason we bought it. To fix it up for profit."

"Is that what you two do for a living? Restore old boats?" Grant took a pull on his beer as he waited for an answer. As he drank, I noticed a strip of untanned skin on his ring finger where a wedding band had once been. *Trouble in paradise?*

I filled him in. "This will be our first boat rehab. We normally flip houses."

Grant's head bobbed. "Mixings things up, huh? Keeping it fresh?"

"Exactly." Buck held his bottle poised at his lips. "Can't hurt to learn some news tricks." He took a slug.

Grant used his hands to lift his left leg up onto the bench to stretch out. *He must have trouble moving it on its own.*

While I would've ignored the elephant in the room—or should I say on the boat?—Buck brought the subject up. Using his beer bottle once again as a pointer, he angled it at Grant's leg. "Boating injury?"

Grant shook his head. "I slipped and fell in a store about six weeks back."

My busybody cousin asked, "Did you break your leg?"

"No," Grant said, "but I banged my knee up pretty good. Got some soft tissue damage, torn ligaments and tendons. I've been going to physical therapy, not that it's helping much. The doc says it won't ever be the same. I had to quit my job. Can't tend bar with a bum leg."

"Shame," I said. It was frightening how something unforeseeable could happen and a person's whole life could change in an instant.

He settled back, turned his head up to the sun, and issued a happy sigh. "Nothing beats lake life, does it?"

Buck took another drink of his beer. "Looking forward to finding out."

Though the fishing boat was long gone by then, I found myself gesturing to the end of the dock where it had departed a few minutes earlier. "The name of your friend's boat," I said. "*Caudal Otta Fish.* What's that mean?"

Grant cleared things up for me. "The caudal fin is another name for the tail fin of a fish."

"Ah." *Mystery solved.*

Jojo stepped to the end of the boat and looked back at Grant, whining softly. "Nature calling, boy?"

Jojo wagged his tail.

When Grant struggled to rise with his cane, I offered to take the dog for a walk so he could relieve himself. "That would be a big help," Grant said. "He nearly pulls me down." He pointed to a leash tied to one of the boat cleats. "There's his leash."

I untied the leash, clipped it to the dog's collar, and stepped with him onto the dock. The dog nearly pulled my shoulder out of the socket as he headed down the dock. He was strong, with that just-out-of-puppyhood energy. He dragged me toward the grassy area by the trees. I had to jog to keep up. He sniffed along the edge of the trees, lifting his leg to mark several of their trunks as we went along. When he stopped to pop a squat, a soft rustling in the woods caught my attention. I looked up to see the man from the johnboat walking away through the trees. There didn't appear to be a trail where he was walking, but maybe he'd spotted a rare bird and ventured off the path to get a better look.

Jojo finished doing his business and I realized I didn't have a poop bag to clean up his mess. Luckily for both of us, I had a disposable latex glove in my pocket. I donned the glove, picked up his droppings and slid the glove back off, turning it inside out as I did. On our walk back to the *Sexy Sheila*, I dropped the doggie doodie into a waste bin.

Sawdust mewed from the back window of the *Skinny Dipper* as Jojo and I approached. I'd expected Sawdust to cower in fear when he saw the dog, but instead he put his paws up on the glass and scratched, as if trying to get through. Jojo stopped and sniffed the air at the back of the *Skinny Dipper*, scenting Sawdust. Before I knew what was happening, he'd leapt onto the back of the boat and dragged me over to the window. He stood on his hind legs and he and Sawdust looked at each other through the glass, Jojo's tail wagging happily all the while. I was glad to see the dog wasn't being aggressive.

Sawdust mewed again, more insistently. He seemed determined to make a new friend. I tied the leash to the railing on the *Skinny Dipper* to limit Jojo's range of movement in case things went south, put Sawdust's life-jacket back on, and opened the back door of the boat to release him. To my surprise, my little fraidy-cat showed no fear, marching right over to the big, wriggly dog and sitting up prairie dog style as if trying to look Jojo in the eye. The dog lowered his front half, his rear end still moving left and right at warp speed, and went nose to nose with my kitty. When Sawdust mewed again, Jojo opened his mouth and licked Sawdust from chest to ear, nearly lifting the cat off the ground with his enthusiastic tongue. Sawdust activated his purr, happy to have made a new friend.

I scooped Sawdust up and cradled him to my chest as I walked Jojo back to the *Sexy Sheila*. "Mind if my cat joins us?"

"Not at all," Grant said. "The more the merrier."

I set Sawdust down and he sniffed his way around the small platform, Jojo tagging along behind him.

Grant's phone chimed with an incoming notification. He pulled it from the breast pocket of his T-shirt and eyed the screen. "Looks like I've got one on the hook."

CHAPTER 3

A NEW FOUR-LEGGED FRIEND

SAWDUST

Sawdust had seen dogs before, but mostly from afar. Normally, he was a fraidy-cat. Dogs were much bigger than cats. They had menacing growls and loud barks and long, pointed teeth. *Scary!* But the way this dog was acting, wiggling around all silly and licking Sawdust with his tongue, the cat could tell he was a friendly sort, what Whitney would deem a "good boy."

Sawdust went snout to snout with the dog, exchanging sniffs. The dog had been nice enough to give him a lick. Sawdust figured he should return the favor. He stuck out his much smaller tongue and swiped the side of the dog's snout. The dog danced around in a circle. What a clown!

CHAPTER 4
ON THE HOOK

WHITNEY

Grant turned his phone to show us the screen. On it was a profile pic of a pretty redhead. She had a nice smile and wore a blue blazer over a white turtleneck in her profile pic, clearly hoping to catch dates with her profile and her pretty face rather than her cleavage or a lusty, come-hither expression. She looked to be in her mid to late forties. It was nice to know that Grant was looking for someone age appropriate rather than someone young enough to be his daughter, like some middle-aged and older men had a tendency to do.

Buck asked, "What dating apps are you on? Bumble? Hinge? Plenty of Fish?"

"No," Grant said. "I'm on Match.com and eharmony. I've got premium accounts."

Buck cocked his head. "You know the others are free, right?"

"Yeah, but you get a better class of people with a paid app. The fee sorts out the riffraff."

Buck snorted. "Well, la-di-da."

Ignoring my cousin's barb, Grant read the woman's profile out loud. "Says she's got an MBA and works as the head of human resources at a national insurance company." He skimmed the rest of her details and summarized them for us. "Plays piano and speaks three languages."

"She sounds like quite the catch." Maybe it was wrong of me, but I wondered why such an accomplished, professional woman would be interested in Grant. He was attractive, sure, and there was certainly nothing wrong with working as a bartender. Most bartenders tended to be younger, though, and if they stayed in the business they eventually worked their way up into managerial positions or even ownership long before reaching Grant's age. *Would Grant and this woman have anything in common?* "You going to try to reel her in?"

"I'd be a fool not to." Grant swiped right and tucked the phone back into his pocket. He turned to Buck. "If it doesn't work out, maybe you and I can hit the bars, be each other's wingman."

"No can do," Buck said. "I'm spoken for. I'll be taking that walk down the aisle in just a few weeks."

"Oh, yeah?" Grant rested an arm along the back of the bench. "What's your fiancée like?"

"Pretty," Buck said. "Fun. Smart. Sweet. Strong. She's a fantastic cook, too. I could go on, but in the interest of time let's just stipulate that she's darn near perfect."

I couldn't resist getting a barb in. "We're all wondering why she puts up with him."

Buck shrugged. "Heck, I wonder that myself." Turning back to our neighbor, he asked, "How long have you lived here at the lake?"

Grant took another sip of his beer. "About four months. Lake life is amazing! So much freedom. Get to fish whenever I want to. Nobody nagging me to get out of bed and mow the lawn."

Hmm. I wondered if the blonde woman who'd come by looking for him before was the source of that nagging. I was tempted to ask, but thought better of it. He might not appreciate me getting up in his business.

Grant's phone pinged. He pulled it from his pocket, read the screen, and grinned. "What do you know? She wants me to meet her for drinks right now." He pulled his wallet from the other pocket of his swim trunks, looked inside, and muttered, "Damn." He looked up at Buck. "I don't have any cash on me. Any chance you could spot me some funds?"

Buck said, "You don't have a debit or credit card you can use?"

"They've been frozen while my divorce is pending."

Aha! A pending divorce explained the strip of untanned skin on his ring finger and his comment about the nagging.

He continued to explain his situation to Buck. "I've got some funds in a savings account. If you can spot me, I'll run by the bank tomorrow and withdraw the cash to pay you back."

Buck hesitated a moment, and I knew what he was thinking. We barely knew this guy, and it was a little presumptuous of him to ask, but it's not like he could run off with Buck's money and disappear when he lived next door, right? Besides, he'd been neighborly, treated us to a couple of beers. Buck took out his wallet and counted the cash inside. "I've got three twenties and a couple of singles. How much do you need?"

"Sixty should do me," Grant said.

Buck handed the cash over.

"Thanks," Grant said. He used his cane to lever himself to a stand. "Sorry to cut things short."

"No worries." Buck stood to go. "Good luck with your date."

I stood, too, and reached down to round up Sawdust. "Say goodbye to your new friend, boy." Sawdust mewed a final time, bidding his new buddy farewell.

Back aboard the *Skinny Dipper*, Buck and I freshened up. He headed off to meet up with his buddies, while I waited for Collin to swing by to pick me up for the movie. I sat on the upper deck with Sawdust, looking out over the water. The gentle lapping of the water against the boat's hull was hypnotic, luring me into a relaxed trance, and the gentle evening breeze was soft and soothing on my skin. *Grant was right. Nothing beats lake life.*

I was yanked from my relaxed stupor by a voice calling, "Hello up there!"

I went to the railing and looked down to see Collin standing on the dock. An avid runner, Collin sported a lean, athletic build, along with dark hair and green eyes. His attractive exterior package was matched by a perceptive mind and a determined demeanor, traits we had in common. We'd met a while back when I'd discovered the body buried in the flower bed at the cottage. Not exactly a meet-cute, but we'd bonded over solving the murder and taking down the killer together. We made a formidable team.

I motioned with my hand. "Come on up and take a look at this view."

Collin stepped onto the back deck and wound his way up the spiral staircase to the upper deck. He stopped and cocked his head. "Is it just my imagination, or is this boat listing?"

"It's not your imagination. One of the pontoons has a leak. Buck's planning to repair it."

Collin came forward and stopped behind the wheel, gazing out over the lake. The sun was just beginning to set, lighting up the surface of the lake as it descended. "Wow," he said on a breath. "Gorgeous. And the view isn't bad, either." He slid me a flirty grin. "Once the boat is fixed up, you and Buck should schedule all of your showings at sunset."

"Good idea."

He turned his head to look up at the sky. The first stars of the night were just beginning to stand out against the darkening backdrop. "I bet it's dark out here at night." Collin was an amateur astronomer and enjoyed stargazing, but the lights of Nashville limited visibility from his backyard. "I should bring my telescope out here."

I pointed to the light poles along the dock. "There's lights here on the pier, but we could take the boat out once the new motor is installed. It would be darker on the water."

"It's a date."

Once he'd looked over the upper deck, I took him downstairs and showed him the living quarters. "We'll need to fix up the furniture, replace the flooring, and paint both the inside and the exterior. But we think we can get everything done in two or three weeks."

"That's good timing with summer coming up."

"Colette wants me to host her bachelorette party on the boat before we sell it."

Collin said, "The boat would be a fun place to host a bachelor party, too."

"Owen could probably use some help with the planning." Buck's younger brother would serve as his best man, which meant he was responsible for the bachelor party. He was also responsible for three young daughters, which left him little time for much else than going to work.

"I'd be glad to help," Collin said.

After double-checking that Sawdust had enough food and water, I gave my kitty a kiss on the head and secured him inside the boat. Then Collin and I headed out to the movie. Jojo woofed at us from the window of the *Sexy Sheila* as we disembarked. I felt bad for the dog, trapped in the small hull of the cabin cruiser. A young mutt like him needed a yard to run around in so he could burn off his energy. I turned to Collin. "Do you think we'd have time to stop at the store on the way to the theater?"

He checked his sports watch. "We can spare a few minutes. Why?"

"I want to buy some tennis balls."

"Taking up a new sport?"

"No. They're for the dog. He's got lots of pent-up energy. Chasing a ball would be a good way for him to get some exercise."

Collin frowned. "His owner doesn't exercise him?"

I explained about Grant's bum leg. "I took the dog out for a walk earlier today, and he nearly pulled my arm off."

"Maybe you should get a Frisbee, too."

"Good idea."

The movie was entertaining, and Collin and I enjoyed a glass of wine on the upper deck of the boat afterward.

Sawdust joined us on the platform, enjoying the cool evening air as it ruffled his fur.

Collin bent down to run a hand over the cat's back. "A cat on a boat is considered good luck."

"It is?" I asked. "Why?"

"It goes back to pirate times. Cats killed the rats that ate the food stores and carried fleas that caused the plague. Rodents chewed up ropes, too. Having cats on board solved a lot of the sailors' problems."

While Sawdust might chase a small spider, I couldn't imagine him going head-to-head with a rat. The poor cat would be terrified. But he nonetheless earned his keep by keeping me entertained and cuddled. He served the same purpose my stuffed animals had when I was a young girl, although he required much more attention from me. I didn't mind, though. The furry little guy had stolen my heart.

After we finished our wine, I walked Collin down the spiral staircase. He left me on the lower deck with a warm kiss that, like the boat, rocked my world.

Later that night, the bobbing of the boat rocked me gently to sleep. I slept like a baby, at least until an angry voice coming through my open window woke me at half past seven Saturday morning.

"Bad dog!" Grant said.

I peered out the open window to see him shaking a finger at Jojo, who'd dropped a fresh pile of poo on the deck. The dog hung his head, ashamed and unhappy about being scolded. But what choice did the poor beast have if his owner didn't take him off the boat for a potty break?

Leaving Sawdust dozing on the bed, I threw a windbreaker on over my pajamas, slid into my slippers, and grabbed the canister of tennis balls I'd purchased the evening before. I opened the vacuum-sealed can, and the air released with a *whoosh*. I took one of the fuzzy yellow balls, leaving the other two in the can. I exited the back of our boat and called over to our neighbor. "Trouble on board?"

He scowled. "Jojo crapped on the deck."

For both the dog's sake and Grant's, I tried to make light of the situation. "Maybe that's where the term *poop deck* originated."

Grant's continued scowl said he failed to appreciate my clever humor. I held up the tennis ball. "I bought some balls for Jojo. How about I take him out on the shore and get him some exercise?"

Grant might not have appreciated my humor, but he appreciated my offer. "That would be great." He hobbled over to retrieve the leash from the cleat and handed it to me as I boarded his boat.

I patted my leg. "Here, Jojo." The dog came over and I clipped the leash onto his collar. He pulled hard on the leash, nearly choking himself as I led him off the boat and down the dock. We made our way down the shore away from the parking lot and road. Once I felt we were at a safe distance, I reached down and unclipped the leash. "Fetch, boy!" I pulled my arm back and threw the ball as far as I could.

Jojo bolted after the bouncing ball and grabbed it out of the air in mere seconds. He ran back and dropped the ball at my feet, his tail whipping back and forth as he danced in excited anticipation for the next throw. We repeated this process approximately eight thousand times over the next few minutes. Throw, fetch. Throw, fetch. Throw, fetch. The young dog was tireless, but my arm wasn't. Lest I injure my rotator cuff and be unable to work on the boat rehab, I figured I'd better call it quits. When Jojo realized our game of fetch had come to an end, he trotted over to the lake's edge and bent his head down to lap at the water. *Slurp-slurp-slurp.*

Once he'd drank his fill, I reattached his leash and walked him back to the *Sexy Sheila.* I handed the dog and the tennis ball over to Grant. "Jojo had a ball."

He offered a mild chuckle at my pun and cast me a hopeful glance, his earlier bad mood seeming to have dissipated. "Would you mind coming back later and taking him out again?"

Though I had a lot to do today, what kind of person would I be if I didn't help out a neighbor and his dog? "No problem." Even as I agreed, I realized my help was only a short-term solution. Grant would need to figure out a way to exercise his dog himself. Some training might also make the dog less rambunctious and more manageable. Turning to other matters, I asked, "How'd the date go last night?"

He grunted. "Terrible. Her profile was very misleading."

"What do you mean?"

"She was dressed like a teenager but smelled like my grandmother. She showed up in ripped jeans and a tank top that showed her bra straps and didn't come down far enough to cover her belly button, which was pierced, by the way. She'd sprayed on so much rose-scented cologne it made me lightheaded. She went on and on gossiping about her coworkers, who I've never even met. I couldn't get a word in edgewise. If that wasn't bad enough, she ordered three glasses of the most expensive red wine the bar served. I barely had enough money to pay our tab."

How strange. Sounded like some sort of bait and switch. Then again, people carefully curated their profiles to make a good impression. From what I'd heard, it wasn't unusual for the real person to fail to live up to their online image. "Oh, well," I said. "There's plenty more fish in the sea."

"You got that right. I met some fun guys at the bar, at least. They're coming by later to spend the day on the lake."

I felt a twinge of jealousy. I'd be spending the day working rather than having fun. Today, Buck and I planned to patch the leaky pontoon. "Sounds fun. See ya," I told Grant. He returned the sentiment and I returned to the *Skinny Dipper.*

After feeding Sawdust his breakfast, I slid him into his kitty life jacket, started the coffeepot, and poured myself a bowl of cereal.

I'd just finished eating when Buck emerged from his berth and trod into the kitchen wearing his bathing suit. "I slept like a log."

"Me, too. Sleeping on this boat is like being rocked in a cradle."

He tossed back a quick cup of coffee. "Let's get to work."

CHAPTER 5

AIR REPAIR

WHITNEY

We stepped outside to see Buck's younger brother Owen pulling up. Owen was a thinner, beardless version of Buck, with a wife and three adorable daughters. Owen spent the bulk of his time assisting his father in his carpentry business, but he helped us out on occasion, too. We'd need him today. It would take the three of us to stabilize the boat and set it straight.

Grant and Jojo watched us from the deck of the *Sexy Sheila* as Buck and I walked out to Owen's van. We each retrieved a blue plastic barrel from the cargo bay. Buck would situate them under the *Skinny Dipper* to hold it up while he removed the pontoon to repair it on dry land. But first, we tied the boat as tight as we could to the moorings to help keep it from sinking. We also placed bumpers between the dock and the boat to ensure Buck would have room to work without getting crushed if the boat shifted.

Though it was a sunny day, it was early in the season.

The lake water was still relatively cold. Grimacing against the chill, Buck slowly lowered himself off the end of the dock and into the lake. "Hoo-ee!" he hollered. "I can hardly feel my legs."

Grant leaned over the side of his boat to call to Buck. "Should've got yourself a wetsuit."

Buck scoffed. "Now you tell me!"

We handed the plastic barrels off the end of the dock and he forced them under the boat to support it, diving under to secure them in place with two-by-fours that served as crossbeams. It was a makeshift system, but necessity was the mother of invention. I held my breath every time he disappeared under the boat but, luckily, he resurfaced relatively quickly each time. Once the plastic barrels were in place, he set about removing the pontoon. It took a good quarter hour, but he finally managed to get it free. He situated the long pontoon in the water at the end of the dock.

The pontoon was divided into three air chambers, each with its own bung hole. Buck unscrewed the tops and determined that only the middle chamber contained water. Using nylon straps and lots of muscle, we wrangled the pontoon up onto the dock and turned it over to empty the flooded chamber.

Using our shop vac, I blew air into the center bung hole at a low psi—pounds per square inch. Buck pushed the pontoon back under the water. A stream of small bubbles rising to the surface indicated where the aluminum had been punctured. Buck marked the spot with a special underwater marking pen I'd ordered online.

After unplugging the vac and moving it out of the way, Owen and I helped Buck lift the pontoon onto the dock once again. We turned it over and drained the minute amount of water that had leaked in during the test.

As Buck and Owen set about patching the pontoon, I went into the boat's kitchen to start measuring the vinyl floor planks for cutting. Sawdust lay on the small countertop to supervise my work. Using a utility knife and a carpenter's square, I cut the pieces, making sure to leave a quarter inch for expansion. I'd been working about half an hour when movement outside the kitchen window caught my eye.

A middle-aged man and woman strode up to the *Sexy Sheila*. The man had dark hair streaked with silver. He wore sunglasses, a casual cotton shirt, khaki shorts, and boat shoes. The woman sported a pair of wedge sandals and a skimpy sundress to show off the fit physique she'd managed to maintain despite the years she'd accumulated. Her light brown hair was shoulder-length and teased to look wild. Copious amounts of cosmetics coated her face, and her fingernails were long and pointed, in line with the current trend, and painted a vibrant pink. A striped beach bag hung from her shoulder. Two rolled-up beach towels, a bottle of rosé, and a copy of *Southern Living* poked out of the bag. Jojo stood on the back deck of the boat and wagged his tail in greeting.

Grant set aside the cold pack he'd been holding to his knee and used his cane to lever himself to a stand. "Hey, Mick. Hey, Sheila."

Aha! This must be the sexy Sheila the boat had been named after.

Mick glanced around the boat as he helped Sheila aboard. "You taking good care of my baby? Following the maintenance instructions I gave you? Noting everything in the maintenance log?"

"Don't worry," Grant said. "The *Sexy Sheila* is in shipshape."

"Can't thank you enough for helping me out like you did." Mick pulled what appeared to be a folded check from the breast pocket of his shirt, unfolded it, and held it out to Grant. "Got your repayment right here."

Repayment? Had Mick borrowed money from Grant? If so, I surmised that it must have been before the divorce proceedings began and Grant's finances got tied up.

Although Jojo raised his snout to sniff the paper, Grant made no move to take the check. He simply stared down at it for a moment before returning his focus to Mick's face. "I can't take that."

Mick seemed to stiffen. "What do you mean? The deal was I'd buy the boat back from you once we got back on our feet."

Grant shook his head. "That wasn't the deal."

Mick thrust the check at Grant. "Yes, it was."

"No," Grant said. "The deal was that I'd sell the boat back to you for a mutually agreeable price at a mutually convenient time. This isn't a convenient time for me."

"Why not?" Sheila snapped.

Grant sighed and looked down for a moment in shame, much as Jojo had earlier. "Because Deena tossed me out. She's filed for divorce. This boat is my home now, at least until we get the property settlement worked out or the insurance company pays the claim for my knee injury."

Mick raised the check and waved it. "This check is for twelve thousand dollars! That's twenty percent more than you paid me for the boat. That's more than enough money to get yourself an apartment until you sort things out with Deena or the insurance company pays up."

"Sorry, man," Grant said, "but with this bum knee I can't work. No landlord is going to rent to someone with no income coming in."

Sheila cut a glance at her husband as a cloud passed over her face. "There's lots of jobs you can do from behind a desk."

"Nothing I'm trained for," Grant said. "I've tended bar since I turned twenty-one. It's all I know. I can barely work a computer."

Sheila frowned. "The labor department could help. They've got retraining programs."

"Retraining takes time," Grant said.

"Time?" Mick snorted. "Looks to me like you've got plenty of that right now."

Grant didn't respond.

Mick exhaled sharply. "What's it going to take?"

"I'd need fifty grand at least," Grant said. "The boat is worth that."

"You don't have to tell me!" Mick snapped. "I bought it new for more. But you only paid me a fraction of its value. I'm not going to buy my boat for full price twice! I'd be better off buying a different boat from someone else."

Grant raised his palms. "Maybe you should consider that."

Sheila gave Grant a look so icy it was a wonder the lake didn't freeze over. She pointed one of her claws at the back of the boat. "My name is on the back. This is *our* boat. If you think we're just going to walk away, you better think again."

Grant shook his head slowly. "I'm sorry, you two. I really am. But I need either the boat or enough cash to ensure I'll have a roof over my head for the next year or two."

The check still clutched in his hand, Mick crossed his arms over his chest and rocked back on his heels. "You're not trying to screw us over, are you? I'd hate to have to get lawyers involved."

"There's no need for lawyers," Grant said, "though if you spoke to one they'd tell you our agreement is too vague to be enforceable. The time and dollar amount aren't stipulated. Who's to say when the boat has to be sold back and for how much?"

Sheila's heavily lined eyes narrowed into sharp, suspicious slits. "How would you know the agreement was unenforceable unless you'd asked an attorney yourself?"

Mick turned and addressed his wife now. "I bet he talked to a lawyer before he even gave us that contract to sign. I bet he purposely had us sign a worthless piece of paper he knew would give us no recourse." He turned back to Grant. "I never should've trusted you."

"Hold on, now!" Grant raised his free hand in a *stop* gesture. "I only found out that the contract was unenforceable when I showed it to my divorce attorney. I never meant to cheat you. I'm *not* cheating you. I'll sell the boat back to you someday. I will! But you've got to meet me halfway here. If I give up the boat now, I'll be out on the streets, living in my car."

Sheila's expression soured. "You mean your fancy Camaro? Boo hoo."

Grant frowned. "It might be a nice car, but it's not big enough to live in." He rubbed a hand over Jojo's head. "Besides, what would I do with my dog?"

The three had reached an impasse. I wasn't sure what to think of the situation. They'd all made good points. It wasn't clear what was fair here.

Sheila turned to Mick, her eyes misty with emotion. "I'm so sorry, hon. This is all my fault."

"No, it's not," Mick growled. "It's his." He jammed the check back into his pocket and stared Grant down. "If you're not going to sell the boat back to me, then you should take over the monthly payments for the slip rental."

"I would if I could." Grant heaved a sigh. "But, like I said, things are really tight for me right now."

Sheila said, "Maybe we'll just stop paying the rental, then."

Grant said, "You could do that. Hell, I wouldn't even blame you if you did. But if you stop paying the slip lease, you'll lose this spot. You'd have to find somewhere else to dock your boat once I sell it back to you. The waiting list for slips is a mile long at every marina on the lake. You wouldn't be able to get another for years."

Mick's shoulders slumped. He appeared defeated. He released a loud sigh.

"I'm sorry about this," Grant said. "I truly am. I appreciate you cutting me some slack. You know how it is to go through a hard time."

Mick and Sheila exchanged a knowing glance, both looking slightly embarrassed for berating the man who'd bailed them out when they'd been in a similar financial bind.

"Tell you what." Grant gestured at Sheila's beach bag. "I can see y'all came out here hoping to enjoy some time on the water. Why don't you go ahead and take the boat out for an hour or two? I'd need her back by two, but until then she's yours. I'll hang out with my new neighbors in the meantime." He gestured toward the *Skinny Dipper*, again being presumptuous. Buck and I had a lot of work to do today. We couldn't exactly entertain guests. Grant cocked his head and eyed Mick. "What do you say?"

Mick, in turn, looked to Sheila.

She said, "It's better than nothing, I suppose."

Grant said, "That's the spirit!" He hobbled off his boat, calling for Jojo to come with him. The dog followed along, his tail wagging, as Grant climbed aboard the *Skinny Dipper*. "Ahoy!" he called.

Sawdust and I met him and the dog at the back door. "Hey."

"Mind if Jojo and I hang out here with y'all? My friends are taking the *Sexy Sheila* out for a bit."

With my cousins and I busy with our tasks, it wasn't the best time for us to be hosting a guest. Even so, I didn't want to be rude to our neighbor or prevent Mick and Sheila from having some fun on their boat. "We need to knock some things off our repair list today, but you're welcome to hang out on the back deck while we work."

"Thanks. Jojo and I will do our best to stay out of your way." He gingerly lowered himself onto the rubber ducky, using the float as a recliner of sorts. While Jojo and Sawdust danced around each other, Grant pulled out his phone. A moment later, the device blared "Rock and Roll All Nite."

Must be the guy's favorite song.

For the next two hours, I continued to measure and cut the vinyl planks, Buck and Owen worked to patch the pontoon, and Grant continued to lounge on the deck, listening to music and scrolling through profiles on dating sites. Once again, movement outside the windows caught my eye as the *Sexy Sheila* returned to the dock with Mick at the helm.

Sheila eased herself over the side of the boat that bore her name and onto the dock, while Grant levered himself to a stand on our back deck. Jojo followed him as he returned to his slip and helped Sheila moor the boat to the cleats on the dock. "You get the bow line!" he called to her, "I'll get the spring and stern lines."

While Sheila handled the ropes at the front of the boat, Grant tied down the ropes along the sides and back. In no time, the boat was secured.

Mick disembarked and joined Grant and Sheila on the dock. "I topped off the tank for you."

He did? That was an awfully nice gesture in light of the argument they'd had earlier.

Grant reached out to simultaneously take Mick's hand and pat his shoulder. "Thanks, man. You did me a solid."

"By the way, Sheila and I thought we smelled gas fumes when we first boarded."

"Gas fumes?" Grant repeated. "I hadn't noticed."

I lifted my nose to the air and inhaled deeply. I caught what could be a faint whiff of gasoline, but that wasn't unusual at a busy dock.

Mick said, "Don't forget to turn off the blowers when you fill up or they could suck fumes into the boat. You might want to have the fuel hoses checked, too. There could be a leak."

Grant gave the man a sailor's salute. "Will do. By the way, you're welcome to take her out again any time."

"I appreciate the offer. We'll definitely take you up on it." With that, Mick and Sheila set off down the dock and climbed into her shiny red Mazda Miata convertible. They lowered the top and drove out of the parking lot.

It seemed the argument had blown over for now. I hoped the friends would be able to work something out that would be acceptable to all of them. I hated to think their dispute would sink their friendship.

CHAPTER 6

SOMETHING FISHY IS GOING ON

WHITNEY

Early Saturday afternoon, my cousins finished repairing the pontoon and replacing it under the boat, and Owen left to spend time with his wife and daughters. Buck joined me inside to work on the flooring.

I'd already spent some time reviewing the study materials for our upcoming boating license test, and quizzed him as we worked. "What are the two types of boat hulls?"

"Uhhhhhh . . ." He glanced around, as if he might find the answer in the boat.

I rolled my eyes. "You haven't even looked at the study guide, have you?"

"I glanced at it."

I shook my head, but shared my knowledge with him. "There are two types of hulls, displacement and planing. Displacement hulls push the water out of the way and need less propulsion. Planing hulls glide on top of the water and need more propulsion."

He nodded. "Displacement. Planing. Got it."

I moved on to my next question. "How many feet of anchor line should you let out relative to the depth of the water?"

Buck scratched his head. "I'm gonna go with three. That sounds about right."

"Nope," I said. "Guess again."

"Four?"

"Nope."

He frowned. "Five?"

We could be at this all day. Again, I gave my cousin the answer. "The correct answer is seven to ten feet depending on the wind and the size of the waves."

My lesson was interrupted when three boisterous men in their thirties arrived and made their noisy way down the dock to board the *Sexy Sheila.* They all wore swim trunks and T-shirts. They'd brought a colorful beach ball, hot dogs, buns, bags of potato chips, and enough beer and ice to host a frat party. Jojo sniffed the packages of hot dogs and danced around in excitement. After the men stashed the ice and beer in Grant's cooler, he untied his moorings, took the helm, and off they went. They were barely past the no-wake buoy when Grant cranked up the onboard stereo. The strains of "Rock and Roll All Nite" filled the air, shattering the peace of the lake. At least the boat was headed away from us, so it would be quieter soon.

Buck and I kept working, and I continued to quiz him until I ran out of questions. Had he been taking the actual test, he would have failed miserably. An hour later, Buck was still working on the flooring inside, and I was filling the plastic garbage bin we'd placed on the back deck for small construction refuse when the woman with the platinum blonde bob returned. Though she wore casual clothing today, her choices were nonetheless tasteful and classic. A pair of salmon pink capri pants paired with a silky tunic, silver jewelry, and low-heeled sandals. A designer purse hung from her shoulder. She stared at the empty slip again, shook her head, and muttered, "That man is never around when you need him."

I didn't want to butt in, but I thought I might be able to help her in some way. "Everything okay?"

She pointed to the empty slip. "Have you met Grant yet?"

That sounds like a loaded question. "I have."

"Any idea when he'll be back?"

I didn't know this woman, so I wasn't sure how much I should share with her. I didn't tell her he'd gone out on the water with new friends he'd met at the bar last night after a disastrous meetup with a woman from a dating app. I settled for saying, "No idea. Sorry." It wasn't a lie.

She cast an irritated glance at the water before setting her gaze on me again. "Whatever you do, don't lend the guy money. You'll never see it again."

Uh-oh. Too late. Buck had lent Grant sixty dollars last night for the date that didn't work out. I recalled the name Grant had given earlier, of his wife who'd filed for divorce. "Are you Deena?"

She threw her head back and mirthlessly barked a laugh. "Ha!" When she righted her head, she said, "No. Deena is wife number five. I was number four."

Whoa. "Grant's been married five times?"

"Yep. His past failed relationships should have been a huge red flag, but Grant can be quite the charmer. I was dumb enough to fall for his flattery and believe his lies. He has an uncanny ability to identify vulnerable women." Her eyes flared with anger, but there was something else there, too. Shame. Sorrow. Loneliness. "I'm not going to stick around," she said. "I've wasted enough time on that man. Just tell him Jackie came by and wants to know where the man cave furniture is. Under the terms of our divorce settlement, he was supposed to make the payments on the furniture, but he didn't. My name was on the sales contract, too, and the collection agency kept hounding me. I ended up having to pay it off to save my credit rating. The furniture should be mine since I paid for it."

"Sounds fair." I gave her a nod. "I'll tell him."

"Let me give you my cell number," she said. "I'm not sure if he still has it. He might have deleted it from his contacts."

"Okay." I whipped out my phone and entered the name "Jackie" as a new contact. She hadn't given her surname, nor did I think I'd need it, so I simply entered "GrantsEx#4" in the space for the last name. As she rattled off her number, I entered the digits in my phone.

Our exchange completed, she thanked me and headed back to the parking lot. She climbed into a light silver late-model Volvo sedan and drove off, her back tires spitting up gravel and dust as she punched the gas.

Five ex-wives and numerous financial problems? Grant clearly has hidden depths.

During the afternoon, the lake filled with boats. Some puttered slowly around the perimeter of the lake, the occupants enjoying the scenery. Others bobbed on the surface as those aboard soaked up the sunshine. One sped across the lake, pulling men on wakeboards and water skis. If I didn't know better, I'd have thought one of the skiers was Grant. The guy appeared to be wearing a bright yellow bathing suit like the one Grant wore when we first met him. But the boat and skier were too far away and moving too fast for me to say for sure. Only the bird-watcher could know for sure. He was back again today, his binoculars aimed at something across the lake. A small flip-up screen stood erect between the lenses. Looked like he had expensive binoculars with a built-in camera so he could record the birds. *He sure takes his birding seriously.*

In the early evening, Buck and I were replacing missing screws on the spiral slide when Grant and his buddies returned to the dock sunburnt, half-drunk, and half-dressed, their chests exposed. Grant backed the *Sexy Sheila* into his slip at an off angle. The boat bounced off the bumpers, jostling the men in the boat and causing Jojo to splay his legs to keep from falling over. Though the dog appeared concerned, the men didn't care. They laughed and whooped. One of them leapt from the boat to the dock, lost his footing, and stumbled across the boards, slamming sideways into the *Skinny Dipper. Bam!* The impact shook our vessel, and the guy dropped his bottle of beer to the dock. *Clink!* Fortunately, the bottle didn't shatter. Unfortunately, it roll-roll-rolled off the side of the dock and into the lake, where it sunk. The men yukked it up over that maneuver.

Buck frowned, stood, and went to the railing to address the man lumbering up the dock. "Watch it, buddy. We're working over here."

The man stopped in his tracks and raised his hands over his head. "Oh, no! It's the boat police! Am I under arrest? You gonna throw me in the brig?"

The men yukked it up some more. *Idiots.*

Buck skewered the man with his gaze. "Just have some manners. Y'all aren't the only people out here."

One of the other men opened the swing gate at the back of the deck on the *Sexy Sheila* and stepped onto the dock to join his friend. Jojo hopped onto the dock with the man, sniffed his way over to one of the light posts, and lifted his leg to urinate on it. Not exactly polite, but I blamed Grant, not his dog. Jojo didn't know he shouldn't make a mess on the dock. He only knew nature was calling.

Grant left the helm and moved sideways around the perimeter of his boat, tossing ropes over the side. He moved without his cane, though he had one hand on the side of the boat at all times to support himself. The men on the dock grabbed the ropes and tied them to the cleats.

While Buck and I finished removing the broken generator and installing a new one, the men hung out on the *Sexy Sheila*, blasting country music so loud Buck and I had to shout to hear each other over it. Buck's admonishment clearly meant nothing to these guys, and Grant made no effort to rein his guests in. They laughed, fed what remained of the hot dogs to Jojo, and tossed the beach ball around until one of them sobered up enough to drive them home.

Once the men had driven off in their pickup, I stepped to the rail to address Grant. "A woman named Jackie came by earlier. She wants to know what you did with the furniture from your man cave. She said she had to pay it off to protect her credit rating."

Rather than answer me, Grant turned and looked off across the lake. His chest rose and fell as he heaved a sigh.

I held up my phone. "She gave me her cell number in case you need it."

He shook his head. I wasn't sure if that meant he already had her number or if he merely didn't want it but, either way, I supposed I'd done my duty.

Buck stepped up next to me. "Got that sixty bucks I loaned you?"

"Shoot!" Grant turned back our way and slapped his forehead. "With my buds coming by, I totally forgot. I'll run by the bank tomorrow and take care of it."

Buck grunted. "Tomorrow's Sunday. The banks will be closed."

Grant swung his arm in a *shucks* motions. "First thing Monday morning, then." He dragged his index finger over the left half of his chest. "Cross my heart and hope to die."

Buck merely grunted again in reply.

Emmalee came by the *Skinny Dipper* on Sunday to check out the boat and make plans for Colette's bachelorette party.

"Wow!" she said as she looked around the place. "This boat is the perfect place for hosting the party."

I told Emmalee what I'd come up with so far. "We've got some chaise lounges on order. They can double as beds the night of the party so we can make it a sleepover. Since we're going to hold the party on the boat, I figured we'd go with a lake theme. Let's make Colette a veil out of a fishnet."

"A fishnet veil?" She barked a laugh. "That'll be a hoot!"

I told her about the drink recipe I'd found online. "It includes Swedish Fish. We can serve it in a punch bowl with a plastic treasure chest at the bottom."

She tapped her index finger on her chin, thinking. "We could use a donut pan to bake cupcakes and frost them red and white to look like life preservers."

"Great idea!"

We sat at the kitchen booth with our laptops and searched for more water-themed ideas.

Emmalee turned her computer to face me. "What do you think about these?" She toggled back and forth between a float shaped like a diamond ring and others shaped like mermaid tails.

"Let's get them!"

We spent an hour nailing down the plans for food, drinks, games, and décor. When we finished, we sprawled on beach towels on the upper deck, basking in the sun, though Emmalee covered her skin in a liberal coating of sunscreen lest her fair skin burn. I could hardly wait for the boat to be done so we could host Colette's big bash. I doubted Owen had put any thought into Buck's bachelor party yet. He probably hadn't had time. *Good thing he has Collin as the party co-captain.*

First thing Monday morning, Grant took off in his Camaro, purportedly to run by the bank. He didn't return all day.

At half past five, one of the men he'd partied with the day before sauntered up the dock. It was the same guy who'd slammed into our boat and given Buck grief. I was working inside the *Skinny Dipper* and saw him through the window. The guy stood on the dock behind the *Sexy Sheila*, cupped his hands around his mouth, and hollered, "Yo! Grant!"

Jojo stuck his nose out the window and eyed the guy, barking in greeting. *Woof-woof!*

When there was no human response from within the boat, the man boarded it and rapped on the door to the cabin. *Rap-rap-rap.* He called out again. "Grant! Hey! Open up!"

I could hear Jojo scratching on the inside of the cabin door. He barked again, the sound muffled this time.

When knocking again did no good, the guy disembarked and made his way down the dock beside the boat, cupping his hands around his eyes now as he attempted to peer inside the vessel. He wasn't likely to have much luck. The windows were tinted with reflective film for privacy.

Rather than allow the guy to continue upsetting Jojo, I called out my window. "Grant's been gone all day."

He scowled. "He said he'd be here now. He owes me a hundred bucks. When's he getting back?"

I was neither my neighbor's keeper, nor did I owe this jerk any more courtesy than he'd shown Buck and me the day before. "Your guess is as good as mine."

The guy muttered a few choice curse words. "I've got places to be. Tell Grant I'll be back in a day or two, and he'd better be here with my money."

Since when did I become Grant's cabin steward? I didn't bother to respond.

The guy left, but not before giving the *Sexy Sheila* a

solid kick that sent the boat slamming into the dock on the other side and Jojo into an uproar. *Woof-woof-woof-woof-woof!*

When Grant finally reappeared that evening, he brought out a cutting board and a sharp knife, and pulled a couple of fish out of the refrigerator in his cabin. He brought the fish out onto the deck to clean them. Seeing him cut off the fish's head, slice open the belly, and remove the entrails had me swearing off seafood forever, but Sawdust, smelling fresh fish, was curious. He stood atop my toolbox, a paw on the rail as he watched Grant prepare the fish for cooking.

When Grant finished, he filled the kettle grill mounted to his boat with charcoal, squeezed a quick stream of lighter fluid onto the briquettes, and struck a match to fire it up. A breeze blew out the first match. He turned the kettle grill in its frame so that the lid blocked the wind and lit a second match. This attempt was a success, and the charcoal whooshed into flames. Once the fire calmed down, he lay the fillets on his grill. While they cooked, he used his cane to hobble to the front of his boat and dumped the fish heads and parts into the lake.

He returned to his grill and sprinkled seasoning from a small jar onto the fillets. He used a spatula to flip the fillets over and sprinkled the seasoning on the other side, too. He shook the jar hard then held it up so that he could eye the clear glass below the label. His frown told me he'd run out. He leaned over the side of his boat and tossed the empty jar into the trash can on our deck. If he'd asked me first, I wouldn't have minded, but since he didn't ask, I was a little put off that he'd used our trash can. He was being presumptuous, yet again. The guy had a poor sense of boundaries.

A few minutes later, Buck emerged from the interior of the *Skinny Dipper*. "Something sure smells good out here."

I hiked a thumb to indicate Grant's boat. "He's cooking fish." I reached into the trash bin and retrieved the empty jar. The label featured a smiling cartoon fish with a hook through its lip like one of those piercings sometimes seen on older millennials. A conversation bubble read "I'm hooked on Gil's Fish Flavoring!" I held the jar out to Buck. "This is the seasoning he used."

"Oh, yeah?" Buck took the jar from me. "I'm going to look for this next time I'm at the grocery store." Shifting his focus from me to our neighbor, Buck called over to him. "Hey, Grant. You got my money?"

Grant cringed. "Sorry, dude! I didn't have a chance to get by the bank today before it closed. I got sidetracked driving all over town putting in job applications. Took longer than I expected."

Buck pressed him for details. "Where'd you apply?"

"Here and there," Grant said. "You know how it is."

"No, I don't." Buck stared him down. "Here and there *where*?"

I was curious myself.

When Grant sputtered, Buck crossed his arms over his chest. "I'm never going to see that money again, am I?"

Grant dropped his jaw. "I'm good for it! Have some patience."

Buck said, "Your obnoxious friends used up all of my patience yesterday." Buck disappeared back into the boat, but emerged again a moment later with a plate and a fork in his hand. He stepped off our boat, circled over to Grant's, and opened the swing gate to climb aboard. He kicked the beach ball aside and used his fork to move a fillet from the grill to his plate. Buck's behavior made Grant's unauthorized use of our trash can seem inconsequential.

Grant threw up his hands. "What are you doing? That's my dinner!"

"What a coincidence," Buck said. "It's my dinner, too."

I fought to keep from laughing. Buck was one of the nicest guys I knew but, as he'd said, his patience had limits and he'd never been one to take being scammed lying down. Considering all the time and money we were putting into this project, I couldn't blame him. Sixty dollars wasn't nothing, and Buck had wedding and honeymoon expenses coming up, too.

Grant held on to the boat and shook his cane in the air. "You wouldn't dare have done that if I wasn't disabled! What kind of man steals dinner from the mouth of someone who's injured and out of work?"

"One who realizes you never had any intention of repaying the sixty bucks you borrowed from him."

I feared the situation might escalate but, before it could, Buck left the *Sexy Sheila* and returned to the *Skinny Dipper* with his plate of grilled fish. Grant started to protest some more, but was interrupted when Jojo began to bark with joy, leaping up and down on his back legs like a canine pogo stick. *Woof! Woof-woof!* The dog backed up and tried to make a running leap over the side of the boat and onto the dock, but there wasn't enough room for him to gain momentum and he ended up skidding into the swing gate.

"Jojo!" called a joyful male voice. "Hi, boy!"

We turned to see a teenage boy sprinting up the dock. His lips were spread in a huge smile that revealed a set of teeth being forced into submission by a set of so-called invisible braces. Raging hormones had turned his face into a bubble wrap of acne. Despite these common awkward-stage nuisances, the kid was cute, his brown eyes bright with excitement. He wore his dark hair short on the sides and shaggy on top, a modern-day modified mullet that was much more attractive than the original version.

On hearing the boy's voice, the dog went bonkers. *Arf-arf-arf! Arf-arf!* Jojo bounced off the boat benches, running back and forth in the small space, thrilled to see the kid. The boy opened the swing gate and Jojo bolted out, knocking him back onto his butt on the dock. But the boy didn't care. He laughed and grabbed the dog in a bear hug. The two rolled about in a rambunctious embrace.

"Careful! Don't roll off the dock!" Behind the boy came a fiftyish woman wearing blue medical scrubs. She had a cardboard box tucked under one arm, and a variety of mail in her other hand. Her brown curly hair was wrangled back into a ponytail at the nape of her neck. She wore glasses and an expression of utter and absolute exhaustion. Remaining on the dock, she held out the mail to Grant.

He reached over the side of the boat to take it from her.

Once he'd laid the mail down on a bench, she handed him the box. Her tone was flat when she spoke. "Here's more cold packs for your knee. Figured you could use them."

"Thanks, Deena," Grant said. "Always the nurse, aren't you?"

She snorted softly. "I don't like to see people suffer."

Grant cocked his head and offered his most disarming smile. "Even me?"

She inhaled a deep breath and slowly released it. "Yes. Even you."

His gaze roamed her face, assessing. "How have you been?"

She seemed too weary to even muster up any ire. "How do you think?"

"I've missed you," Grant said. "A lot."

She rolled her tired eyes. "Cut the crap and sign the settlement, Grant. Please. I'm begging you. It's more than fair. We barely reached our first anniversary. I can't offer you any more money or I'd have to dip into my retirement and I'd be charged a penalty on my taxes. If we have to hash things out in court, you're likely to get even less. Just sign the papers so we can move on."

"I'm sorry, Deena," Grant said, "but I can't. I'll be out of work for who knows how long, and I've got to pay the boat expenses so I have somewhere to live. The medical bills for my knee are adding up. Plus, there's the insurance on my car, and vet bills and food and stuff for the dog."

"Give Jojo to us, then," she pleaded. "We'll cover his expenses."

"He's *my* dog," Grant said. "I'm the one who brought him home from the shelter."

"You might have brought him home, but he was the family's dog. Tanner's the one who took care of him."

Grant swallowed hard before softly saying, "I need him. He's all I have now."

"And whose fault is that?" Deena said. Not bothering to wait for an answer that wasn't likely to come, she said, "Jojo would be happier with a yard to play in. It's selfish for you to keep him here on this boat."

Grant's jaw flexed and his grip tightened on the handle of his cane. "You feel sorry for a dog living on this little boat, but not me? That's how it is?"

The woman slumped and put her face in her hands. She spoke through her fingers. "There's just no reasoning with you, is there?"

The boy leapt to his feet to defend his mother. "You're such a butthead, Grant!" The dog turned to look at Grant, as if agreeing with the boy.

Grant opened the swing gate, grabbed Jojo by the collar, and dragged the dog back onto the boat. He closed the gate behind him. "It's best y'all go. My life is hard enough without you harassing me."

Hard life? He'd spent the weekend going to bars on Buck's dime, and having fun on his boat, drinking beer and eating junk food he hadn't paid for. Besides, they'd hardly harassed the guy. Heck, his wife had brought him cold packs for his knee.

Deena swiped a tear from her eye and waved for her son to follow her. "Let's go, Tanner. This was a waste of time." She walked off down the dock.

Tanner followed her for a couple of steps, but when Jojo stood on his back legs to look over the side of the boat and sent up a heartbreaking wail, the teen turned back around. His body jerked as he choked back a sob. He swallowed hard and turned again to go. As he passed

Buck and me, he shook his head. "Mom really knows how to pick 'em."

He followed his mother to her car and stopped at the door to look back one last time at Jojo. The dog was whining and wailing inconsolably, scratching at the back gate on the deck, trying to get free. My heart broke for the poor dog. He missed his boy. I felt heart-sick for the boy as well. Meanwhile, my opinion of our dockside neighbor was getting worse and worse.

CHAPTER 7

THIS CALLS FOR KITTY CUDDLES

SAWDUST

Sawdust had enjoyed the bits of fish Buck had fed him earlier. So yummy! With his tummy full, he'd usually be tempted to flop down on the deck and take a nap. But he couldn't. He could hear the dog's sad wails and whimpers coming from the boat next door. His new friend felt heartbroken that the boy had left. Sawdust knew that feeling. He felt it every time Whitney left him alone at their cottage. But at least Sawdust knew Whitney would always come back. The cat sensed the dog didn't know if he'd ever see his boy again. He wished he could go over to the other boat and cuddle up with the dog, offer him some consolation.

CHAPTER 8
FISH FOOD

WHITNEY

Deena and Tanner climbed into her red Toyota Rav4 and drove off. The car made almost no noise. *Must be a hybrid.*

That evening, Grant left Jojo tied on the deck rather than taking him into the cabin. *Poor dog.* He had little latitude with the short rope. I feared he might go over the side and hurt himself. He seemed lonely, too, with only the beach ball to keep him company.

Jojo's whining continued long into the night. Buck was lucky his berth was on the other side of the boat. Mine was on the side that faced the *Sexy Sheila*, and I found it impossible to sleep with the dog's desperate and incessant cries. Even Sawdust seemed to have trouble sleeping, and he was a virtual pro, spending the bulk of his days catnapping. He put one ear against the mattress and crooked his paw over the other to block out the sound.

Around midnight, the whining finally settled down

to a soft rhythmic whimper. I'd finally fallen asleep when a different sound replaced the whine and jerked me from my slumber. *Thump-thump-thump.*

Is that Jojo's tail? As I sat up in bed, a shadow passed in front of the light pole on the dock. I eased myself across the bed to the window, quietly slid it open, and peered out through the screen, careful to stay a few inches back so I couldn't be seen. The shadow formed a human shape and approached the back of the *Sexy Sheila. Is someone trying to steal Jojo?* I'd heard of unscrupulous people stealing pets and then demanding a ransom from owners. Pets could be stolen for other nefarious reasons, too. *Has the party guy returned to get his hundred dollars? Is he going to take Jojo as canine collateral?*

Nobody would be stealing Jojo on my watch. *Though if it's Tanner . . .*

I grabbed my cell phone and slid out of bed. I debated waking Buck, but I figured once the would-be dognapper realized I'd spotted them, they'd take off and leave Jojo behind. No need to wake my cousin.

Sawdust padded along behind me as I went to the living room and bent down to access my toolbox. I unfastened the clasps and grabbed my largest wrench. It was heavy and made of metal, the perfect improvised weapon, just in case. I quietly opened the back door of the houseboat and stepped out onto the deck. I used my bare foot to force Sawdust back inside. No way did I want my little guy coming out here and getting into the fray. I had no intentions of leaving the *Skinny Dipper* to physically confront the dog-napper, but you never knew what a startled person might do.

I could see the dark shadow reach over the swing

gate on the deck of the *Sexy Sheila* to release the inside latch. Using my left hand, I punched in the code to unlock my cell phone. By then, the would-be pet thief had leashed the dog, lured him out through the gate, and started up the dock in my direction.

I tapped the flashlight icon and a beam of light burst from my phone, illuminating a startled teenage boy and his beloved dog. Tanner gasped and threw up a hand to block the light, blinking against the glare, his face contorted in panic. As quickly as I'd turned the light on, I turned it off. It took a second for my eyes to adjust again to the dim light, but when they did, I motioned for Tanner to keep moving. "I was sound asleep," I whispered. "I didn't see a thing."

He spoke on a sob. "Thanks! I'll take good care of him."

"I know you will." I gave him a smile and motioned again. "You better get going." The last thing we needed was Grant waking up and finding Tanner taking Jojo away and me doing nothing to stop it. I wasn't an accessory to the crime, nor was I aiding and abetting, but I wasn't exactly an innocent bystander, either.

Tanner scurried down the dock and loaded Jojo into the SUV his mother had been driving earlier. I felt happy for both of them. I only hoped Grant wouldn't find a way to get the dog back. If he wanted a pet, he should go to the pound and get one that was lazy and calm, maybe an older dog who'd love nothing more than to lounge on a boat.

Though the SUV's hybrid engine made virtually no noise, I knew Tanner must have started the car because it began to move. He drove quickly across the parking lot, waiting until he reached the road before turning on his headlights. *Smart move.* That way, the lights wouldn't alert Grant to his presence.

I went back inside the *Skinny Dipper*, returned my wrench to my toolbox, and scooped up Sawdust, carrying him to my berth. We settled back in. A few minutes later, my mind was in that dusky twilight that precedes sleep when my ears detected another sound coming from nearby—a metallic clang. I didn't bother sitting back up to look out the window. I was too sleepy. Besides, the sound was one heard often around a marina, the sound of a rope against the aluminum mast of sailboat. *Nothing to be concerned about, right?*

On Tuesday morning, Buck and I got up bright and early to get to work. Today, we'd paint the *Skinny Dipper.* With moisture rates being high in the mornings, it wasn't a good time to apply primer or paint, so we'd wait until afternoon for that. But there was plenty to do beforehand that would fill our morning.

In preparation for painting the boat, I'd performed quite a bit of research to ensure we did things right. I'd learned that there were two general types of paint for boats. There was bottom paint for the part of the boat that went underwater. Bottom paint contained antifouling agents to prevent marine growth such as algae, or barnacles in saltwater, from adhering to the surface. Topside paint was designed for the part that remained above the waterline. Of course, boats could be constructed of wood, fiberglass, or aluminum, and there were different paints and primers for each material. Different types of rollers worked best for each type of surface and paint, too. Smooth rollers were best for some, while carpet-texture rollers were a good choice for fiberglass or when a textured surface was desired. There was apparently an entire world of boat-related paint to contend with.

Luckily for us, the paint on the underside of the houseboat was in good condition, so we only had to worry about painting the upper part. Good thing, because hauling the large boat out of the water would have been time-consuming and a hassle. It was much easier to work on the boat in place in the slip.

Buck and I had quite a bit of prep work ahead of us. First, we had to sand the rust off the exterior, hose off the dirt and cobwebs, apply epoxy to the dings and gaps, and install tape around the windows and doors to protect the trim. We also needed to lay tarps over the deck in case the primer or paint dripped.

After coffee and a quick bagel, Buck and I stepped outside to start working. I purposefully worked on the far side of the houseboat so that I wouldn't have to deal with Grant when he finally dragged himself out of his bunk and discovered his dog was gone. I'd keep my promise to Tanner not to tell Grant who had taken Jojo. But even if I kept my mouth shut, I was afraid my face might betray me. I tended to wear my emotions on my sleeve. I hadn't told Buck anything about my nighttime adventure, so he wouldn't need to lie.

Buck went to his van to round up his random orbital sander. Though I could only see him from the knee down as he stood behind the open cargo bay doors of his van, I could hear his voice clearly. He issued a groan and muttered a light curse.

I stepped off the boat and walked over to his van. "What's wrong?"

He held up a plastic-wrapped package. "I grabbed the

wrong-size discs for my sander. These are four-and-a-half-inch. I need six-inch."

"No worries," I said. "I can run to the hardware store. I need to get some rubber washers for the kitchen sink. I noticed it has a slight leak around the left handle. Couldn't hurt to get some more dust masks, too. Anything else?"

"I think that covers it."

I rounded up my keys and purse, told Sawdust to be a good boy while I was gone, and headed out to my SUV. The closest hardware store was a half-hour drive away, but fortunately they had everything we were looking for. I placed the bag of supplies in my passenger seat and headed back to the marina.

On the return drive, I drove up on a silver pickup truck pulling an empty boat trailer. The road curved quite a bit as it wound along the lakeshore. On the curves, my eyes caught a glimpse of a small red convertible in front of the pickup. *Is that Sheila's Miata?* It wasn't until the car and truck slowed and turned into the parking lot for a public boat ramp that I could be certain. It was indeed Sheila's Miata. Even in profile, there was no mistaking her fashion runway–ready makeup and teased hair. Her passenger seat was empty. *Wait. Is that Mick driving the truck?* I turned back to look over my shoulder, but it was too late. Between the tinted windows on the truck and the additional distance I'd driven, I couldn't be certain.

I returned to the *Skinny Dipper*, handed the sanding discs to Buck, and bent down to greet Sawdust, who was mewing pathetically as if he'd thought I'd abandoned him forever. "I missed you too, boy."

After reassuring my cat that he was immensely loved

and that I would always come back any time I went away, I got to work.

Around half past ten, Grant's voice called out from the *Sexy Sheila*. "Jojo? Where are you, boy?" There was a short pause before he addressed my cousin, his anger and annoyance over last night's stolen fish apparently forgotten in worry. "Hey, Buck. Have you seen my dog?"

"Not since yesterday," Buck replied. "Wasn't he inside with you last night?"

"No," Grant replied. "He wouldn't stop whining so I put him on the deck."

I detected an undertone of guilt and regret in his statement.

Buck said, "Maybe he got off the boat somehow and chased a rabbit or squirrel into the woods."

"Could you help me look for him?"

"Sure."

A moment later, Grant hobbled up the dock and Buck stepped off the back of the *Skinny Dipper* to join him. Buck looked my way. "Jojo's missing. Come help us look for him."

"Sure." I set my sandpaper down. "Let me put Sawdust in the boat first." I picked up Sawdust and placed him inside, glad that neither Buck nor Grant had specifically asked me whether I'd seen Jojo. I'd feel bad lying outright, though I was willing to do it for the dog's sake. Still, I'd rather commit a crime of omission by failing to share information rather than directly stating a falsehood.

We walked over to the woods, all three of us calling the dog's name. I cupped my hands around my mouth. "Jojo! Come here, Jojo!"

As we walked down the shoreline, futilely calling into the woods, we came across the man with the binoculars again. As we approached, he looked down at his guidebook. All we could see was the top of his sunhat. He barely glanced up when we stopped right in front of him.

"Excuse me," Grant said as he leaned on his cane. "Have you seen a loose dog? Black lab mix?"

"Nope. Sorry." The man promptly returned his attention to his guidebook.

Grant frowned at the man's terse, unconcerned reply. We continued past him, still calling Jojo's name. We'd been at our search for a quarter hour when Grant gave up. "He's not here. If he was, he would've come back by now. I never thought he'd figure out how to get the latch open on the gate or I never would have left him on the deck. He must've nudged it with his nose." To Grant's credit, he seemed genuinely remorseful. His shoulders slumped and his eyes were dull. "Maybe someone found him and took him to the pound."

A twinge of guilt made me stiffen. Grant was too busy focusing on the uneven ground in front of him to notice, but Buck did. He looked my way and discreetly raised his brows in question. I mimed twiddling my thumbs and whistling. In other words, *I know something but this is not the time or place for me to share it with you.*

Grant used his cane like a golf club to hit a stone out of his path. "Jojo's got one of those microchips. If he ends up at the pound, I suppose they'll call me."

We returned to our respective vessels to find Mick and Sheila waiting on the dock. The beach bag hung again from Sheila's shoulder. I turned to see Sheila's

Miata in the parking lot. The silver pickup and trailer that had followed her into the public boat launch earlier were nowhere to be seen. *Hmm.*

Mick gave Grant a smile. "'Mornin', captain. Mind if we borrow the boat for a couple of hours?"

Grant shook his head. "Sorry, Mick. It's not a good time. My dog's missing. I need to be here when he gets back. Plus, I've got a date coming by tonight for drinks. I've got to get the boat cleaned up."

Sheila frowned. "But you said we could use the boat any time."

"I didn't think you'd just show up," Grant said. "I figured you'd call or text me first to arrange it."

Mick harrumphed. "Can't you just wait for your dog on the dock?" He pointed to the *Skinny Dipper.* "Or on their boat?"

Sheesh! They were just as presumptuous as Grant.

Buck joined the conversation. "Sorry, but that's a no go. We're sanding the outside today. It's going to be noisy and dusty, not to mention dangerous."

If Jojo wasn't missing, I might feel glad that our construction noise would be giving Grant a taste of his own medicine. But with the dog gone, I wasn't about to gloat. My mind went again to earlier. Had Sheila and Mick left the pickup and trailer at the public boat dock so that they could steal the *Sexy Sheila* back? Maybe they planned to drive the boat over to the public launch, load the boat on the trailer, and drive off with it. As they say, possession is nine-tenths of the law. Maybe they figured they could hide the boat somewhere and put pressure on Grant to accept the check they'd offered him. Then again, maybe it hadn't been Mick driving the pickup. Maybe he'd been at the public boat ramp for some other reason. He could've taken an early morning ride on another boat with a friend, and then had Sheila drive there to pick him up. That scenario seemed unlikely though.

I was debating whether to mention that I'd seen them turn into the public boat ramp earlier that morning when Grant shut the conversation down.

"Look," he said. "Today's just not good, all right? I'm happy to let you use the boat another time. In fact, how about tomorrow? Why don't you two come by around this same time?"

Mick and Sheila exchanged a look before Mick turned back to Grant. "Okay. Tomorrow it is."

With that, they returned to Sheila's Miata and drove off, but not before Mick cast a steely look back at Grant. Grant didn't notice. His eyes were on the woods. I thought he was keeping an eye out for Jojo, but when I followed his gaze, I realized he was staring at the bird-watcher with an expression of anxiety and apprehension on his face. *What's that about?* I decided I must be misinterpreting things. Maybe he wasn't even looking at the bird-watcher at all. Maybe he was merely looking into the trees.

Grant sat on his deck all morning, keeping an eye out for Jojo. His vacant, far-off expression told me that leaving Jojo on the deck overnight likely wasn't his only regret.

When I went into the boat to refill my coffee mug, I spotted him through the window. He was looking over some paperwork he'd pulled from a manila envelope. *Is that the property settlement Deena had referenced? Is he considering signing it now?* I supposed it was none of my business, but it would be nice to see their conflict be resolved. Even so, part of me couldn't blame Grant for holding out with his future up in the air due to his leg injury.

Movement in the parking lot caught my eye as a car turned into the marina. The next thing I knew, Grant practically dived below deck, shutting the cabin door behind him. The guy who'd partied with Grant on Saturday and come by yesterday looking to recoup the hundred bucks he'd loaned Grant was back.

He boarded the *Sexy Sheila* and rapped on the door to the cabin cruiser. *Knock-knock.* When there was no response, he knocked again, louder, and called, "I know you're in there, Grant. I see your Camaro in the parking lot. I want my money."

When there was still no response, he performed the same routine he had yesterday. He disembarked and walked down the dock, cupping his hands around his eyes to try to look into the cabin windows. He slammed a fist down on top of the cabin. *Bam!* "Get your ass out here, Grant!"

I hoped the guy wouldn't come over and ask me and Buck whether Grant was in the boat. I really didn't want to get involved. Fortunately, we didn't have to. The manager of the marina appeared at the end of the dock, heading toward the *Sexy Sheila*.

He raised a hand in the air and waved. "Excuse me, sir! Sir!"

Grant must have called the marina office. He probably figured the manager could get out here faster than law enforcement.

The angry guy turned to look at the approaching man,

but held his fist a few inches above the cabin, ready to bring it down again.

The manager stopped at the back of the boat. "This is a private marina! I'm going to have to ask you to leave."

The guy had fifty pounds on the manager and much more muscle. He looked the man up and down and snickered. "You can ask all you want, but I'm not leaving until Grant gives me my money."

The manager pulled his phone from his pocket. "Well, then. You've left me no option but to call the authorities."

When the guy lowered his hand and began to stalk toward the manager, Buck, who'd been working outside, cleared his throat loudly. "Be cool, bro. It's only money. Don't do something you'll regret."

The guy cast a look at Buck, sized my cousin up, and decided that maybe he had a point—or at least that he didn't want to wrangle with a guy holding an electric sander that could remove three layers of his skin in two seconds flat. He used a flat palm to slap the top of the *Sexy Sheila* and hollered, "You can't hide forever, Grant!" Having delivered his threat, he strode past the manager, checking the older man so hard with his shoulder that it sent him stumbling backward a few feet. Fortunately, the marina manager didn't fall off the dock.

The guy drove off, but not before squealing his pickup truck's tires in the parking lot and sending up a cloud of burnt rubber, dust, and an acrid smell. *Squeee!*

A few seconds later, Grant peeked his head out his cabin door. "Is the coast clear?"

"It is." The manager frowned. "But I can't have you luring unsavory types like that to the marina. If this happens again, you'll have to find a new place to dock your boat."

I didn't blame the man. After all, he'd taken a direct blow to the shoulder while Grant holed up in the boat. It wasn't fair for him to bear the brunt of Grant's mistake. He shook his head and headed back to the administrative building.

Just after noon, the *Caudal Otta Fish* trolled up. The same man was at the helm, and the same passenger sat in the other seat up front. Grant ambled to the end of the dock and climbed aboard. The three puttered off in search of a good fishing spot. Meanwhile, I decided to fill Buck in on last night's visitor to the *Sexy Sheila*.

Buck said, "Grant's stepson took Jojo, huh? The dog'll be better off. He was too high-energy to be cooped up on a boat all the time."

"That's what I thought, too. That's why I didn't tell Grant what I saw. Do you think that was the right thing to do?"

Buck let out a long breath. "It's a gray area. But your heart was in the right place."

"In my throat, you mean?"

Buck tried to relieve my worry and guilt. "It's best we stay out of it. It's up to Grant's ex-wife to decide what to do now."

Deena wasn't Grant's ex yet, but there was no point in correcting Buck. He was right. I should leave it up to the parties involved. Besides, I was feeling less sorry for our neighbor now. He'd put the marina manager at risk earlier. Buck, too. Maybe even me. If they'd gotten into an altercation, I would've felt obliged to grab a wrench and jump into the fray.

Sawdust lounged in the sun in his life jacket on the deck, lying next to the rubber ducky, while Buck and I finished the prep work. We'd just opened and stirred our first can of primer when the *Caudal Otta Fish* stopped at the end of the pier to drop off Grant. They'd been out on the lake only a couple of hours today, but they must have found a good fishing spot. Grant's string held three sizable fish.

The boat eased away as Grant wobbled up the dock on his cane, the fish hanging from his other hand, their tail fins—*caudal* fins—nearly dragging on the deck.

Buck eyed the fish. "Oh, good. You brought lunch. Looks like there's enough for your friend from earlier, too. Why don't you give him a call? Invite him back?"

Grant cast my cousin a look of irritation that only served to make Buck chuckle. While we rolled the primer on the side of the boat, our neighbor retrieved his cutting board and knife from inside his cabin, brought them out onto his deck, and set about gutting and beheading his catch. Once the fillets were ready, he pulled a new jar of Gil's Fish Flavoring from his pocket, removed the clear plastic seal, and sprinkled the seasoning over the fish. After rounding up his small bag of charcoal, the bottle of lighter fluid, and a box of matches, he opened his grill, and peered inside. A layer of half-burnt briquettes remained.

Grant added a few new briquettes and was about to squeeze lighter fluid onto them when Buck stopped him. "Would you mind taking your boat out onto the water to grill your fish? If the smoke blows this way, it'll mess up our paint job."

Grant frowned, but then seemed to remember we'd helped him look for his dog that morning and get rid of the guy pounding his fists on his boat. He owed us at least this small favor. "All right. I'll go out on the lake. At least that way you can't steal my dinner." He cut Buck a look.

Buck and I untied the ropes mooring the *Sexy Sheila* to the dock. Once the boat had been freed, Grant took the helm and slowly pulled out of his slip. The motion caused the beach ball to roll to the back of the deck. It spun to the side as he turned to head out onto the lake. Though he was on the other side of our boat and we could no longer see him, we could tell when he stopped because his motor went silent.

As Buck rolled primer onto the front of the boat, he said, "Don't tell Colette, but Grant's fish seasoning was even better than her blend. I just might ride the ducky out there and steal some catfish from him again."

"Poor guy," I said. "Between you stealing his dinner and his stepson stealing his dog, he can't hold on to anything."

Buck's mouth opened in a laugh, but I couldn't hear it over an unexpected, eardrum-shattering *KABOOM!* The lake and surroundings pulsed with the energy of the explosion, and the percussive force rocked the *Skinny Dipper.* Buck and I fell backward onto the dock, landing hard on our butts. Sawdust slipped off the deck and into the water with a small splash. The floating dock surged below us, riding the waves created by the blast. Propelled by the explosion, a beach ball appeared in the air above, descending toward us like a brightly colored meteor. The ball bounced off the top of the *Skinny Dipper*, bounced once again off the dock, and landed in Grant's empty slip.

Deafened by the explosion, I moved on autopilot. I

pushed myself to a stand and rushed to snatch Sawdust out of the water before he could be crushed between the rocking boat and dock. *Thank goodness for his life jacket!* It had kept him from going under. Sawdust opened his mouth to mew but, still, I could hear nothing. Clutching my drenched cat to my chest, I turned and ran back to join Buck at the end of the dock. As I approached, his raised his hands to his head in horror and helplessness.

I stopped next to my cousin and looked out at the lake. The *Sexy Sheila* was ablaze, fully engulfed in fire. Flaming pieces floated atop the water surrounding it. Oddly, the smoke rising from the wreckage was yellow in color rather than black or gray. There was no sign of Grant in the smoke and flames. *Oh, my gosh. He's dead, isn't he?* As the realization struck, I felt my knees give way and I melted down onto the dock with my cat in my arms. Fortunately, after a beat or two, my wits gathered themselves. I whipped out my phone to call for help. "A boat exploded on Old Hickory Lake!" I cried, naming the marina to give first responders a location. "There was one man on board!" While Grant had spent the afternoon gathering fish to eat, I feared he now served as food for them.

While I spoke to the emergency dispatcher, Buck glanced around frantically. We had yet to replace the motor on the *Skinny Dipper*, so he couldn't take the boat out to try to help. He darted to the back of the boat and grabbed the life ring. He kicked off his boots, ran, and dove off the end of the dock in his coveralls and socks. *Splash!* When he surfaced, he swam as fast as he could, dragging the life ring behind him.

By the time Buck reached the buoy marking the no-wake zone, several other boats had pulled up as close to the conflagration as they dared, the occupants looking over the sides into the water, searching for survivors who might be in the lake. They didn't appear to be finding any. They fanned the smoke from their faces and coughed as they continued to look around. The wind carried some of the smoke my way, and it tickled my nose and throat, too.

Seeming to realize that those on the boats were in a much better position than him to help Grant—assuming the guy was even still alive—Buck turned around and swam back to the dock. With his clothing soaked and his frantic swim having zapped his energy, he had a hard time lifting himself up. I reached down an arm and helped pull him onto the boards. He stayed on all fours for a moment while the lake water ran and dripped off him. When he was able to catch his breath, he turned his head and looked up at me. "What happened out there?"

All I could do was shake my head. I had no idea what had made Grant's boat burst into flames. I only knew we were damn lucky the boat hadn't been at the dock when it happened or we might not have lived to wonder.

CHAPTER 9

CAPSIZED CAT

SAWDUST

Sawdust's heart beat so fast his entire body shook. *What had just happened?!* First there was that horrible loud noise that hurt his ears and made it hard to hear the calming words Whitney was whispering to him now. Then the boat tipped and dumped him in the cold water. He hated water! And if that wasn't already bad enough, an enormous fish with the longest whiskers Sawdust had ever seen darted out from the shadows under the dock and nibbled at his tail! It terrified the poor kitty. Cats were supposed to eat fish, not the other way around!

He tucked his head into Whitney's armpit to hide from the horror.

CHAPTER 10

HOOK, LINE, AND SINKER

WHITNEY

As I cuddled my soaked, shaking cat, a red boat from the fire department raced up to the inferno. The other boats backed off to give the firefighters room to work, though many stopped fifty or so yards away to watch them extinguish the blaze. The smoke billowing from the *Sexy Sheila* gradually turned from that odd yellow to a more-typical dark gray.

Woo-woo-woo! An ambulance raced into the parking lot of the marina. The cargo bay doors opened and two EMTs emerged. They grabbed various pieces of equipment and ran down to the end of the dock to be ready if the firefighters on the boat brought them a patient. I feared they would not. *Thank God Jojo hadn't been on the boat, too!*

Eventually, the firefighters managed to get the blaze under control. Little of the *Sexy Sheila* remained, just the lower hull and part of the front cabin. Debris floated in the water all around. The rest of the boat had apparently sunk. Two other fire department boats arrived. While some worked with nets on poles to gather the pieces of flotsam, others stabilized what remained of the boat and tied it to one of their vessels. I assumed they planned to tug it ashore for examination.

After a few more minutes, the EMTs returned to the ambulance, stashed their things back in the cargo bay, and closed the doors. When the ambulance rolled off with no patient inside, I knew for certain that Grant had lost his life.

Sawdust was shivering from cold and I was shivering with shock when a large red SUV pulled into the marina parking lot and took a spot near Grant's Camaro. The fire department logo was emblazed on the side, along with the words FIRE INVESTIGATION underneath the emblem. They certainly hadn't wasted any time. I supposed when evidence could be destroyed by heat and flames, it was critical to start looking into matters as quickly as possible.

The driver's door opened and a woman in khaki pants and a blue golf shirt with the fire department logo on the chest climbed out. She wore thick-soled black work boots suitable for walking through dangerous rubble, and had thick hair as red as the flames that had destroyed Grant's boat. She closed the door and took a look around, assessing the area. Her gaze eventually locked on me and Buck, and she headed in our direction, an old-fashioned spiral notebook in her hand.

We met behind the *Skinny Dipper.* Up close like this, I could see she wore little makeup, though her skin was nonetheless colored with a multitude of reddish-brown freckles. She looked to be around forty. She extended a hand as she introduced herself. "Deputy Fire Marshal Melanie Landreth."

I shifted Sawdust to the crook of my left arm, took the woman's hand, and introduced myself. Buck followed suit.

She pulled a cheap ballpoint pin from the coil on the spiral and used it to point out at the lake, where the crews continued to pull wreckage from the water. "It's standard procedure for the fire department to gather information after an explosion, get our ducks in a row."

It was an ironic statement. Any real ducks in the area had scattered.

"We saw the boats searching the water," I said. "Did they find Grant's body?"

"Not exactly." Her chest heaved as she took a deep breath. "But we did find evidence that indicates he perished."

Yeesh. I was grateful she didn't elaborate.

She cast a glance out at the water before returning her focus to me. "People tend to sink pretty quickly after an incident in the water. We've got divers looking for him now but it's not always an easy job, especially when a body isn't intact."

Ugh. She'd elaborated after all and now I was left with the thought that Grant had been blown to bits, parts of him strewn all over the muck on the bottom of the lake. He'd been reduced to little more than chum.

Buck said, "I heard there's towns under the water. Houses and streetlights and everything."

"Not in Old Hickory Lake," Landreth said. "You're thinking of Percy Priest and Dale Hollow." She turned back to me. "If the divers don't find him, or at least most of him, we'll send regular patrols through the area.

Once a body starts to decompose, gases build up inside and bring it to the surface."

I swallowed hard, almost sorry I'd asked about the man. "How long does that take?"

"Two, maybe three days. Given the apparent force of the blast, it could come up anywhere in this area."

The thought that Grant—or parts of him—might surface near the *Skinny Dipper* made my head go woozy. Buck grabbed me by the arm to steady me.

Landreth looked from one of us to the other. "You two see what happened?"

My ears had only just stopped ringing. "Actually, it's more like we heard it. A sudden explosion and then a lot of yellowish smoke."

Her brows rose slightly. "The smoke was yellow? You're sure?"

"Yes," I said. "After a while it turned gray, like normal smoke."

Buck and I pulled out our cell phones and showed her the footage we'd captured. She directed us to forward the videos to her cell phone. I suggested she also check with the marina to see if their security cameras might have captured the explosion.

"I talked to the marina management on my way in," she said. "The only functioning security camera is an interior model mounted over the entrance to the marina office. They said they had an exterior system in the past but it was exposed to the weather and constantly broke down so they didn't continue to maintain it."

I looked up at the light posts that stood at intervals along the dock. Although cameras were mounted on a couple of them, the cameras hung askew from their base plates, clearly no longer in service. What's more, the plastic camera casings were brittle and cracked. The summer sun and heat could be relentless. Nashville suffered cold winters, too, with snow and ice. The seasons had taken their toll. The lens on the camera closest to the *Skinny Dipper* bore weblike cracks across the surface. Even if the camera had been functioning, the fractured image would have likely been useless.

The investigator opened her notebook, jotted a note, and looked from me to Buck. "You two familiar with the boat that went up?"

"We are," Buck said. "It was called the *Sexy Sheila*." He pointed to the slip next to ours, which contained nothing but the ironically cheerful-looking beach ball. "It was docked right there not long ago until we asked the owner, Grant something-or-other—"

"Hardisty," I supplied.

"Yeah," Buck said, "Grant Hardisty."

She raised a finger in the give-me-a-moment gesture as she wrote the name down on her pad, repeating it slowly and drawing it out as she did so. "Grant. Hardisty. Okay. And the boat was the *Sexy Sheila*? Got it." She looked back up at Buck. "Go on."

"Grant went fishing earlier today with a couple of older guys on another boat. When he got back, he cleaned the catfish he'd caught. He was about to fire up his grill when I asked him to take the boat out on the water first. We're in the process of painting our houseboat and I didn't want the smoke from his grill to mess up the finish." He gestured to the can of primer still sitting open on the dock, forgotten and drying out. "He drove out a hundred yards or so and dropped anchor. Then, ka-boom!" He put his hands up next to his temples and flicked his fingers to simulate an explosion.

Landreth cocked her head. "Was Grant Hardisty the only person on the boat?"

"Yes," Buck said. "It was just him."

"Did either of you notice whether his grill was a gas grill? Was there a tank attached?"

"No tank," I said. "He used charcoal."

"Gotcha." She made a note in her notebook. "Do you know if Mr. Hardisty had any flammable substances on his boat?"

I said, "He had lighter fluid for the grill."

"How much lighter fluid?" she asked.

"Just the one bottle, as far as I know." I looked to Buck and he nodded to indicate the single bottle was all he'd seen, too.

She made another note in her spiral notebook. "Any idea when he last filled the gas tank on his boat?"

"Saturday," I told her. "He's not the one who filled it, though."

Her brows knit. "He's not?"

"The guy Grant bought the *Sexy Sheila* from came by Saturday morning. Grant called him Mick. Mick's wife is Sheila."

"She the one the boat was named after?"

I nodded. "Grant and Mick had a dispute over the boat. Apparently, Grant bought it from Mick under the condition that Mick could buy it back at some point, but the terms weren't nailed down well." I told her about the spirited debate I'd overheard, how Mick had offered Grant a check and that Grant had refused the payment. "When they first arrived at the marina, Mick asked whether Grant was taking care of the boat and updating the maintenance log. Grant told Mick that the boat was in 'shipshape.'"

"Did Grant show Mick the log? Give him a look around the boat to verify that it was being maintained?"

"No," I said. "But Grant let Mick and Sheila take the boat out. When they brought it back, Mick told Grant he'd topped off the tank." Something else Mick said came back to me, too. Something portentous. "Mick also said that he and Sheila thought they smelled gas fumes when they'd first boarded the boat. He reminded Grant to turn the blowers off when he gassed up, and suggested he get the fuel hoses looked at to make sure they didn't have leaks."

"Did Grant do that? Get the hoses checked out?"

"Not that I know of. I didn't see him take the boat out for repairs, and I didn't notice a boat mechanic come by. What about you, Buck?" I looked to my cousin.

He shrugged and raised his palms.

Landreth said, "Sounds like he might have failed to maintain the vessel properly. Dangerous gases can build up in the bilge if a boat isn't taken care of." She paused a moment. A cloud seemed to pass through her eyes, though she didn't say what she was thinking. Instead, she asked, "Other than today, when Mr. Hardisty moved the boat at your request, has he used the boat since Mick fueled it up?"

"He took some men out Saturday afternoon." I told her what Grant had told me. That he'd met the guys in a bar and invited them to spend Saturday afternoon on the boat. "They were out on the water for around three hours. We're pretty sure we saw them water skiing." I had no idea how much gas a boat burned, but the trip had probably depleted only a nominal amount of the fuel store. If the boat's gas tank had been filled recently, that would explain why the explosion was so big and why the fire got out of control so quickly. The tank on our houseboat held two-hundred gallons of fuel. The cabin cruiser's tank was likely similar in size. *That's an awful lot of gasoline.*

"Any idea who the men were?" she asked.

"No," I said, "but he told us he'd met them at the bar where he'd gone to meet a woman he'd connected with through Match.com. He showed us her photo on his phone app." Of course, I also remembered how he'd said she looked nothing like her photo when she'd shown up, how it seemed like she'd pulled a bait and switch.

Buck added, "One of the men has come by twice since Saturday, trying to collect money he loaned to Grant. He's been pretty forceful about it. The marina manager had to throw him off the property earlier today."

Buck didn't mention that Grant owed him money, too. Of course, this was America, where people have the right not to incriminate ourselves. Besides, Buck had nothing to do with the explosion. Mentioning the money he'd loaned Grant would only muddy the waters.

After making another note in her spiral, she asked, "Did Mr. Hardisty scuba dive?"

"Not that we know of," I said. "Why? Can the oxygen tanks explode?"

"Contrary to popular belief, scuba tanks contain other gases in addition to oxygen," she replied. "The better term is *air tank*. It's extremely rare for the tanks to explode, but it's not unheard of. That said, when they explode they simply burst open. They don't cause fires on their own. But if a tank exploded on his boat, it could have damaged a propane tank in his galley if he had a propane stove, or it could have punctured a fuel line and ignited a fire. There's lots of possibilities. I'm hoping the wreckage will provide some clues, but that might not pan out given the strength of the explosion and the severity of the fire. There doesn't appear to be much of anything left."

The thought that someone could be blown to smithereens and essentially disappear from the face of the earth made my stomach twist.

"I'll need to notify Mr. Hardisty's next of kin," Landreth said. "Do you know if he was married?"

"He was," I said. "His wife's name is Deena."

"Any idea where they lived?"

"He lived on the boat," I said. "I'm not sure where she lives. They were in the middle of a divorce. They hadn't been married long. Only a little over a year."

She paused for a beat or two. "I see. Do you know if she took his last name?"

"She did," I said. "She came by here yesterday to talk to Grant. She works at Vanderbilt University Medical Center. She was wearing scrubs and an employee badge with her name on it. It said 'Deena Hardisty.'"

"Good. That'll help me track her down." She closed her notebook and pointed her pen at the *Sexy Sheila*'s slip. "For now, let's keep the identity of the boat and the occupant between us, all right? At least until I notify his wife. Don't talk to reporters, either. Okay? We need to process the scene and determine what happened. It can be difficult for us if inaccurate information gets out."

Buck and I agreed to keep mum.

She slid her pen back into the rings on her spiral notebook and tucked it under her arm. "Thanks for the information, folks. Depending on what the lab turns up, I may or may not be back."

With that, the investigator gave us a final nod and left us to our project and our thoughts. Naturally, our thoughts immediately went to the people in Grant's life and how they'd react on hearing the news that he'd perished in an explosion.

Deena might be horrified by the manner of Grant's death, but I doubted she'd miss the guy. With him now blown to bits, there'd be no need for a property settlement. She'd get to keep her assets. She'd probably get his Camaro, too. *I wonder if she'll let Tanner drive it.* Jackie would get no satisfaction, I supposed, but I don't think she'd truly expected to. I think she'd only come by to give her ex a little hell and even the score a bit. Mick would never have the chance to buy back the *Sexy Sheila*. The captain of the *Caudal Otta Fish* would have lost one of his fishing buddies, but at least he still had the other guy. Unsuspecting women on the dating apps would be spared the humiliation of being fleeced by the gold-digging Prince Charming. It was sad to think that Grant Hardisty's death was a net positive for others but, then again, he'd been the one to create that equation. I only hoped that, when I passed, the math worked out differently.

CHAPTER 11
SMOKE SIGNALS

WHITNEY

Shortly after Landreth departed, my cell phone blared and jiggled in the pocket of my coveralls. I set the primer-covered roller down and pulled out my phone. The screen read COLLIN FLYNN. I tapped the button to accept the call and put the phone to my ear. "Hey, Collin."

"Are you okay?" he asked. "I heard there was some sort of explosion at Old Hickory Lake."

"There was. Remember the guy I told you about? The one in the slip next to us?"

"The one who plays 'Rock and Roll All Nite' twenty-four seven?"

"Yeah. That's the one." *He won't be playing the song anymore. I might almost miss it.* "His boat blew up."

I swear I could hear Collin's jaw come unhinged. "It blew up right next to you? Are you hurt?"

"Fortunately, no," I said. "Sawdust was thrown off the boat but he was only scared, not injured."

He released a loud breath. "Thank goodness."

"Grant was about to start up his grill to cook some fish he'd caught, but Buck and I were priming the boat, and Buck asked him to take his boat out on the water so it wouldn't mess up our paint job. He was about a hundred yards from us when his boat exploded." I told him about the caustic yellow smoke.

"Yellow, huh? Sounds like it could have been an incendiary fire."

"Incendiary?" I wasn't familiar with the term.

"Intentionally set," he clarified. "An accelerant might have been used."

Could it be true? Had someone blown up the boat on purpose? "An investigator from the fire department came out. A woman named Melanie Landreth. You know her?"

"I've met her before. We attended training together on active shooter and mass casualty situations."

What a sick, messed-up world we live in. "She questioned Buck and me briefly. She said they're going to examine the debris and, if anything looks suspicious, she'll be back." I swallowed the lump in my throat. "There's no sign of Grant. Not alive anyway. If the explosion wasn't an accident, I wonder if you'll be assigned to work the homicide."

"It's unlikely," Collin said. "When someone dies in a fire or explosion that was deliberately set, the murder falls under the fire department's authority. Metro PD will help if requested, but otherwise we stay out of it."

Though Collin and I made a great crime-solving team, I was glad we wouldn't be investigating Grant Hardisty's death. I'd come across bodies before, but I'd never actually witnessed a death taking place. Seeing someone lose their life was exponentially more horrifying than finding them already deceased.

Collin realized I'd be upset. "Why don't I come by tonight and take you out to dinner? It'll take your mind off things for a while."

"I'd love that, Collin. Thanks."

We arranged for him to swing by around six o'clock.

Buck and I continued to apply the primer, working in silence. Normally, Buck would play his favorite country tunes while he worked and sing along, and we'd engage in idle conversation or good-natured ribbing. But not this afternoon. The day felt somber, and making noise would seem disrespectful. I found myself occasionally glancing over at Slip 27, finding it difficult to believe that the *Sexy Sheila* had been floating there only hours before. Now, the empty rectangle seemed to be a watery grave.

At half past five, while Buck worked at the front of the boat, a fiftyish woman wandered up the dock. She wore a sheath dress and heels, fresh from an office job. Her dark hair was pulled up into a sleek twist. Unlike many women her age, who still sported the thin brows that had been in vogue when they were younger, her brows were thick and full. My guess was she'd had them enhanced with microblading for a more contemporary look. She carried one of those open woven totes that was equal parts bag and basket. A pair of flip-flops peeked out of the top, along with a bottle of suntan oil, nestled among a towel and what appeared to be beach-type attire. She stared at the empty slip that had—until a few hours ago—housed the *Sexy Sheila*.

She looked my way and pointed at the empty slip. "Is this where a guy named Grant usually keeps his boat?"

My stomach churned. This must be another woman he'd met on a dating app, the one he'd told Mick and Sheila he needed to clean up the boat for. I stepped off our boat and onto the dock so I could address her privately. "It was," I said. "I'm sorry to have to tell you this, but there's been an accident. A bad one."

"An accident?" She turned and looked out at the fire boats on the lake. Her eyes went wide as she turned back to me. "Did something happen to Grant?"

"Unfortunately, yes. His boat exploded."

Seemingly thrown off-kilter by the news, she reached out a hand to grab the pedestal where our electrical connection was plugged in. She put the other hand to her chest as if to slow her heart. She turned to gaze again at the empty slip. Her face puckered as she mused softly aloud. "I wonder whether Jackie caused it," she said under her breath.

Or at least that's what I thought I'd heard. "Did you say 'Jackie'?" I asked. *Could Grant's ex-wife number four have done this?*

A look of panic skittered across the woman's face and she shook her head vehemently as she removed her hands from her chest and the pedestal, straightening. "No, no, no. I said I wonder what *exactly* caused it."

Had I truly misheard her? Or was she trying to cover something up? "It's under investigation. I'm sure the authorities will figure it out." I cocked my head and eyed her. "Were you two dating?"

"No. I hadn't met Grant in person yet, but we connected on a dating site and we've been chatting by e-mail and text for a couple of weeks. He invited me out to his boat tonight for drinks and a cruise on the lake. He confirmed with me earlier today." She took a few breaths to calm herself.

It was a horrible, awkward situation. I had no idea what to say, but figured I couldn't go wrong with, "I'm sorry. I know he was looking forward to meeting you. He mentioned that he was going to clean up his boat for your date."

Her mouth formed a shape that was half-smile, half-grimace. "Thanks. I guess I should . . . just go?"

I nodded. *What else was there for her to do?* "Take care."

She returned to her sporty Audi coupe, opened the door, and wrangled the tote into the tiny backseat. As she drove off, I spotted the bottle of suntan oil lying in the parking lot. It must've fallen out of her carryall. No sense leaving it on the asphalt where it would likely get run over. I left the boat and walked out to the parking lot to retrieve the bottle. I noticed it was the same brand that Grant used. *That's a coincidence.* It was full, too, apparently brand new. I had no idea who the woman was and, thus, no way of returning the bottle to her. But I wouldn't let it go to waste. Though I usually bought a higher-SPF lotion, it had an eight sun-protection factor. I could use it on days when I didn't expect to be outside for extended lengths of time.

I slid the bottle into a pocket on my coveralls and returned to the boat. After putting the top on my can of primer, I rinsed my roller and brushes, and went into the boat. I stashed the suntan oil in the bathroom cabinet, and set about cleaning myself up. Sawdust watched from atop the toilet seat as I slid into a pair of jeans, sandals, and a girly top, and gave my hair a quick curl. I put on earrings and applied light makeup to my face. I turned to my cat. "Do I look okay?" He stood, purring, and looked up at me as if he thought I was the most beautiful being who'd ever lived. Say what you will about cats, but my Sawdust was good for my ego. I reached out to stroke his ears. "Thanks, boy. I needed that."

Knock-knock. I looked up to see Collin standing at the door. I grabbed my purse and stepped out onto the deck. Buck was priming the upper deck now. I called up to him as we left. "I'll be back around nine!"

"It's gonna be a hot one tomorrow," he called. "Pick up some Gatorade."

"Will do!"

Collin and I drove to a Thai restaurant in northeast Nashville. I ordered fried rice and a glass of chenin blanc. Collin got the pad Thai and a Singha beer. Over dinner, I told him about the plans Emmalee and I had come up with for Colette's bachelorette party. "How are the plans coming along for Buck's bachelor party?"

"Owen and I thought we'd order some pizza and get a keg of beer."

"That's it?" I rolled my eyes. "You men are so lazy."

Collin shrugged. "Pizza and beer pretty much describes every bachelor party I've been to."

"At least come up with a signature cocktail for the party and some games."

He mused aloud. "Best cannonball off the upper deck? Pool-noodle races? Beach-ball volleyball?"

"That's more like it. In fact, I'm going to steal the beach-ball volleyball idea."

We finished our meal and climbed back into his car

to return to the *Skinny Dipper.* It wasn't until we were nearly back to the marina that I remembered Buck asking me to pick up some Gatorade. We were far from any full-service grocery story, but the Get-N-Git sat only a short way ahead.

I pointed to the store as we approached. "Pull in there right quick. I need to run in and get some drinks."

"Better hurry." Collin rolled to a stop and pointed to the posted hours. The store would close at nine.

Collin's dashboard clock read 8:58. I had two minutes to get in and get out. I leapt from his car and hustled inside. An attractive sixtyish woman stood behind the counter. Her dark brown hair framed her face in feathery layers, a style that had been popular in the disco era and seemed to be making a quiet comeback. She wore a colorful bohemian tunic over leggings, her outfit stylish but easy to move around in.

"I'll be quick," I said.

"No worries," she said. "Take your time."

The fact that she would rather have my business than close on time told me she might own the place.

"Anything I can help you find?" she asked.

"Sports drinks."

She pointed to the far left of the refrigerated cooler. "Back there. You can't miss them."

"Thanks!" I scurried to the back of the store and gathered a half dozen bottles of Gatorade in my arms. As I was heading up the aisle, my eyes spotted a jar of the fish seasoning Grant Hardisty had used on his catfish, the one Buck had also liked, Gil's Fish Flavoring. The whiskered cartoon catfish eyed me from the jar. I'd earlier thought the fish looked like he was smiling, but after what happened today it looked more like he was screaming. Hearing that explosion and witnessing the aftermath had really done a number on me. I grabbed a jar of the seasoning, too, hoping I wouldn't drop anything before I made it to the checkout.

I plunked the merchandise down on the counter. The woman rang it up for me and placed it in a heavy-duty paper bag with a handle. "Thanks for shopping at the Get-N-Git. You got what you came for." She pointed at the door, grinning. "Now Git!"

It was a silly shtick, and one I presumed she used often. Nevertheless, I found myself chuckling at her mock rudeness. I really needed a laugh about then. "Thanks!"

She circled around the counter as I exited the door. I heard the click of her locking it behind me as I headed to Collin's car. Once I was seated, she turned off the outdoor and indoor lights, though the neon beer signs over the refrigerated coolers provided dim illumination inside.

Collin started his car and pulled out of the parking lot. When we arrived at the marina, Collin carried the bag to the *Skinny Dipper* for me. Buck sat on the upper deck, having finished applying the primer and now enjoying the cool evening. Sawdust lounged on the spiral staircase, reaching out a paw to swipe at bugs who flew by on their way to gather in a frenzied mob under the dock lights.

I called up to Buck. "Got your drinks, Cuz! Got you a surprise, too."

His face appeared as he looked down over the railing. "What is it?"

I reached into the bag Collin was holding and pulled

out the fish seasoning. I held the jar up and shook it. "It's that seasoning you liked. The one you said was even better than Colette's."

Collin gasped loudly in jest. "He didn't!"

"He did."

Buck frowned. "You two better keep that to yourselves. Colette will take a wooden spoon to my backside if she hears I said anyone's cooking was better than hers. She'd never feed me again, either."

Buck was in no danger of starving to death. Since he and Colette had begun dating, he'd put on a few pounds, even more after she'd opened her café. He'd better watch it or he might not fit into his tux for their wedding. Of course, I was one to talk. My waistline had expanded since she and I had moved in together, too. She kept the fridge stocked with fresh food and ready-made meals that only had to be popped into the microwave. I realized then that, once she moved out, my roommate Emmalee and I would be back on our own, having to do our own grocery shopping and cook our own meals. *Sigh.*

After I stashed the drinks in the refrigerator and the seasoning in the pantry, I walked Collin back out to the deck. There, he pulled me to him and held me for a long time, gently stroking my hair much like I stroked Sawdust. "You okay?" he asked.

"Getting there," I said softly. It had been an awful day, but I'd suffered no personal loss. Still, I'd feel much better once we knew for certain whether the explosion had been an accident. I hoped it had been. It was bad enough that a man had lost his life in such a gruesome manner, but it was even more horrifying to think that someone could be so cruel and callous as to kill Grant on purpose in such a showy way. I prayed that wasn't the case.

My prayers went unanswered.

Over coffee on the deck the next morning, Buck said, "I almost miss the blaring music and the scent of coconut tanning oil."

"Me too."

I logged into my computer to see what had been reported about the explosion. Though there were multiple links to websites for various local TV and radio stations, they contained very little information. A boat had exploded on Old Hickory Lake. The cause was under investigation. One person was presumed dead. But while the reports contained little in the way of facts, they were accompanied by a half dozen sensational videos recorded by witnesses on their cell phones. Most only showed the aftermath, but one had even captured the explosion itself, in the background of a video of a man reeling in a large catfish. The videos were accompanied by audio tracks wherein the witnesses cried out and exclaimed, said prayers, or, in some cases, cursed in surprise. *"Did you see that boat go up? Holy* bleep*!"*

At half past eight, Melanie Landreth walked up the dock.

We went to stand but she motioned for us to keep our seats. "No need for formalities," she said.

"Cup of coffee?" I asked. Though I told myself I was being mannerly, my true motive was likely to put off hearing the bad news she'd likely come to share. After all, if the explosion had been an accident, there'd be nothing more to discuss, would there?

"Coffee would be great," she said. "I take it black."

I went inside and poured coffee into a mug for her. When I returned, I found her sitting on a lower step on the spiral staircase, dangling her keychain in front of Sawdust. He batted the keys around, happy to have found a new playmate. I handed her the warm mug.

She thanked me and took a sip before getting down to business. "The lab report came back first thing this morning. Traces of ammonium nitrate were found on some of the debris and in the water samples that were taken. I suspected as much yesterday when you told me about the yellow smoke. Ammonium nitrate burns yellow."

"I've heard of that stuff." Buck's eyes narrowed. "Is that what's in fertilizer? Like what was used in the Oklahoma City bombing?"

"Mm-hmm," she said. "Ammonium nitrate isn't generally combustible itself unless exposed to intense heat, but it can act as an accelerant and can be dangerous if it's not properly stored or if it comes in contact with fuel. It's been involved in several accidental explosions and fires at fertilizer factories. There was an explosion in Texas a few years back, and one more recently in Winston-Salem, North Carolina. That particular fire burned for days. They had to evacuate a large area around the fire because the smoke and fumes were making people sick. There was a huge explosion in Beirut a few years back that involved ammonium nitrate, too. Two hundred and twenty people were killed."

"The chemical has exploded unintentionally, then," I pointed out. "Does that mean the explosion on the *Sexy Sheila* could have been an accident?"

"Only if Grant Hardisty had a good reason for having large quantities of ammonium nitrate on his boat, and I can't think of one. He has no lawn out here, no need for fertilizer."

"Maybe he'd bought some to put on the yard at his wife's house," I said. "He seemed to be trying to win her back. Maybe he thought he could do something nice, spruce up the yard, and she'd forgive him."

"If that's the case," Landreth said, "why not store the fertilizer in her garage rather than on his boat?"

She had a point. I was only trying to figure out whether there was any other logical explanation for what had happened.

"That said," she continued, "our crime scene techs will check his car for any trace of ammonium nitrate. If he'd bought it himself, there might be traces in his trunk. For now, though, I'm going on the assumption this was an intentional explosion." She drank the remainder of her coffee in one long gulp, then sat the cup down on the deck. Much to Sawdust's disappointment, she returned her keys to her pocket and pulled out her notepad.

Landreth's gaze shifted between me and Buck. "Did you two see anything suspicious out here? Anyone nosing around the boat before the explosion?"

"No," Buck said. "I didn't see anyone other than the guy we told you about, the one who was raising a ruckus about the money Grant owed him. But I wouldn't call what he was doing *nosing around.* He was hardly being subtle."

If he'd had something to do with the explosion, he would've tried to be sneakier, wouldn't he?

"I'm planning to obtain Grant's communications from the dating site and see if I can determine which bar he went to Friday night. Maybe someone there can identify the man you're talking about."

"He drives a silver pickup," Buck told her, not that it would likely be much help. Neither he nor I had noticed the make or model, and pickup trucks were fairly common vehicles.

Landreth turned to me and inquired if I had seen any other suspicious persons around. I shook my head, but that only made another thought, an awful one, fall into place. I had indeed seen someone nosing around before the *Sexy Sheila* blew up. Tanner. *If the boat explosion wasn't an accident, could Tanner could have had something to do with it?* It seemed coincidental that he'd come by the night just prior to the explosion and taken the dog. Maybe he wanted to get the sweet, energetic pooch out of harm's way. But maybe he'd only come to get Jojo because he loved his pet and knew the dog would be happier at their house. I wasn't about to implicate the kid, not until I spoke to him myself first and felt him out.

Landreth tried another tack. "Do you know of any other particular person who might have wanted to blow up the boat or kill Grant?"

"Wait." My head cocked of its own accord. "Blow up the boat *or* kill Grant? You're distinguishing the two?"

She raised a shoulder. "Sometimes arsonists only mean to destroy property but people get accidentally hurt or killed in the process. Collateral damage."

My thoughts went to Mick and Sheila, how they'd wanted to buy the boat back but Grant had refused. I reminded Landreth about the conversation I'd overheard among the three. She asked me to run through the argument again in more detail.

I did my best to remember the exact exchange. "Apparently, when Mick sold the boat to Grant it was subject to some sort of buyback agreement, but they got into a dispute over the exact terms. Mick wanted to buy the boat back now, but Grant argued that he needed the boat to live in, at least until his divorce was finalized. Well, actually, he told Mick he needed either the boat or fifty thousand dollars. Mick said he wasn't about to pay Grant that much for the boat when Grant had paid him much less for it. Grant told Mick he'd sell the boat back to him once his financial circumstances improved. That's where they left things."

Landreth angled her head in one direction, then the other, as she mulled over what I'd told her. "That situation could go either way. Mick might have figured that if he didn't get to enjoy his boat, nobody else should, either. He might have been motivated to blow up the boat out of spite. But if he truly thought he'd get the boat back one day, it wouldn't be in his interests to destroy it."

I remembered the icy look Sheila had cast at Grant. It had been cold enough to freeze water. Maybe she was the metaphorical iceberg that sunk the *Titanic*. "Sheila apologized to her husband. She said the situation was her fault."

"Do you know what she meant by that?"

"No," I told Landreth. "She didn't say. You think Sheila could have done it? Maybe she didn't like to see her husband be humiliated, or maybe she wanted to get revenge?"

"Could be," Landreth said.

"Something else about them has been bothering me, too," I said. "If they smelled gas when they boarded the boat, why would they take it out on the water? Seems like they'd know the situation could be dangerous."

A wry smile pulled at Landreth's lips. "I had the same thought the first time you mentioned it."

Aha. That explains the dark look that had passed through her eyes when we first spoke about it. I wondered if Mick and Sheila had mentioned the gas smell in the hopes of getting it on the record, so to speak. They might have realized I could hear them through the kitchen window and wanted someone to note that they mentioned the alleged gas smell. Maybe, while they'd had the boat, they'd somehow sabotaged it, punctured a fuel line or something like that. But wouldn't that pose a risk that they'd blow themselves up before they made it back to the dock? And why would they want to destroy the boat they'd so desperately wanted to buy back? I wasn't sure things made sense.

Landreth interrupted my reverie. "I'll talk to Mick and Sheila. Any chance you know their last name?"

"No. It didn't come up."

"No problem. I can get it from the boat registration records." She made a note on her pad before looking up again. "Anyone else you might consider a possible suspect?"

"Grant's ex-wife Jackie," I said. "She came by looking for him. She had some sort of beef over furniture that he'd been awarded in their divorce and was supposed to pay for but hadn't. She ended up paying off the account so it wouldn't ruin her credit."

"Don't suppose you've got a last name for her either? If not, I can check the marriage records."

"No, I don't have a last name," I said, "but I do have her phone number. She gave it to me so I could relay it to Grant in case he'd deleted it." I pulled up my contacts list and held up my screen to show her the number I'd entered for "Jackie GrantsEx#4."

Landreth jotted the number down in her spiral, glancing back and forth between my screen and her notebook to double-check that she'd written it down correctly.

A bird flew overhead, casting a moving shadow across the boat and cawing loudly. "There's someone else," I said. "He doesn't have anything to do with Grant Hardisty or the *Sexy Sheila*, but he might have some evidence that could help you. He's a birder. He was out here nearly every day for hours at a time watching the ospreys. He had a camera and binoculars, fancy ones with a built-in video recorder. Maybe he caught something on video that would help. I don't know who he is, but I could keep an eye out for him and get his contact information when he comes back."

"That would be great." She fished a business card out of her pocket and held it out to me. "You can give him this, too." She wrote another note in her spiral before looking up again. "What did Mr. Hardisty do for a living?"

I felt my mouth screw into a wry twist. I hated to speak ill of the most-probably dead, but I didn't want to mislead the investigator, either. "He mentioned that he used to work as a bartender, but he never said where. From what I gleaned, most of his support came from his wives. Seems he married well and often." I told her that, based on what I'd seen and heard, I pegged him as a gold-digger who targeted professional women. "He fell a few weeks back and hurt his knee, and hasn't been able to work since. He used a cane to get around."

She made another note and looked from me to Buck. "Anything else you can tell me about him?"

Buck grunted. "His favorite song was 'Rock and Roll All Nite' by Kiss. He must've played it five dozen times since we came out here to fix up the *Skinny Dipper*."

She chuckled. "Well, it is a classic." As she'd done before, she slid the ballpoint pen into the rings on her notebook and tucked it under her arm. "Thanks, folks. If you think of anything else, don't hesitate to call."

After she left, I gathered up the kitchen trash and went to add it to the bin on the deck so I could lug the whole lot down to the marina's dumpster for pickup. As I went to upend the smaller trash can, my eyes spotted one of Grant's cold packs in the garbage bin. He must have tossed it in when we weren't looking. I gasped when I saw the list of contents. The first ingredient was ammonium nitrate.

CHAPTER 12

TOO LITTLE, TOO LATE

WHITNEY

I grabbed the cold pack and pulled it from the trash. It was ambient temperature now, the chemicals that caused the chill having long-since played themselves out. "Buck!" I called. "Come here!"

He'd gone inside to change into his coveralls, and came out wearing them. "What are you hollering about?"

"This!" I held up the cold pack and pointed to the list of contents.

He stepped over and read aloud. "Ammonium nitrate." His eyes shifted from the package to me. "Uh-oh."

"*Uh-oh* is right. This is one of the cold packs Deena gave to Grant. She brought him an entire case. I thought it was nice of her, especially since they're divorcing—"

"But maybe it wasn't nice at all," Buck said. "Maybe she was filling his boat with ammonium nitrate so he'd blow sky-high."

I weighed the cold pack in my hand. "This isn't very

big or heavy. It seems like it would take a lot of these to blow up a boat."

"Maybe there were more on the boat than just the one case we saw her bring to Grant. Tanner could've put a bunch of those cold packs around the boat when he came to dognap Jojo."

Could he? I wasn't sure there'd been enough time between me waking up and glancing outside for him to load the boat with cold packs. Then again, the live well, a built-in bin where fishermen could keep their catch alive in water, was empty. Tanner could've easily and quickly filled the well with the packs. It would take only a matter of seconds to dump a bunch of them out of a box or bag.

Buck frowned. "You've got to tell Landreth."

"But I promised Tanner I wouldn't tell anyone I saw him taking the dog."

Buck grimaced. "You can't keep your promise to that kid, especially now. You need to call Landreth back and tell her what you found."

"I will," I said, "but I'd like to talk to Tanner and Deena first, feel them out. We don't know if either of them even knew there was ammonium nitrate in the cold packs, or that it could be used to cause an explosion. Besides, it seems a little odd they'd just leave the stuff on the boat without detonating it, doesn't it? Grant could have found the cold packs before they blew up and their plan would go up in smoke."

"Maybe they'd set a timer."

"Wouldn't that require some sophistication? Some technical knowledge?"

Buck snorted. "All it would require is an internet search."

I decided to test his theory. I carried the cold pack inside, booted up my laptop at the kitchen table, and searched for how to make ammonium nitrate explode. It didn't sound quite as easy to improvise a detonator as Buck implied. It would still require some technical know-how, as well as some luck to make sure the detonator functioned correctly. Nevertheless, it was doable.

So long as I was on my computer, I searched for "ammonium nitrate explosions involving cold packs." On reading a couple of links that noted the chemical had been extracted from medical cold packs to be used in explosions, my heart grew as cold as the packs themselves. It was possible the cold packs had caused the explosion. The only question remaining was, if the cold packs had been involved in the explosion, had they been intentionally or inadvertently involved?

Leaving the cold pack on the kitchen table, I closed my laptop and went back outside. "I'm still not entirely convinced. The two of them would be rid of Grant once the divorce was final. There'd be no need to kill the guy. They were clearly frustrated with him, but is that enough motive to end someone's life and risk spending the rest of your own in jail? And if they'd set a timer, they'd have no assurance Grant would even be on the boat at the time. Plus, they'd have to know they were risking hurting or killing other people. You and me, specifically. Would they really be so cold-hearted?"

Buck exhaled sharply. "You want to go talk to them and find out more before you say anything to Landreth, don't you?"

My cousin knew me well. "Yes."

"All right. But I'm not about to let you go alone."

"Aww." I gave him a punch in the arm. "You love me, don't you, Cuz?'

"I can't hardly stand you," he teased. "I just need someone to help me finish this boat."

"Let's go to their house this evening. Tanner will be home from school then, and maybe Deena will be home, too." I hoped she wouldn't be at work. I'd prefer to speak to them both at once.

Buck and I spent the day applying the shiny white paint to the outside of the boat, starting on the upper deck and working our way down. I couldn't risk Sawdust getting fur in the paint, so I'd left him inside today. He had to settle for watching us work through the window. All the while, I wondered what Tanner and Deena would tell us. Did the cold packs have anything to do with the explosion? Was Deena's apparent concern and generosity nothing more than a charade, a way to get dangerous chemicals onto to Grant's boat? Had Tanner taken Jojo Monday night to get him out of harm's way? Had he planted more of the cold packs about the boat then?

I was pondering these questions when I was jarred from my mental meandering by an "Excuse us!"

I turned to see Mick and Sheila standing on the dock. Mick was dressed in nice shorts and a short-sleeved cotton shirt. Sheila wore her wedge sandals again, though this time she'd paired them with a pair of skin-tight capri leggings in a leopard print and a fitted black tank top. As before, her face was spackled with copious amounts of makeup and her hair had been teased so hard it looked as if she'd stuck her finger in a socket. I greeted them with a "Hello."

Mick pointed to Slip 27. "Do you know when Grant will be back?"

Um . . . never? Apparently, Landreth hadn't spoken to these two yet. She probably hadn't had time yet to search the boat registration records and get out to their house. Or maybe she'd focused first on Jackie. I hated to be the one to give them the news, but there was no way around it. I walked down the deck and stepped off the boat to address them eye to eye. "I'm sorry to say this, but Grant won't be back. Ever."

Mick's face turned purple and his fists clenched at his sides. "Are you saying Grant moved my boat off the lake? If he's trying to hide my boat from me I'll ki—"

I stopped his tirade with a raised palm. "No. That's not what I'm saying at all. There was . . ." *An accident? An explosion? A murder?* I decided to go with "an incident."

Sheila scoffed. "*An incident.* What does that mean?"

"It means the *Sexy Sheila* was destroyed and Grant was killed."

"Killed?" She jerked her head back as if she'd been slapped. "What? What the hell happened?" Before I could answer, she cut a furtive look at her husband. He cut her an equally furtive look right back.

"The boat caught fire," I said, being intentionally vague to see if they might slip and mention an explosion.

"How?" Sheila asked.

"The cause hasn't been determined yet."

Mick cleared his throat, seemingly upset by the news. "Was Grant trapped in the cabin?"

Though I knew, or at least suspected, that Grant had been on his desk lighting his grill, I continued to keep my cards close to my vest. "I don't know all the details. Sorry."

Sheila was already on her cell phone, typing with thumbs tipped in long, pointy nails painted metallic purple. She tapped the screen and appeared to be skimming over news reports. "Says here a boat exploded on Old Hickory Lake yesterday. The cause is still under investigation." It could have been my imagination, but her faced seemed to pale under all her makeup.

"Explosion?" Mick snarled. "I bet Grant let gas build up in the bilge. That guy couldn't even take care of himself. I never should have trusted him to take care of my boat!"

Mick seemed much more concerned about the boat than his deceased friend. Or course, that so-called friend had screwed the guy over. Maybe he thought Grant had gotten what he deserved. *Or maybe Mick made sure Grant got what he deserved.*

Sheila stared at her husband for a couple of beats, her forehead furrowing in question. Was she, too, wondering whether her husband might have intentionally killed the guy he'd considered to have stolen his boat from him? Was she also wondering whether the buildup of gas in the bilge was a convenient explanation intended to mislead others into thinking the explosion had been an accident? If Mick had been the one to blow up the boat, maybe he had assumed the boat would sink entirely and that any trace of the ammonium nitrate would be washed away.

I eyed them closely. "What brings you by?"

"I planned to make Grant an offer on the boat." Mick reached into the breast pocket of his shirt and pulled out a folded check. He unfolded it to show it to me. The check was made out to Grant Hardisty in the amount of $20,000. The preprinted names on the check read RAYMOND AND SHEILA MCNEELY, the last name no doubt giving rise to Mick's nickname. According to the information on the check, the two lived in Nashville. I quickly memorized their street address. He refolded the check and slid it back into his pocket.

"Twenty grand is quite a bit more than y'all had agreed to, isn't it? I overheard you tell Grant earlier that when you sold him the boat he'd agreed to sell the boat back to you for twelve thousand." Of course, that figure hadn't made it into the written contract Grant subsequently prepared.

Sheila scowled and put her hands on her hips. "You were eavesdropping on our conversation? That's rude."

Is she really trying to make me *the bad guy here?* "No, I wasn't eavesdropping. I just happened to overhear it." I gestured to Slip 27. "There's not much space between these slips and you three weren't exactly speaking quietly, if you recall." If anyone had been rude, it had been them, shouting and carrying on with Buck and me trying to work peacefully just ten feet away.

The two exchanged glances again. Mick had the sense to look at least a little ashamed. He cast a final glance at Slip 27 before turning back to his wife. "Let's go."

They walked off without saying another word, let alone a goodbye. As they departed, I wondered whether our interaction here had been a charade. Had they killed Grant for refusing to sell the boat back to them, then come by today to try to make themselves look innocent? I had no way of knowing, but those odd looks the two gave each other told me they hadn't likely worked in cahoots. In fact, each of them had appeared slightly suspicious of the other.

As soon as they drove off, I retrieved Landreth's business card and called the cell number listed on it. "Mick and Sheila just came by," I told her. "I've got a last name and an address for you if you haven't already dug it up."

"I haven't," she said. "I started with the ex."

"Jackie? You've talked to her?"

"I did."

"What did she say?"

"That she had nothing to do with what happened to Grant," Landreth said. "She was quite cooperative. She allowed me to look around her place and review her computer browsing history. There were no red flags. She even let me check the location history on her car's tracking system. The last time her car was at the marina was when she spoke with you."

"Could she have come back in a rented vehicle? Or maybe a car she borrowed from a family member or friend?"

"It's possible," she said, "but renting a car would have left a paper trail and borrowing a car would mean the owner could implicate her. She didn't strike me as a woman who'd be dumb enough to leave a paper trail or potential witnesses."

Jackie hadn't struck me as stupid, either. Then again, she'd been senseless enough to fall for a gold digger like Grant. But even intelligent people could fall victim to a romantic ruse. The heart could be much more vulnerable than the mind. *Hmm.* Returning the conversation to other suspects, namely Mick and Sheila, I rattled off their full names and the address that had been on the check he'd shown me earlier.

"Thanks," Landreth said. "How'd you happen to get this information?"

I told her how the couple had come by, purportedly to make a better offer on the boat. I told her that Mick had mentioned gas buildup in the bilge as the possible reason for the explosion, and that the two had exchanged odd looks. She said she'd get in touch with them. With any luck, she'd find some evidence to implicate one or both of them, and the case would be closed quickly. I hated to think Tanner or Deena could have been involved, or that the two of them might have plotted to kill Grant together. What would become of Jojo if the mother and son were arrested?

CHAPTER 13

COINCIDENCE OR CONSPIRACY?

WHITNEY

At six o'clock Wednesday evening, Buck and I stepped up onto the porch of Deena Hardisty's house. It was a well-kept brick Colonial. The flower bed in front was filled with spring flowers, annuals that had recently been planted, and surrounded by a bed of aromatic cedar mulch. I had the canister of tennis balls in my hand and my cousin by my side. I rang the bell. *Ding-dong.*

Jojo immediately erupted in barks. *Arf-arf-arf! Arf-arf!* From behind the door, we could hear Tanner's voice. "Down boy! Quiet!" Judging from the scratching sounds on the other side of the door and the continued barking, Jojo had obeyed neither command.

Deena's voice faintly called, "Who is it?"

A couple of seconds went by and we heard Tanner call back to her. "Those people from the houseboat."

We heard shuffling sounds, and a moment later the door opened. The smell of spaghetti sauce and garlic bread wafted out. *Mmm.* Deena stood there in yoga pants and a fitted tee, her son behind her. Jojo bolted out the door and jumped up on me. *Arf! Arf-arf!*

I reached down and ruffled the dog's ears. I might be more of a cat person, but I could definitely see the appeal of a pooch, especially one as sweet as Jojo. "Hey, boy."

"Down, Jojo!" Deena scolded. Again, he ignored her, probably because I was giving him ear scratches now. She looked to me. "Sorry. He's barely out of the puppy phase."

"No worries," I said. "I'm glad he likes me." I held up the can. "I bought these for Jojo. Thought I'd bring them by." There were only two balls left, of course, one of them having gone up—or down—with the boat.

Tanner circled around his mom to take them from me. "Thanks!"

"We were wondering about something." Still ruffling the dog's ears with one hand, I used the other to pull the now-tepid cold pack from my pocket. "How many of these cold packs did you supply to Grant?"

"A couple of cases," Deena said. "Last time we had a mediation meeting, Grant kept wincing in pain. I figured he could use them."

"A couple of cases," I repeated. "How many are in a case?"

"Twenty-four. Why?"

Ignoring her question, I posed another of my own. "If you two were in the middle of a contentious divorce, why would you care if he was in pain?"

She frowned slightly. "Because I'm not a monster. I might not want to be married to the guy anymore, but

I don't like to see anyone suffer. It's why I became a nurse."

Is she telling the truth, or had she formulated this response and kept it at the ready should anyone ask? I couldn't tell.

"Besides," she added, "the sooner he recovered from the fall, the sooner we could proceed with the property settlement. It was in my own interests to help him recover as quickly as possible."

Now that's a reason I can believe. I shook the pack back and forth in my hand. "Do you know what's in this?"

Deena's brow formed a V. "In the cold pack?" She lifted a shoulder and let it fall. "Some sort of gel and granules."

"Yes," I said, "but do you know exactly what chemicals are inside?"

"No." She gestured to the pack. "But if you turn it over, the contents should be noted on the back."

"Are you saying you don't know the specific contents, then?"

"No." She cocked her head, her face tight with concern and curiosity. "Why?"

I looked to Tanner. His face bore a similar expression.

I found myself slipping my hand into my pocket, where I'd hidden my big wrench. I grasped the handle, ready to whip it out in self-defense, if necessary. Next to me, I noticed Buck slide his hand into the pocket of his coveralls as well. He'd secured a claw hammer in his pocket. "The reason I'm asking is because these cold packs contain ammonium nitrate."

While Tanner's expression didn't change, Deena's

expression grew slightly more confused. "Ammonium nitrate? So . . . ?"

Did she not understand the significance of the chemical, or was she playing dumb? "Ammonium nitrate can explode under the right circumstances."

Her expression became even more confused until her face itself seemed to explode. Her eyes went wide and her mouth gaped. "Are you saying the cold packs I gave Grant made his boat explode?" She put a hand over her mouth in horror. "Oh, my God!" After a few seconds, she lowered her hand to her chest. "We use them at the hospital all the time. I had no idea they posed any sort of risk."

Tanner looked to her, his eyes narrowing slightly.

"Ammonium nitrate is generally safe," I explained. "It's only when it comes in contact with a fuel source or flame that there's a problem."

Buck told them what he'd told me earlier. "There's all sorts of websites on the internet that give instructions on how to make a bomb out of the stuff."

It was Deena now who took an involuntary step back. Her gaze cut to her son. No doubt he was a typical teenager and spent untold hours online, doing homework, playing games, watching TikTok videos, and who knew what else. *Is she wondering whether he might have found a way to make the cold packs explode?*

When neither of them said anything further, I prodded them. "Good thing Jojo wasn't on the boat when it exploded." I looked down at the dog, who was still rubbing himself against my legs. "Right, boy?"

Deena seemed to realize what I was insinuating, and she didn't like it. She reached out, grabbed Jojo by the collar, and pulled him off me. "If we'd lost Jojo, too, it would have been even worse." She turned to her son. "Take Jojo out back and throw a ball for him."

"Okay." Tanner patted his leg. "C'mon, boy!" The two trotted off toward the back of the house.

Deena jerked her head toward the kitchen behind her. "Thanks for bringing the tennis balls, but we were just about to sit down to dinner. Is there anything else?"

I figured I had nothing to lose by being blunt. "I don't know if Tanner told you or not, but I saw him take Jojo from Grant's boat. We even spoke briefly. Did you know Tanner was going to steal the dog?"

She exhaled sharply. "You can hardly steal your own dog. My son and that dog are joined at the hip. Tanner took good care of him and took him on runs and to the dog park. Grant never lifted a finger, for Jojo or anyone else. Besides, a small boat is no place for a large, energetic dog."

Clearly, she was avoiding the subject and trying to minimize what her son had done.

"You didn't answer my question," I said.

She stiffened and hesitated a moment, as if considering her words before speaking. "No, I didn't know Tanner was going to take Jojo, but I also don't blame him one bit. The thought crossed my mind, too. But the fact that he took the dog the night before Grant's boat exploded is just a coincidence. Do they even know for certain that ammonium nitrate caused the explosion? That woman from the fire department told me it could have been an accident, that gases can sometimes build up in a boat."

Landreth had informed Deena of Grant's death the day of the explosion, before the cause was known.

Apparently, she hadn't yet given Deena an update. I wasn't sure whether I should say more, confirm that the ammonium nitrate was the cause, though I'd already implied as much. "If you want more information, you should talk to Melanie Landreth. You have her number, right?"

"I do. She left her business card. She told me she'd let me know once they had some answers."

"Well, then," I said, "she must not have any yet." I switched topics. "Mick and Sheila McNeely came by the dock today. They had a check for Grant. They were going to offer him twenty thousand dollars to buy the boat."

Deena's shoulders slumped. "It was worth much more than that. At least fifty thousand. Grant bought it for only ten grand. He ripped them off, took advantage of them."

"He did?" I prodded.

"Grant and Mick were friends. Mick owned a restaurant where Grant once tended bar. Mick and Sheila ran into some money trouble last year and Grant offered to lend Mick ten grand with the boat as collateral. It was only supposed to be a short-term deal, but I think Grant manipulated Mick with his false charm, just like he manipulates everyone else. I wouldn't blame Mick for being furious at Grant."

Was she trying to throw suspicion off herself and her son and onto Mick? Or was she simply speaking the truth? "Was the boat insured?" I asked.

"Yes," she said. "I made sure the insurance was always paid up. Grant wasn't the most responsible person, and he didn't have much experience with boats. I was afraid something would happen, that someone might get hurt or he'd run into a pier or another boat."

"Have you filed a claim yet?'

She shook her head. "The thought hadn't even crossed my mind. I've been trying to come to grips with things, and to make plans for his remains. He didn't have any children or siblings. His father has already passed on and his mother has Alzheimer's. She lives in a nursing home. She's a sweet woman, but Grant was her only child and she spoiled him. At least she won't grieve her son. She hasn't recognized him in over a year."

This bit of information was simultaneously sad and comforting.

From her kitchen came the sound of the oven timer. *Bzzzzz.* She glanced back at the kitchen. "That's the garlic bread. I better get it before it burns. Thanks again for the tennis balls." With that, she closed the door on us.

Buck and I returned to my SUV, where I removed my wrench from my pocket and he removed his hammer from his. I was glad we hadn't had to use the weapons, but I was disappointed we hadn't gotten any real answers.

I mulled things over as we drove back to the marina. "What do you think?" I asked Buck. "I thought she seemed genuinely surprised that the cold packs contained a potentially explosive substance."

"She might have been," Buck agreed. "Maybe it was Tanner who figured it out and blew up the boat."

I recalled how she'd grabbed the dog and sent Tanner out back to play with him. "She certainly didn't like us questioning her son."

"Understandable," Buck said.

"Did you think she was pointing fingers at Mick and Sheila?"

"For sure," Buck said.

"Do you think she could be right? That Mick or Sheila blew up the boat?"

"I do. Mick must've trusted Grant or he'd never have signed the boat over to him. Nobody likes to feel like a fool. That said, you've got to tell Landreth about the cold pack you found in our trash. You know that, right?"

I sighed. "I do. But I'll wait until morning. It's been a long day and I don't want to disturb her personal time." I knew from dating Collin that crime investigation was hardly a nine-to-five job, and that the work often took precedence over all else. Still, the trash wasn't going anywhere. Landreth could take a look in the morning.

We pulled into the marina a few minutes later and parked. The beach ball had floated to the open end of Slip 27. I walked down to the end of the dock, rounded it up, and brought it inside the *Skinny Dipper.* Sawdust greeted me with a mew and proceeded to perform figure eights around my ankles. I set the ball on the floor in the living area and he strolled over to sniff it. He reached up a front paw and raised up on his hind legs. When the ball rolled away and he fell to all fours, he seemed to feel empowered by his ability to move something so much larger than himself. He swished his tail proudly and batted at the big ball, rolling it around the room. It bounced off the cushion-less furniture frames in a slow-motion game of pinball. It felt as if the same game was playing in my head, my thoughts bouncing back and forth in my mind. I could see why many of the suspects would have reason to kill Grant Hardisty. But who had actually done it?

CHAPTER 14

CAT TOY

SAWDUST

Sawdust missed his new doggie friend. They'd just gotten to know each other, and now he was gone. Sawdust could smell the dog's scent on the big ball Whitney had brought into the boat for the cat to play with. He hoped he'd see his friend again one day.

The ball was a blast! His other ball toys were much smaller, about the size of his paw, and easy to bat around. But this one was huge! Even when he stood on his hind legs, he couldn't see over it. But it didn't weigh much. He could push it around the boat like he was a big, strong lion rather than the runt of his litter. So much fun!

CHAPTER 15

A LITTLE BIRDIE TOLD ME . . .

WHITNEY

Thursday morning, I was wakened by Buck muttering in the kitchen. "Darn it!"

"What's wrong?" I called.

"We're out of coffee."

I'd used the last of the grounds the day before and had intended to pick some up at the grocery store. But in the all the excitement of Landreth's revelations, Mick and Sheila coming by the marina, and our visit to Deena and Tanner, I'd totally forgotten. I slid out of bed. "I'll run to the Get-N-Git and pick some up."

I threw on my coveralls, brushed my teeth, and splashed some water on my face. After pulling a brush through my hair and donning my work boots, I grabbed my purse and headed out to my SUV. I noted that the passenger door on Grant's Camaro was open. The back end of someone in khaki pants stuck out of it, a crime scene technician, no doubt. The trunk was open, too.

A female tech in khakis and a red shirt was applying some type of tape or film to the carpeting inside the trunk, probably trying to lift any granules of ammonium nitrate that might have been left behind if Grant had transported the chemical in his trunk.

I pulled out my cell phone, called Landreth, and told her about the cold packs I'd found in our trash the day before. "They contain ammonium nitrate. Grant's wife brought him an entire case of the cold packs just a few days ago. I see that there's a crime scene team here looking over Grant's car. Should I tell them about the cold packs so they can collect them, too?"

"I'll get in touch with them," she said. "I'm coming out there. Stay put. I might have some questions for you."

"I was just on my way to grab some coffee at the convenience store down the road. We're all out. Okay if I run to the store first?"

She huffed but said, "Make it quick."

I climbed into my car and drove down the road to the Get-N-Git. Several vehicles were already in the lot, most of them with boats on trailers behind them. Looked like there were lots of fishermen planning to get an early start on the water. All the boats had punny names painted on the back. *Bad Buoy. Fishin' Impossible. Shameless Hooker.*

The bells on the door jingled as I walked inside. The same woman who'd rung me up before for the sports drinks and fish seasoning stood behind the counter, ringing up items for a customer. I continued on, glancing down the aisles for coffee. When I spotted several bags on a shelf, I turned and headed down the aisle. A man was on his knees farther down, sliding bags of nuts and sunflower seeds onto metal pegs. He looked vaguely familiar, though I could only see him from the side.

He glanced up at me. "Can I help you find something?"

I held up the coffee. "Found what I came for. I was just thinking you looked familiar. Are you the owner of the *Caudal Otta Fish*?"

"Yup, that's me." He cocked his head. "Have we met?"

"No," I said. "My cousin and I own the *Skinny Dipper*. We're docked in Slip Twenty-Six at the Marina."

"Ah. Next to the *Sexy Sheila*." His face fell and he sat back on his heels. "Horrible what happened, isn't it?" He shook his head.

"It was awful." I extended my hand and introduced myself. "I'm Whitney Whitaker."

He stood and took my hand. "Billy Underhill." He released my hand and angled his head slightly. "Were you there when it happened?"

"I was. My cousin, too. We were totally shocked."

"Good thing the boat didn't blow up at the dock or you might have been a goner, too. It's bad enough Grant and his dog died."

"We were certainly lucky," I agreed. Billy apparently hadn't noticed that Jojo wasn't on the *Sexy Sheila* when he'd picked up Grant to take him fishing or when he'd later dropped him off. Grant must not have mentioned the missing dog to him, either. I decided not to correct him. He might find the situation as suspicious as I had, and realize Jojo's disappearance pointed to Tanner. Then again, Billy might not even be aware that the explosion was deemed suspicious.

Billy did the same thing Deena had done before. He looked over my shoulder, as if looking into the past. His voice caught when he said, "I'm gonna miss that guy. He was one of my favorite fishing buddies."

"Had you and Grant been friends long?" I asked.

"No," he said, returning his focus to my face. "Two or three months, maybe? He started coming in here a lot when he and his wife split and he moved onto the boat. I felt sorry for him. He was quite the sad sack, seemed like he could use a friend, so I invited him to go fishing with me and another buddy. Eventually, it became a regular thing."

"What do you think happened?" I asked, curious whether he might have a theory that could help me figure things out.

He shrugged. "Could've been a problem with his propane stove in the galley, or could've been a faulty fuel line. Who knows? Grant didn't seem to know much about boats. The *Sexy Sheila* was his first. Wouldn't surprise me if he accidentally started a fire somehow and it got out of hand before he could stop it."

An image in the circular security mirror mounted in the back corner caught my eye. It was the woman at the register, looking in our direction. I turned and caught her eye over the top of the shelf, which stood about four feet high. She offered a small smile. "Careful now," she called, "or Billy will talk your ear off. My husband has never met a stranger."

He chuckled and called back to her, raising a hand in the air to point to me. "She and her cousin are fixing up a houseboat at the marina." He addressed me again. "Grant told me about it. You're going to repair it and resell it, right?"

"That's the plan," I said. "We've rehabbed other properties with mixed success." I was being a little modest.

Although our first flip hadn't quite worked out as we'd hoped, we'd made a decent profit on our second flip, a traditional house in a neighborhood not far from the airport, and we'd made a pretty penny refurbishing an old motel near downtown and turning it into upscale condominiums. Even so, there were no guarantees the houseboat would make us much money. Only time would tell.

"Well, good luck to you. When you're ready to sell, feel free to post a flyer on our bulletin board." He gestured to a wide corkboard mounted on the back wall near the restrooms. All sorts of items were posted there for sale. Kayaks. Jet skis. Boats. Paddle boards. Even a water bike. People had posted photos of available vacation rentals, too, and offered various services ranging from boat repair to fishing guides.

"Thanks! I'll do that." As I carried my bag of coffee to the checkout counter, I caught a whiff of coconut. I turned to see a display of sunscreen, suntan lotion, and suntan oil on an endcap. One of the oils was the brand Grant had used, the one that make his skin glisten and smelled good enough to eat. I'd be tempted to buy some myself if I didn't already have a full bottle of the stuff thanks to the woman who'd come to the marina to meet him, the one with the nice eyebrows and the Audi who'd dropped her bottle in the parking lot.

I carried my coffee to the checkout. As I placed it on the counter for the woman to ring up, I got a better look at her. While she'd seemed bright and spry before, she appeared haggard today. Her eyes were red and droopy as if she was sleep deprived, and she slouched, seemingly pulled down by unseen weight. "Are you all right?" I asked quietly, hoping my question would be taken as sincere concern and not an insult.

She bit her bottom lip and averted her eyes for a moment before turning back and offering a feeble smile. "I didn't sleep well last night. I'm worried about my mother. She tripped over her slippers and took a bad fall."

Looked like Grant Hardisty wasn't the only one who'd taken a tumble. In light of the fact that Billy's wife appeared to be in her early sixties, her mother would likely be in her eighties. Maybe even nineties. Women that age were prone to osteoporosis and could easily break a hip. "Nothing broken, I hope?"

"Luckily, no. Just some bruising."

"Glad to hear it."

She rang me up and I used the machine to pay with my debit card. As she handed the bag of coffee to me, she offered the same shtick she had the other night, though it lacked her earlier enthusiasm. "You got what you came for." She pointed at the door. "Now git!"

I bade her a good day and headed out to my SUV to drive back to the marina. In the distance on the lake, I could see a fire department boat trolling slowly by, several people on the deck, probably looking to see whether Grant's body—or parts of it—had resurfaced. *Eeep.* I returned to the *Skinny Dipper* where I made a pot of coffee, drank two cups in quick succession, and slid Sawdust into his life vest so he could lounge in the morning sun on the deck.

Melanie Landreth drove up a few minutes later. She stopped to speak to the technicians still working on Grant's car, and one of them handed her a pair of latex gloves and several clear plastic evidence bags. She walked over to the *Skinny Dipper* and donned the gloves. "All right, Whitney. Show me what you found."

I held out the cold pack I'd discovered in the bin the day before. She took the pack from me, placed it in a clear evidence bag, and used a marker to document the date, time, and location the evidence had been found. Turning back to me, she said, "Can you get me another trash bag? I'm going to have to look through the rest of this can."

I scurried inside, grabbed a clean trash bag, and returned to the deck. At her direction, I held the new bag open. She leaned over and began to sort through the trash can, placing any unrelated refuse into the bag I was holding. Packaging for the paint rollers and brushes. Used sandpaper. An old pair of flip-flops I'd discovered in the closet of the berth where I was staying.

As she lifted a bottle of tanning oil, it slipped right out of her gloved hand and clunked to the bottom of the bin. "Slippery sucker."

"That oil was Grant's, too." He'd used the stuff by the gallon.

"Smells good," she said. "Makes me crave a big piece of coconut cream pie."

I wasn't sure whether she'd share information with me, but I figured it couldn't hurt to ask. "Did you have any luck getting information from the dating apps?" I asked. "Were you able to identify the bar where Grant met his date and the guys who came out to water ski?"

"No," she said, "or at least not yet. Grant had some preliminary conversations through the dating sites with dozens of women, but then they must have moved to communicating via e-mail or text. I looked at their profiles.

Several of the women had red hair. I have to prioritize suspects, and I think it's more likely that someone close to Grant killed him rather than some guy he met only recently and borrowed money from. Blowing someone to smithereens seems like an extreme overreaction to being stiffed a hundred bucks. If nothing else pans out, I'll contact the women and see if I can determine which one met him last Friday and where."

She had a point. Still, the guy hadn't exactly been reasonable when he'd come out to the marina to recoup his funds. Had he been able to get his hands on Grant, I could imagine him giving the guy a beating.

As she wrapped up the evidence collection, I told her about Tanner dognapping Jojo.

Landreth pursed her lips. "This happened the night before the boat went up?"

I nodded.

"And you didn't tell me about this earlier because . . . ?" She circled her hand as if trying to pull the information out of me.

"Because I'd promised the kid." I cringed in contrition. "But also because I didn't think it was relevant until I saw the cold pack."

She cast me a sour look. "Better late than never, I suppose. Anything else you're keeping from me?"

I'd better come clean. "Buck and I went to see them last night. I had a can of tennis balls I'd bought for their dog when he was still living on the boat, and I took it to them."

She cast me a second, even more sour look. "Did you mention the cold pack you'd found?"

I cringed again. "It might have come up."

She shook her head but, luckily for me, she didn't

give me the chewing out I deserved. "Looks like I've got some folks to visit." With that, she was gone.

The crime scene team wrapped up their work on Grant's Camaro as Buck and I prepared our paint and brushes. My cousin worked on the far side of the boat, while I worked on the side next to the empty slip that had once housed the *Sexy Sheila*.

Our boating exam was coming up soon, and I had yet to see Buck study. I quizzed him through the open windows of the boat. "In a boating emergency, what are the four rescue techniques?" The answer I was looking for was *reach, throw, row, and go.* You could *reach* out to the victim with an oar, fishing pole, towel, or arm, and pull them to safety, though offering an arm posed the risk that you could also be pulled into a dangerous situation and was not the preferred method. You could *throw* them a personal floatation device. You could *row* out to them if a smaller craft such as a rowboat, kayak, or dinghy was an option, and use the oar to help them aboard. Finally, you could *go* for help from someone trained in lifesaving.

"Well, you could toss them a life ring."

"That counts as a *throw*," I said.

"You could jump in and pull them out yourself."

"It's better to use some sort of device to pull them in. That's the *reach* method. The others are *row* and *go*." As I went to dip my roller into the paint, my eyes spotted the bird-watcher. He was wearing his camo gear again. He stood on the bank near the far end of the long dock, his binoculars to his eyes, appearing to be scanning the horizon.

I gently set my roller down and circled around the back of the boat, scratching Sawdust under the chin along the way. I peeked around the corner. "The birder is back. I'm going to talk to him." I'd get his name and number and give him Landreth's contact information. I still felt a little guilty about speaking to Deena and Tanner without consulting Landreth first. Putting her in touch with the birder would make up for that, at least a little.

I began heading the man's way. As I did, he turned his binoculars in my direction. I wasn't entirely sure whether I was in his field of vision but, in case I was, I raised my hand and waved to let him know I was heading for him. He didn't wave back. Instead, he swung his binoculars back in the other direction. *He must not have seen me.* He lowered his binoculars and began to walk into the woods. *Darn!* If I didn't catch up to him quick, I might not catch him at all.

I cupped my hands around my mouth. "Hey there! Could you wait, please? I need to talk to you!"

He must not have heard me, either. Rather than stopping, he ducked in among the trees and disappeared in the thick, shadowy woods. *Ugh!* I ran as fast as I could along the uneven bank, calling, "Sir? Sir? I need to speak with you please!" But he was nowhere to be seen. The woods seemed to have swallowed him.

I ventured down a narrow footpath, calling out. "Hello? Bird-watcher? Hello? I need to talk to you, please!" There was no response. I stopped and slowly scanned the woods. The only movement I saw were tree limbs swaying in the breeze and two squirrels scampering up a tree trunk. With a resigned sigh, I turned and walked back to the *Skinny Dipper.*

Buck looked up as I stepped back onto the boat. "Did he have any information?"

I raised my palms. "I didn't catch him. He went into the woods and I couldn't find him."

Buck frowned. "He couldn't have gotten far. Did you call out to him?"

"Several times." Either he didn't hear me or he ignored my pleas. I had an eerie feeling it was likely the latter. If so, maybe it was just as well I didn't find him in those thick, dark woods.

Twenty minutes later, I was back at work, running my paint roller up and down the side of the boat, when the man emerged from the trees. I was hidden from his view, but I could see him through the boat's windows. He slunk along the edge of the woods before making a break for the marina. He walked at maximum speed to cross the distance quickly, but he didn't run. He seemed to be trying to avoid arousing suspicion which, ironically, made me more suspicious of him. *He's avoiding me, isn't he? Could he have something to do with what happened to Grant?*

I set my roller down and took off running toward the small marina office. It might be risky but, unlike the woods, at least there were people around who would see us in the parking lot. He'd be crazy to try something when there would be eyewitnesses, right?

Buck called after me, "Where are you going now?"

There was no time to explain. I turned and hollered over my shoulder, "Keep an eye on Sawdust!"

The man disappeared behind the building. I ran as fast as I could and circled around the corner just in time to see him drive off toward the exit in a basic light gray sedan. Luckily for me, two cars approached on the main road, one from either direction, and he had to wait for them. I'd never be able to reach his car in time to stop him, but I could at least get his license plate number so that we could identify him. I whipped out my cell phone and snapped a pic. Though the license plate number was blurry when I enlarged the photo, it was nonetheless readable.

Panting from the exertion, I turned to walk back to the *Skinny Dipper* only to find Buck sprinting toward me. He slowed as he reached me. "Are you okay?"

"I'm fine. Just a little out of breath." I explained that I'd taken off to try to catch the bird-watcher. "It seemed obvious he was avoiding me."

"Maybe it's good you didn't catch him, then," Buck said. "He could be dangerous."

"You think the whole bird-watching thing could have been a ruse? You think he's been spying on Grant all this time? Maybe he was trying to figure out Grant's routine so that he could get onto the boat to plant the explosives."

"Could be," Buck said. "He seemed to be trying to hide his face the day we helped Grant look for Jojo. It's like he didn't want us to get a good look at him. Maybe he hoped we wouldn't be able to identify him in a police lineup, if it came to that."

"I'll call Landreth when we get back to the boat. I was able to snap a photo of his license plate. She can run the number and figure out who he is."

Buck gave me a rare compliment. "Smart thinking."

"All of my thoughts are smart."

"No, they're not. Remember the jelly bean and fruit punch soup you made that one summer when we were kids? That wasn't smart."

"I was only seven!"

"Still," Buck insisted, "stupid idea."

"As I recall, you ate two bowls of it."

"Also a stupid idea. Maybe even stupider."

We returned to the boat. Buck had put Sawdust inside for safety, and the cat was sitting in the window with an anxious expression on his furry little face. He put a paw to the glass. I went inside and scooped him into my arms. "Sorry I worried you, boy."

I placed Sawdust on the kitchen table and took a seat in one side of the booth. Before I could dial Melanie Landreth's number, my phone sprang to life with an incoming call from Collin. I tapped the screen to accept the call. "Hey."

He wasted no time with a preamble. "Remember how I said I wouldn't be involved in Grant Hardisty's murder investigation?"

"Yeah?"

"I was wrong. I'm all in now."

Sawdust rubbed his face against my phone, nearly knocking it out of my hand. I turned away to put my hand out of reach of his head. "You are? So Landreth asked you to assist her?"

"Not exactly," he said. "I'm in it because someone came down to the station first thing this morning and confessed to blowing up Grant Hardisty's boat."

I gasped as my hand involuntarily tightened on my phone. "Who was it?"

CHAPTER 16

THE ELECTRONIC ENEMY

SAWDUST

Sawdust was jealous of Whitney's cell phone. Sometimes she paid more attention to it than she did to him. It wasn't fair! He gave her love and kisses and cuddles, and the phone didn't do anything but make annoying noises and jiggle unexpectedly, which gave him a start. If he ever had a chance, he'd knock the darn thing off a counter and hope that it would shatter into a million pieces.

Sawdust butted Whitney's knee with his head. When that didn't work, he rolled over in front of her, exposing his belly. While that maneuver had a near-perfect success rate, it didn't work today. Whitney still ignored him. His furry little heart broke. He hopped down from the kitchen table and walked off, but not before casting her a final look of resignation and hurt from the doorway.

CHAPTER 17
CONFESSIONS AND CONFUSION

WHITNEY

Sawdust shot me a pathetic look from the doorway, making me feel guilty for ignoring him, but I had bigger things to deal with the at moment. Someone had confessed to killing Grant, and Collin was about to reveal their identity.

"It was Deena Hardisty," Collin said.

I gasped. "Deena confessed to killing her husband? Whoa."

"Surprised?"

"Yeah, I am. I mean, I thought she could be guilty, but I figured the fire department would have to try to build a case against her. I never thought she'd come right out and admit it." I'd suspected she could be guilty after I'd discovered the cold packs she'd provided to Grant contained ammonium nitrate, but having my suspicions confirmed caused a painful tug in my heart. The woman had a teenage son, after all, and he needed a mother—especially since it sounded like he and his biological father might not get along very well. I recalled his sarcastic comment about his mother's choice in men. *She really knows how to pick 'em.* Turned out she really knew how to kill 'em, too. "Why did Deena confess to you and not Landreth?"

"She didn't understand the jurisdictional arrangement. Most people don't. Even though Deena knew Landreth was an investigator for the fire department, Deena thought Landreth's sole goal was to determine the cause of the fire. She thought the police department would take things from there and handle the murder investigation."

I could understand Deena's confusion. I hadn't understood the delineation myself until Landreth and Collin explained it to me.

"At any rate," Collin continued, "she said you're the one who convinced her to come clean. She said you went by her house last night to question her about a cold pack you'd found in your trash bin."

"I wasn't sure it was important," I said in my defense, knowing he would have preferred I passed the information on to law enforcement and let the professional investigators handle things. Still, he seemed to have accepted by now that I couldn't help but stick my nose where it didn't belong. After all, more times than not, my nosiness had paid off. "I noticed the cold pack had ammonium nitrate it in, but I didn't know whether Deena was even aware of its contents. I use products all the time in my work and I have no idea what's in some of them."

"It was a reasonable question," Collin said, cutting me some slack. "At any rate, she admitted to giving

Grant a large supply of the cold packs since he got hurt six weeks ago. She says she was trying to get as much of the ammonium nitrate on the boat as possible. She showed me two e-mail receipts from a medical supply store, each for a twenty-four-count case of cold packs."

I performed some quick math in my head. Grant told us he'd fallen and hurt his knee six weeks earlier. I'd seen him use several of the cold packs since I'd met him, so all forty-eight cold packs would no longer be on the boat. Exactly how many remained was unknown. But would there be enough of them left to cause such a huge blast?

When I posed this question to Collin, he said, "She told me she also pilfered cold packs from the hospital where she works. She said she took dozens at a time. She hid them in her purse and lunch bag so she could smuggle them out of the hospital undetected."

"How did she get the additional cold packs on the boat?" I asked.

"She claims that it was her idea for her son to remove Jojo from the boat. Once Tanner was back home with the dog and had fallen asleep, she returned to the marina and filled the life jacket bins with more cold packs. She said she doused them with a flammable fluid intended for use in camp stoves."

Even with the ammonium nitrate and camp fuel on the boat, it wouldn't go up without something triggering a reaction. "How did she detonate the materials?"

"She says she put a manual push-button spark igniter in the bin with the fuel and ammonium nitrate. The igniters are used for grills and fire pits. She said she got the idea from the fire pit they have in their backyard. They had to replace the igniter recently when it stopped working. She inserted a sponge under the edge of the cushioned bench top to prevent it from fully closing, but she used a thin one so it wouldn't be obvious that the bin wasn't entirely closed. She knew Grant would sit down on the bench. When he did, he'd inadvertently press on the spark igniter button, cause a spark, and the boat would blow."

"It's scary how simple it sounds."

"You don't have to be an evil genius to set off a bomb," Collin agreed. "You just have to be evil."

"It seems risky, though," I said. "One wrong move and she could have accidentally killed herself."

"That's true," Collin said. "I suppose that was a risk she was willing to take."

Although I could imagine being angry at an ex who'd treated me poorly, I couldn't imagine risking my life to kill him, especially if it would mean leaving my child motherless. *Had she lost all sense of reason?* "Where did she buy the camp fuel and the igniter?"

"She said she bought them at a small hardware store for cash weeks ago. She doesn't remember the date or the exact location or name of the store. She said she purposely went to a store some distance from her home so that she wouldn't run into anyone who might recognize her."

"Sounds like she really thought things through."

"She's a bright woman. She might have even gotten away with it if not for the evidence you provided. We owe you."

I knew Collin was trying to make me feel good for helping law enforcement resolve the case, but rather than feeling proud I felt sick to my stomach. It was nice to know that justice would be done, but justice came at a price. That price would be paid by Deena's son. Maybe Jojo, too.

We ended the call and I summoned my cat back to the kitchen. "Sawdust! Come here, sweetie!" The cat came running, and I gave him the attention he'd been vying for while I'd been on the phone. As I ran my hand over him, I found myself in disbelief. Despite Deena's confession, despite the fact that she had a motive for killing her estranged husband, I thought it was senseless of her to kill Grant given the risk that she'd be sentenced to many years if not life in prison and wouldn't be able to finish raising her son. Then again, there were plenty of mothers who put themselves before their children. Self-centered narcissists, drug addicts, and others. *So sad.*

I gave Sawdust a kiss on the head, stood, and went outside to give Buck the news.

His jaw went slack. "Deena confessed? Really?"

"Really. Collin just called to let me know."

"I can hardly believe it." Buck scratched his head, as incredulous as I was. "At least we don't have to worry about the bomber coming after us now because they thought we might have seen something."

"I suppose." Were we safer now? I wasn't so certain. I couldn't shake the feeling that the woman behind bars might not have been the actual culprit.

Clunk-clunk-clunk. The sound of hard heels clunking their way over wood drew our attention to the dock. Jackie strode up. She wore a business suit, this one in taupe, paired with a pale blue silky tank. She stopped in front of Slip 27 and stared at the empty space for a moment before looking out at the lake, her eyes scanning the water. She appeared to be having a hard time believing that Grant was gone.

Even though she and Grant had split, it would likely be difficult to learn that a man you had once loved and planned to spend your life with had met such a horrific fate. Sensing she might need some emotional support, I stepped off the back of the *Skinny Dipper* and walked over to stand beside her. She was silent, but her face contorted with barely contained emotion.

"I hope you're doing okay," I said. "You probably haven't heard yet, but his current wife is in custody. She confessed."

Her mouth gaped. "Deena said she killed Grant?"

I nodded.

"Have you met her?" Jackie asked.

"Yes," I said. "She came by recently to speak with Grant about signing the divorce settlement. I wasn't intentionally eavesdropping, but I could hear their conversation from our boat."

"Let me guess," she said, sourly. "He refused to sign until she offered him more money."

"That's right."

I thought once Jackie gathered her wits, she might express some sort of regret or sadness as a matter of common decency even if she didn't actually feel a deep sorrow. The last thing I expected her to do was burst into laughter. Yet that's exactly what she did. She slapped a thigh, then tried to cover her delight by putting her hands over her mouth, but her shaking shoulders betrayed her. I wondered if her odd reaction was some sort of strange psychological behavior. Denial, maybe? Or just an extreme case of schadenfreude? "Are you okay?"

She removed her hands and shook her head hard, as if to regain control of her senses. "I am. It's just that . . . well . . . an explosion was the perfect way for him to go.

Poetic justice. Isn't that what they call it? He's blown up so many other people's lives. It was only a matter of time before someone blew up his in retaliation." She chuckled again, though this time it was without mirth. Her mood had shifted, and she looked past me, just as Deena and Billy had, as if seeing Grant at a different time, as someone else. Her voice was soft when she spoke again and her tone held a hint of melancholy. "That man could make you feel so special when he wanted to. Then he could make you feel so ashamed for falling for his tricks. He was a user. It was all take, take, take, and he gave little in return once he'd hooked you and reeled you in."

A fishing metaphor. Hmm.

She sighed. "I suppose I'll never get the furniture now. I didn't ever expect to, really. He probably sold it off for cash when he was between sugar mamas and needed some money. I just wanted to give the man a little hell after all he'd put me through, maybe embarrass him a little."

"Even the score?" I asked.

She nodded. "At least now I'll get the life insurance money."

"You still have a life insurance policy on Grant?" *That's odd, isn't it?*

"I got it when we were married. Pointless, I suppose, since life insurance is intended to replace income that the deceased person would have earned, and Grant hardly worked once we'd walked down the aisle. He wanted to be a kept man. So self-centered and lazy." She rolled her eyes. "I only kept the policy because the premiums were cheap and I had a feeling something like this might happen, that he'd piss off the wrong woman one day."

Looked like Deena had been that wrong woman. "How much is the policy for?" I asked.

"Fifty grand. It's not going to make me rich, but it will reduce the sting of what he did to me." She closed her eyes and heaved a deep, long breath, as if to cleanse herself of the man once and for all. When she reopened her eyes, she said, "Guess I'll be going now."

"Take care, Jackie."

Once Jackie had gone, I debated whether I should notify Landreth and Collin that she had come by and what she'd said. With Deena in jail, having confessed to the crime, there seemed to be no need to interrupt their day. Still, part of me wondered if Jackie had come by to see the empty slip and gloat. Don't they say that criminals like to return to the scene of their crimes, to relive the event and revel in their glory? Her laughter had been only a step away from the *mwa-ha-ha* issued by cartoon villains. But if she had been the one to blow up the boat, would she have been so direct with me, so cold and blunt? Then again, maybe being so bold and brazen was her way of trying to throw off suspicion.

After a few moments, I told myself to stop wasting time pondering the matter. With Deena Hardisty having confessed and in jail, it was all a moot point now, right?

On Friday, updated online news reports noted that Grant's body had surfaced—most of it anyway. While he was mostly intact, some parts of him had been found about the lake and even on boats at the marina, where they'd landed after the explosion. A finger here. A big toe there. My stomach churned at the thought that the man had been partially reduced to chum. I was glad that none of him had surfaced near the *Skinny Dipper.* I'm not sure I could've handled it.

Fortunately, the boat project took my mind off things. Buck and I finished painting the exterior of the *Skinny Dipper. What a transformation!* The once dull, rusty boat now gleamed in the sun, looking like it was a brand-new boat straight off the showroom floor rather than a used vessel that had been manufactured forty-five years ago. The new generator and motor still needed to be installed, and the inside needed a fresh coat of paint, new bedding, and new furniture cushions, but we'd made significant progress this week. Buck and I felt proud, especially when several people stopped to admire the boat and the adorable cat lounging atop the rubber ducky on its rear deck.

Buck said, "The *Skinny Dipper* will be up for sale soon. Bring your offers."

A couple of them asked for our contact information so they could get in touch once the boat was for sale.

"See?" Buck said. "I told you a houseboat would make a good flip project."

"We haven't sold it yet," I reminded him. "Don't count your chickens before they're hatched. Or your fish before they're hooked."

Collin, Buck, Colette, and I had a double dinner date planned on the boat for Friday night. In preparation, Buck and I situated the new outdoor furniture on the upper deck in the late afternoon. We engaged in the usual debate, but finally settled on placing the round table and four chairs in the center of the deck, with the lounge chairs positioned along the railing.

It felt good to have a reason to get out of my paint-splattered coveralls and clean myself up for a change. I showered and shaved my legs in anticipation of baring them for the warm evening. After my shower, I slid into a pair of denim shorts and a tank top under an open, gauzy blouse. Rather than lotion, I decided to use the coconut suntan oil on my legs. The oil would not only soften my skin and smell good, but it would also make my legs look shimmery.

I retrieved the bottle from the medicine cabinet, unscrewed the top, and poured a generous amount into my hand. Lifting my foot up onto the toilet seat, I bent over and applied the oil to my calf. *What the . . . ?* The oil was so sticky I could barely spread it over my skin. It felt heavier than I'd expected—and looked much darker, too, like brown polyurethane glue or maple syrup or molasses. *Wait. Is it molasses?* I lifted my sticky hand to my nose and sniffed. The substance had a faint scent of coconut, but not nearly as strong as the bottle Grant had been using. The coconut smell could have been merely from residue. Instead, this stuff had a very faint sweet scent, with maybe a hint of caramel undertones. *Had the woman who'd dropped it in the parking lot purchased a defective bottle that somehow escaped the factory's quality control? Could suntan oil even go bad?* I had no idea. I only knew I wanted this tacky goo off my skin ASAP. I wet a washcloth, added some soap, and scrubbed the mess from my leg and hand, being careful to make sure I got all of it from between my fingers lest they continue to stick together.

I opened the door and summoned my cousin. "Hey, Buck! Come here!" When he arrived in the doorway, I said, "Hold out your hand. I need your opinion."

He held out a hand, palm up, and I poured an ounce or so of the suntan oil into it. A shadow passed over his face when he seemed to realize the thick liquid pooled in his hand wasn't what he'd expected. He moved his hand up and down a few inches, as if weighing the fluid, then tilted his hand side to side to see how it moved. "This doesn't feel like suntan oil. It's too thick, like it coagulated or something. What is it? Some sort of liquid adhesive?"

"That's what I'm trying to determine." I held up the bottle. "This is the bottle that woman dropped in the parking lot the day the *Sexy Sheila* blew up."

He cocked his head, confused. "Strange."

Strange, indeed.

CHAPTER 18

DECKED OUT FOR DINNER

WHITNEY

Colette arrived at six, ready to get off her feet after a long day at her café. Nonetheless, she looked fresh and pretty in a polka-dot romper and sandals. She glanced around at the boat. "Things are really coming along. This will make someone a nice vacation home."

Buck said, "They could even live here full time if they wanted to."

On that note, I asked Buck and Colette where they planned to live once they tied the knot in late June. We'd been so busy planning the wedding, bridal shower, and bachelorette party, I hadn't even given thought to their future living arrangements. "If y'all want to take over the cottage, Emmalee and I can find a new place to live."

Buck had installed an extensive raised garden in the backyard of the cottage, and Colette had invested a lot of time and effort into planting and cultivating fruits and vegetables in the beds. She often used fresh produce from the backyard in the meals she cooked at home. Buck had invested a lot of his savings in the place, too. With his money tied up in the cottage, he'd have less of a down payment to put on another place for them. He currently lived in a single-wide trailer on three acres north of Nashville, not far from the Kentucky border. While the place made a nice bachelor pad, Colette could never be happy with the trailer's small kitchen.

"I'm planning to move into Buck's place after the wedding," Colette said. "The commute from there to the café is easy. But once the wedding is behind us, we're going to meet with an architect and have a custom house plan designed just for us. I'll want a huge kitchen, of course."

Buck chuckled. "You'll get no objection from me." He loved Colette's cooking. In fact, the old saying that the fastest way to a man's heart is through his stomach applied to the two of them. He'd fallen in love with her cooking before he'd fallen in love with her. She'd then seen how much he enjoyed her food and had fallen for him in return. "The only thing I want is an extra-large garage with a built-in workshop, or maybe a separate outbuilding to keep the noise down so it doesn't wake our babies." He shot a wink at Colette.

Colette shook her head but smiled. "Once the house is built, we'll sell the trailer and have it moved off the property."

I was glad Emmalee and I could stay put for the time being. "I call dibs on your room." Colette's room was the master. I'm sure Emmalee wouldn't mind that I'd claimed it. We'd offered her a lower than market rent for her room. She was getting a good deal, and we'd gotten a good roommate in return.

I motioned for Colette to follow me. "Come here. I want your opinion on something."

I led her down the hall to the bathroom. Buck trailed behind us and waited in the passageway rather than crowd into the tiny bath. I unscrewed the top from the bottle of suntan oil and held it out to her. "Do you have any idea what's in this bottle?"

She eyed the label. "It's not suntan oil?"

"I think the oil was swapped out for something else. I tried to put some on my leg and it was as sticky as glue. I'm wondering if it's pancake syrup or molasses."

She took the bottle, poured a dime-sized amount in her left palm, and set the bottle on the side of the sink. She touched her right index finger to the substance and lifted it a few inches. The thick goop dripped slowly from her finger. "It's way too thick to be an oil." She raised her palm to her face and sniffed. "It doesn't smell like pancake syrup or molasses. It looks and smells like the dark corn syrup I use in my pecan pies." She turned to wash the goo off her hand and finger. As she dried her hands on the towel, she asked, "Where did you get it?"

I told her about the woman who'd come to the dock, the one Grant had been purportedly communicating with after meeting her on a dating app.

Colette cocked her head. "Why would she have a bottle of corn syrup disguised as suntan oil?"

I raised my palms. "Your guess is as good as ours."

Collin arrived at half past six with two bags filled with Indian food. Samosas. Aloo methi mutter. Chana masala. Baingan bharta. Delicious naan. We gathered at the table with the food and a bottle of white wine.

Once we'd all served ourselves, I turned to Collin.

"Grant's ex-wife came by again today. The one I told you about before. Jackie."

After plopping a big dollop of food on his plate, Collin passed a food container and spoon to me. "What did she want?"

I spooned some food onto my plate, too. "At first, I thought maybe she was looking for closure. But when she burst out laughing, I realized she'd actually come to gloat."

"She laughed?" Colette's upper lip pulled back in distaste as she took the container from me. "That's crass."

I picked up my glass of wine. "I thought so, too. She basically said Grant got what he had coming to him. But she said something else that I found quite interesting. She still has an insurance policy on the guy even though they've been divorced for several years."

Collin's brow furrowed. "She does? Did she tell you how much it's worth?"

"Fifty grand." I took a sip of the wine, enjoying its crisp, slightly citrusy flavor. "She said it was a cheap policy and she had an inkling that Grant might piss off the wrong woman one day, so she decided to keep it in effect."

Collin issued a "Hmm."

I placed my napkin on my lap, picked up my fork, and asked, "How was your day?"

"Interesting." He took a sip of his wine as if to steel himself. "Three other people turned themselves in for killing Grant Hardisty."

I nearly dropped my fork. "What?!"

Buck asked, "Who?"

Colette wanted to know "Why? Didn't Grant's wife already confess? I thought the case was closed."

"Melanie Landreth and I thought it was closed, too," Collin said. He proceeded to tell us that both Mick and Sheila McNeely had offered confessions. Sheila had come into the station in the late morning, after having her hair freshly cut and colored and getting a mani-pedi so she'd look her sexy best in her mug shot. He held up his phone and showed us her photo. She stood before the wall with the height measurement demarcated, holding a board with a number on it. She smiled as if posing for a headshot, her lips bright and shiny with a fresh coat of lipstick.

My lip quirked. "She smiled in her mug shot? Who does that?"

"Psychopaths, generally," Collin said. "Though some people do it out of habit. It's an automatic reaction when you're in front of a camera."

Buck snorted. "Does the photographer tell them 'Say cheese'?"

"Nah," Collin said, fighting a grin. "It's 'pleas.'"

"As much as I'm enjoying your comedy routine," I said, "I want the details and I want them now. What did Sheila say?"

"That she knew Grant used dating apps to meet women, so she made a fake profile on one of them and lured Grant away from the boat. While he was gone to meet this fictitious woman, she snuck onto the boat and placed two sticks of dynamite under the hood of his stove so that they'd go off when he lit the burners."

I cocked my head in confusion. "How does she claim she got into the galley of Grant's boat to plant the dynamite? The door would have been locked, wouldn't it?"

Collin said, "She still has a key to the cabin door. She showed it to me."

"Are you sure it's the right key?" I asked. "With the boat blown up is there any way to verify that it fit?"

"The recovery team found Grant's keys when they were collecting the wreckage. He'd attached a floating keychain to them. A lot of boaters use them in case they drop their keys overboard. Sheila's key matched one of the keys on Grant's keychain."

"So, she could get into the galley," I said, "but where in the world could she get two sticks of dynamite?"

"She claims she got them from a demolition supplier, but she refused to say which one because she supposedly 'doesn't want to drag them into this.'" He made air quotes with his fingers.

Buck asked, "Is that possible?"

"Possible," Collin acknowledged, "but not likely. Both federal and state permits are required to buy explosives. Most dealers have multiple steps built into their sales systems to ensure explosives don't fall into the wrong hands. They don't want the liability if their explosives are used for nefarious purposes. The permits and safeguards are why most criminal bombers have to improvise their devices."

I thought aloud. "Dynamite doesn't explain the yellow smoke and the traces of ammonium nitrate the lab found, either."

"It doesn't," Collin agreed. "Landreth kept that detail from the media, and Sheila doesn't seem to be aware that the chemical was on the boat. She couldn't show me the fake profile, either. She claims she deleted the account, but my guess is she made up the whole story."

Colette scooped up a forkful of rice. "Why?"

"Because she thinks her husband killed Grant. She

feels guilty because she's the one who nearly bankrupted them. She went through a severe midlife crisis a while back and spent gobs of money on clothing and shoes and makeup, spa treatments to firm her body and skin, cosmetic surgery, that kind of thing."

I took another sip from my glass. "She does look amazing for her age. I'll give her that."

"That's true," Buck said. "She's still sexy as hell."

Colette pursed her lips. "Do you want me to marry you or not?"

Buck slid her a roguish grin. "Sheila might be sexy, but you're a million times sexier."

Colette gave him a nod. "That's more like it."

Collin went on. "Because of Sheila's spending, her husband felt like he had no choice but to sell his boat to Grant so that they wouldn't lose their house. When Grant refused to sell the boat back to Mick like they'd agreed, Mick killed Grant—or so goes the theory I'm working. Sheila doesn't want her husband to go to jail for killing Grant, because she believes that it's her fault Mick lost his boat in the first place."

I scooped up another forkful of food. "Grant never mentioned to me that he'd been stood up by a prospect he'd met online."

"Me neither." Buck spooned more rice onto his plate. "Of course, he might not have mentioned it because he was embarrassed about it. What about Mick? What's his story? How did he say he blew up the boat?"

"He didn't give many details," Collin said. "He simply said, 'I did it. I killed Grant.' When we pressed him for more information, he just said, 'Your investigators know what I did. There's no need for me to confirm it.'"

Hmm. "That's a little strange, isn't it? If he's confessed and is willing to go to prison for killing Grant Hardisty, why not provide the details of the crime?"

"Good question," Collin said. "Either he's just being uncooperative or obstinate, or—"

"He doesn't know how the explosion happened," I said, finishing Collin's thought while also rudely interrupting him. Fortunately, he took it in stride, knowing my outburst was the result of my interest in the case and in crime solving rather than an attempt to steal his thunder.

"Exactly," Collin said. "I'm not sure which. I asked Mick why he'd blow up a boat he was trying to buy back. He said he didn't believe Grant ever intended to sell the *Sexy Sheila* back to him. He said Grant made him feel stupid and used and manipulated. He didn't like feeling like a victim. He wanted to even the score, get back some of his self-respect."

Buck tore off a piece of naan. "Sounds like a good motive to me. Grant made him feel like less of a man. There's nothing more masculine than blowing something up."

Colette looked askance at Buck. "You've watched too many action movies."

Buck's head bobbed in agreement. "Probably."

Turning back to Collin, I asked, "Did he tell you that he filled up the gas tank on the *Sexy Sheila* when Grant let him and his wife use it last Saturday?"

"He did," Collin said. "He even showed me the receipt for the gas. He spent over four hundred dollars to fill up the tank."

"That's fairly damning evidence, isn't it? Why else would he spend that kind of money?"

As usual, Collin played devil's advocate, looking for reasonable explanations that would make otherwise guilty behavior appear entirely innocent. He'd told me he had to look for holes in his cases to be prepared for what defense attorneys would throw at him. But in this case, where a suspect had confessed, was it necessary to look for holes? Collin said, "It takes time to stop for fuel. Maybe Mick and Sheila wanted the boat to be gassed up and ready to go the next time they used it so that they wouldn't have to waste time at the pumps. Or maybe Grant got to him, made Mick feel sorry for him."

"Grant did have a way of disarming people." I recalled Mick and Sheila's ashamed looks when he reminded them that he was going through a hard time, not unlike the one they'd gone through when he'd bailed them out by giving them cash on the spot for their boat.

Now that Collin had told us Mick's story, I had another pressing question. "Who else confessed? You said there were three people, and two of them were Mick and Sheila. Who was the third?"

Collin scrolled through the images on his phone before showing me another mug shot. This one made my heart sink faster and farther than the *Sexy Sheila*. Tanner stood against the wall, his eyes bright with terror. Unlike Sheila, he wasn't smiling. In fact, his lips were pressed together, as if he was trying to keep them from quivering. His eyes appeared moist, too. *Had he been crying?*

I sat back in my chair, flabbergasted, my appetite instantly gone. "Tanner confessed? What did he say? Was he in cahoots with his mother? Did the two of them kill Grant together?"

"No," Collin said, "at least that's not how he tells it. He says it was all him, that he put cold packs all over the boat when he came here to dognap Jojo."

"But he was only here for a few minutes," I said, adding less assuredly, "at least I think he was only here for a few minutes. I saw him drive away with the dog." He'd been smart enough to leave the headlights off until he reached the road so that the lights wouldn't catch Grant's attention.

"He claims he pretended to leave after he spoke with you so that you wouldn't see him planting the cold packs. He says he drove a little way down the road, waited a few minutes for you to go back inside the *Skinny Dipper* and fall asleep, then came back to put the cold packs on Grant's boat."

Could Tanner have returned without me waking up again and spotting him? I supposed it was possible if he stayed low so that I didn't notice his shadow and worked quietly. His mother's hybrid SUV was very quiet. I hadn't heard the engine when he'd arrived to claim Jojo or when he'd departed with the dog. I wouldn't have heard it if he returned, either. "How'd he start the fire?"

"He says he made his own improvised explosive device from information he found on the internet. He said he used an electrical repair kit and a kitchen timer, plus some gunpowder."

Colette's eyes went wide. "It's that easy?"

"Unfortunately, yes," Collin said, "for people with some technical skill. Even then, it usually takes some practice to get things right."

My gut wrenched as an image of the boy and his dog rolling around happily on the dock filled my mind. If

Tanner went to jail, Jojo would be miserable without his boy. "What else did Tanner say?"

"Precious little," Collin said. "I was in the middle of questioning him about the explosion, how he triggered it, when his father showed up with a criminal defense attorney. The lawyer shut down the interview right away even though Tanner objected and said he wanted to talk."

The boy's father might not be up for a dad-of-the-year award, but at least he had stepped up at a critical moment. Desperate to find another explanation, I asked, "Is Landreth absolutely sure the explosion wasn't an accident? Was ammonium nitrate was found in Grant's Camaro?"

"Not a trace," Collin said. "The only item of interest they found in his car were some printouts from dating sites."

"Let me guess," I said. "All of the women were professional types, slightly older than him."

"Bingo."

Looked like Grant the gold digger was already seeking a new means of support. I told Collin about the woman who'd come by just a few short hours after Grant's boat exploded, the one who'd left the bottle of suntan oil behind, which I'd later discovered didn't actually contain suntan oil. I retrieved the bottle from the bathroom and showed it to him. "Colette thinks it might be filled with dark corn syrup, but we're not sure."

Like Colette, he sniffed the substance and poured a small amount in his hand to examine it. "It's certainly sticky."

"What do you think it means?"

"Who knows?" he said. "Maybe the woman has children or an ex who doesn't like her dating and filled it with corn syrup as a prank when they realized she was going to meet a new man."

In other words, maybe the odd substance had nothing at all to do with Grant Hardisty. I chewed my lip, pondering the situation, and circled back to the more concrete evidence collected by law enforcement. "Did the search team find packaging for cold packs in the debris?"

"No," Collin said, "but the fire destroyed most of the evidence. What the fire didn't ruin sank to the bottom of the lake."

"What now?" I asked.

Collin raised his palms. "I've never faced a situation like this before, where there's multiple confessors. They can't all be guilty but, at this point, the only one who clearly seems to be lying is Sheila. Providing a false statement is a crime in itself. My money's on Deena Hardisty. Her story is the only one with no holes in it. We're holding all four of them for the time being. Maybe a night in jail will convince one or more of them to recant."

My gut tied itself in a tight knot. "Tanner's in jail?" The thought of the young boy in a cell with hardened criminals made me queasy.

"He's being held in juvie," Collin clarified. "For now, anyway. Under Tennessee law, a child of any age can be transferred to the adult criminal justice system if they're charged with murder or attempted murder. If he were found guilty of first-degree murder, he wouldn't be eligible for parole for at least fifty-one years, at least under current law."

"Fifty-one years?!" I cried. "He'd be a senior citizen by then!"

"The law has been a point of contention." Collin tipped his head one way then the other, as if balancing a scale. "Families of the victims and victims' rights groups say the law is fair, that their loved ones won't ever be coming back and that they shouldn't have to fight to keep killers in prison. Advocates of criminal justice reform say mandatory minimums don't take the circumstances into account, such as the age of the offender at the time the murder was committed. Juvenile offenders are subject to the mandatory minimum just like adult offenders."

While there were certainly two sides to the issue, I still felt heartsick. Tanner was a boy who dearly loved his dog. Could he also truly be a killer?

CHAPTER 19
ROCK-A-BYE BABY

SAWDUST

Sawdust liked sleeping on the boat. The gentle waves made the boat rock softly. Normally, Whitney slept well on the boat, too. But that night, Whitney turned over and over and over, unable to sleep. She kicked off the covers, then pulled them back up over herself. She seemed anxious about something. Sawdust wished he could relieve her worry. To that end, he'd curled up against her and purred. It hadn't seemed to help.

As much as Sawdust loved Whitney, she was making it impossible for him to sleep. He was already hours behind on his daily sleep time. He'd been awake most of the day, watching the birds fly around the lake and keeping an eye out for the occasional fish who would flip up out of the water. Whitney had taken off running at one point, and he'd stepped to the edge of the boat to see where she was going. Buck had grabbed him and put him inside before Sawdust could determine what was going on. There'd also been that woman who'd come by the boat, the one who laughed and laughed. Then tonight, Colette and Collin had come for dinner. It had been a busy day, and the cat needed his sleep so he could be refreshed.

Sawdust slid down from the bed, padded into Buck's berth, and leapt up beside the big man. After testing out several spots for comfort, he settled for sleeping in the cozy triangle formed by Buck's crooked knee. He was soon in dreamland, where fish flipped out of the water all day long, throwing themselves onto the deck of the *Skinny Dipper* like gifts from a lake god.

CHAPTER 20

MORAL DILEMMAS AND OBLIGATIONS

WHITNEY

Saturday dawned bright, not a cloud in the sky. After we'd downed our morning coffee, Buck and I set off to the Hermitage Branch Library to take the exam for our boating licenses. We were put in a room with several other people our age or younger. A monitor read a new mystery release while we applicants answered the questions. Having studied in every spare moment, I earned a near-perfect score. The only question I missed was one about noise levels. A motorized vessel's noise level was not to exceed 86 decibels at a distance of 50 feet or more. I'd mistakenly thought the distance was 100 feet.

Buck scored far lower than I had, but achieved the bare minimum to pass. As we left with our new boating certifications, he ran a hand over his forehead and pretended to toss the sweat. "Phew!"

"You should've studied more."

"Why?" He held up his license. "I got my card, same as you, with a lot less work."

"That's a lazy approach to life."

"It's worked well for me so far."

Buck climbed into his van to drive into Nashville. The generator he'd special ordered for the houseboat had arrived at the boat supply. We'd install it as soon as he returned. In the meantime, I swung by the upholstery shop to pick up the new cushions they'd made for the houseboat's living room furniture. They were covered in a navy blue-and-white all-weather fabric that would stand up to wet bathing suits and the inevitable spills that would take place in a house that moved up and down.

On my drive to the marina, I made a quick stop at the Get-N-Git for a loaf of bread and a jar of peanut butter so that I could make an easy lunch later. We'd need sunscreen for both Colette's bachelorette party and Buck's bachelor party. *Might as well stock up now.* It would be one less thing to worry about later. As I headed to the checkout counter, I reached down and grabbed two bottles of the coconut-scented oil. To ensure they hadn't gone bad like the one I'd attempted to use the evening before, I shook them to verify their viscosity. They seemed fine.

Billy was working the register today rather than his wife. He greeted me with a smile. "'Mornin'. How's your day going?"

"Great so far," I said. "Just took my boating test and passed with flying colors."

"Congratulations!" He rang up the bread and peanut butter, and picked up one of the bottles of suntan oil.

I recalled that, the last time I'd been in the store, his

wife had appeared weary and worried, and had mentioned that her mother had fallen. It only seemed right to ask about the woman's well-being. "How's your mother-in-law?"

Billy didn't skip a beat as he scanned the barcode on the back of the bottle of oil. "She's fit as a fiddle. Why do you ask?"

"Last time I was in here, I noticed your wife looked upset. I asked if she was okay and she told me her mother had tripped over her slippers and gotten bruised up."

He fumbled with the second bottle of suntan oil before getting it into the paper sack, and slapped a palm against his forehead. "I'd plumb forgotten about that. All that time fishing in the sun must've fried my brain." He offered a cringe followed by a tentative grin.

Is he covering for his wife? Maybe all of the false confessions had me feeling suspicious of everyone, but I had to wonder if Billy's wife had lied to me about her mother. Might she know something about what happened to Grant? Be involved somehow? Is that what she'd actually been upset about? As quickly as I had the thought, I dismissed it. What reason would the woman have had to kill Grant Hardisty and destroy his boat?

I thanked Billy and picked up my bag. He gave the same schtick as his wife. "You got what you came for." He pointed to the door, the grin still on his face. "Now git!"

I drove back to the *Skinny Dipper.* After eating a peanut butter sandwich for lunch, I installed the cushions on the couch, love seat, and armchair. They looked fabulous! The nautical stripe had been a good choice.

I puttered around inside the boat, replacing pieces of missing or damaged trim. After putting the life jacket on my cat, I left the back door open so Sawdust could meander in and out at will. He climbed atop the rubber ducky and flopped down for a nap. The ducky seemed to be his favorite place to catch a comfy catnap.

Buck returned with the generator later that morning. I helped him wrangle it out of his van and onto a dolly so he could move it onto the boat. Before we did any work on the generator, we made sure every electrical appliance in the boat was turned off and disconnected. Buck stepped out onto the dock and walked over to the pedestal to disconnect the boat's big yellow power cord from the shore power supply. *Better safe than sorry.*

For safety reasons, generators were positioned as far away as possible from the sleeping quarters. In our case, the generator was situated behind a panel on the back deck. It took us a solid hour to take out the old generator. First, we had to remove the rusty soundproofing enclosure from around the unit. Next, we had to disconnect all of the connections to the boat's electrical system, which the generator was made to operate while the boat was out on the water.

As we disconnected the wires and cables, my mind went back to Tanner. Could he have actually designed a working device to detonate the explosives on Grant's boat? I wondered. I supposed he might have taken computer-aided design or electronics classes in school. High schools offered more of these types of specialized classes now than they had when I'd attended years ago. Maybe electronics were simple to him. Still, even though I had worked in a construction trade for years and had a natural knack for mechanical design, electrical stuff still sometimes puzzled me. Luckily, where my skills fell short, Buck's took up the slack.

Once my cousin and I got the foam-lined metal soundproofing box out of the way and made sure there were no more connections in place, Buck removed the bolts. It took both of us to wrangle the generator out of the space and onto the dolly. We rolled it out to his van and heaved it up into the cargo space so that he could take it to the dump later.

When we returned to the boat, I rounded up the vacuum, a nontoxic cleaning spray, and some old rags to clean dust, dirt, and cobwebs from the space before we installed the new generator. Meanwhile, Buck got down on his knees to unbox the new unit.

The vacuum whirred loudly as I used the hose to suck the lint and dust from the empty space. A small spider who'd been living in the space ran for its life. I hoped the spider would build a new web outside where it could take care of the pesky mosquitos that came around at dusk.

I felt a tap on my shoulder and turned, expecting to see Buck. Instead, Tanner stood on the deck. I sprang to my feet without turning off the vac and instinctively held the hose in front of me, as if he were a small spider I could suck up in self-defense. Realizing how ridiculous I must look, I reached over and turned the vacuum off. As it whirred to a stop, Buck glanced up and noticed Tanner for the first time, too. My cousin stood, his expression wary. He discreetly leaned over and retrieved his claw hammer from his open toolbox should it be needed.

"Hi, Tanner," I said.

The boy managed to choke out a raspy, "Hey." His eyes were bloodshot from crying and lack of sleep, and his acne-riddled cheeks were tear-stained. His hair looked like it hadn't been combed in days. His shoulders slumped inside his wrinkled T-shirt.

Buck eyed the kid. "They let you out, huh?"

Tanner nodded, his lip quivering. "My lawyer got me out. They don't think I did it."

My cousin cocked his head. "Did you?"

"No," Tanner said, almost sounding remorseful that he hadn't been the one to kill his stepfather. "I hated Grant, but I didn't kill him. I made up a story about how I blew up his boat, but the police and fire department didn't believe me."

I watched him closely. "If you didn't do it, why did you confess?"

"Because of my mom," he said. "I don't want her to go to prison. I figured they'd go easier on me since I'm a kid. I thought they could only keep me in jail until I turned eighteen."

"I hate to tell you this," I said, "but kids who commit murder can be tried as adults in Tennessee. They can go to prison for life."

"I know that now. The lawyer my father hired told me." He gulped down a sob. "You have to help my mother, Whitney. She didn't do it, either. I know she didn't! She only confessed because she thought I killed Grant. She didn't want to see me get punished when she's the one who brought him into our lives."

Buck and I exchanged a glance before I returned my focus to the teen. "But your mother had a motive and the means to kill him. The cold packs."

He fisted his hands at his sides and glared at me, his eyes sparking with fury. "She only confessed because of you! You told her that you saw me go onto Grant's boat to get Jojo. Then you mentioned the cold packs and that they contained ammonia nitride." He'd gotten the name of the chemical wrong, but there was nothing to be gained by correcting him. He fumed and sobbed at the same time. "She thought you'd tell the police you saw me take Jojo and that they'd come and arrest me. If you had never come to our house, she'd be free right now! You have to get her out of jail. It's all your fault!"

His accusation hurt. I hadn't been trying to get an innocent person in trouble. I'd only been trying to find out the truth. I took an involuntary step backward and bumped into the railing. "Look, Tanner. I only came to your house to speak to you and your mom so I could try to figure things out. I never thought anyone who was innocent would confess as a result."

"But she did!" He brought his fists down, as if slamming them on an imaginary table in front of him. "The police aren't even looking for the real bad guy anymore. You have to find out the truth so they'll let her go!"

I didn't want to reveal that I was dating the homicide detective and knew that his mother had provided clear and convincing details on how she'd committed the crime, so I eased around the subject. "I know this is hard to take, Tanner. But your mother must have convinced them she was guilty or they'd have released her, too. If there were any holes in her story, they would have let her go."

He burst into sobs, his shoulders shaking. Despite the fact that he stood at least five feet eight, he looked like a young child, so lost and confused and powerless. I felt horrible.

I gently took him by the shoulders. "Does your mother know you've been released?"

Too choked up to talk, he lifted the shoulders I held to indicate he didn't know.

"I know all seems lost right now, Tanner," I said. "But the detective and the fire investigator will want to make sure they've got the right person. Just give it some time." The only thing I thought time would do was make it easier for the boy to accept that his own mother was a killer, but the platitude was all I had to offer.

Buck added, "If your mother didn't do it, she'll probably withdraw her confession once she knows you've been released."

I cut my cousin a stern look. I knew he meant well, but he shouldn't get the kid's hopes up. Even if Deena recanted, she wouldn't necessarily be released. After all, Collin had said her story checked out. She'd even described the clever device she'd used to cause a spark and ignite the inferno. There wasn't any coming back from that, was there?

To my dismay, Tanner appeared buoyed by Buck's comment. His eyes brightened, and he straightened.

I held up a palm. "Even if your mother recants, they might not let her go."

Fresh fury ignited in his eyes. "Then you better do something!" The fire in his eyes dimmed and he choked on another sob. "Please!"

Tanner and I held each other's gazes for a long moment. The desperation and grief in his eyes made my insides squirm. I'd caused it. But Deena was very likely guilty, right? And even if I wanted to help free Deena, what could I do? Was there any stone unturned? I could think of none . . .

Except the woman with the sticky suntan oil and the bird-watcher. They were long shots, but I'd see if I could track them down. At the risk of giving Tanner even more false hope, I said, "I'll see what I can do."

As soon as Tanner had driven off in his mother's car, I whipped out my cell phone and called Collin. "Tanner was just here at the marina, begging for me to help him free his mother."

"Poor kid," Collin said. "He couldn't keep his story straight. First, he claimed he'd searched the internet for information on IEDs from his own laptop, and then when we checked his browser history and found no such sites, he claimed he'd searched on his phone. He says he bought more cold packs from a pharmacy near their home and that he'd paid cash for them, but the manager checked their sales for the last six months and there was no bulk purchase of cold packs. When we asked Tanner what type of accelerant he used, he was totally confused. He didn't even understand the question. We also got some wires and a timer from a hardware store and set them down on the table in front of him. We told him to show us how he'd connected the wires to the timer, but he didn't have a clue what to do. That kid's never made a bomb."

"He told me and Buck that he'd confessed so that his mother would be freed. He thinks she only confessed to keep him from being arrested." It was a vicious circle of sorts.

"I can understand why he wouldn't want to believe his mother is guilty," Collin said, "but Deena's story is entirely plausible."

My stomach felt sick. "Are you certain?"

"Certain enough. More certain than I've been in many other cases. Either she's guilty or she's a damn good liar who's done her homework."

Speaking of homework . . . "What about *her* computer?" I asked. "Did you check her browsing history, too?" If she'd performed searches on explosives *after* Grant died, it would indicate she was gathering information to concoct a story to exonerate her son.

"She'd cleared it," Collin said.

"Can your tech team recreate it somehow?"

"They probably could," he said. "They've done a system restore for me before in another case. But their time is valuable and they're backlogged. With her having confessed, I'm not sure it makes sense to add this to their plate."

Seemed the police labs were always backlogged. *So many crimes, so little time.*

"By the way," Collin added, "Tanner wasn't the only suspect released today. We let Sheila McNeely go, too. She'll face charges for providing a false statement, but we don't think she had anything to do with the explosion on the boat. We don't have enough evidence to build a case against her, anyway."

"You've still got Mick in custody, then?"

"Yep," Collin said, "and he's being as tight-lipped as ever."

"You think he could be taking the fall for his wife?"

"I can't rule it out."

"Does he know Deena Hardisty is also in custody? Maybe he'd say more, or recant his confession, if he knows she's on the hook."

"Landreth and I decided to keep that information under wraps for now," Collin said. "If he's guilty and we mistakenly release him, it would be a public relations nightmare."

"Has he hired an attorney?"

"No. He says he doesn't want one."

A stupid move, for sure. "What about Deena?"

"She's got a lawyer. A good one, too. But there's not much the guy can do at his point since she's already confessed. She withdrew her confession once she knew Tanner had been cleared, but there's a lot of evidence pointing her way. I'm sure her attorney will advise her to plead 'not guilty' at her arraignment. He'll probably try to get the confession set aside. I doubt he'll have much luck, though. We recorded it. She was lucid and spoke clearly and intelligently. He's got his work cut out for him."

I thought back to Tanner, of his desperate, grief-stricken face. *I have my work cut out for me, too.*

CHAPTER 21

WORKING BEHIND THE SCENES

WHITNEY

I didn't tell Collin or Landreth about my plans to track down the woman with the sticky suntan oil or the bird-watcher. They might tell me to butt out, and I didn't want to go back on my word to Tanner. Besides, it couldn't hurt to have another person working the case, even if I was only an amateur investigator. If I came across any incriminating evidence, I'd turn it over to the professionals and let them take things from there. What's more, they were both working multiple cases and were stretched thin. I had only Grant's murder to look into.

There was work to be done, so I couldn't pursue either the woman from the dating app or the bird-watcher right away. I decided to start with the bird-watcher, though. After all, I had a solid lead for him—his license plate number.

I got online and ran a search. I had to pay a small fee

and check a box to attest that I was requesting the information for one of a limited number of legal purposes, but I got a name and address. Hugh Montaigne. The car was registered at an address in the nearby town of Mt. Juliet. I decided I'd pay Mr. Montaigne a visit. He'd be more likely to offer me a look at those images or video if I made my request in person. It would also be easier for me to gauge his reaction if I spoke with him face-to-face. If he had something to do with Grant's death, his expressions and demeanor might betray his guilt.

As Buck and I installed the new generator and the soundproofing box that had come with it, I continued to engage in a debate with myself. *What is my moral obligation here?* If Deena had confessed as a result of my visit and she was truly guilty, I'd saved law enforcement some time and effort. Some might call me a minor hero. *Yay me!* It certainly appeared that was the case. But it was an entirely different matter if Tanner was right and his mother was innocent, if she'd only confessed because she feared I'd rat out her son to investigators, tell them I'd caught him dognapping Jojo the night before the boat exploded. What's more, Mick was also in jail for the crime. They couldn't both be guilty, could they? Neither had claimed to be working with the other. One or the other of them was being held unjustly, or both, even if they'd caused the injustice. *Ugh!*

Though I felt horrible for Tanner and wanted to help Collin sort things out, I determined my ultimate ethical obligation was not to any particular person, but to the truth. I'd do whatever I could to ensure the truth came out. To that end, I carefully considered the details of Deena's confession, searching for any weak points.

She'd said she'd driven to the marina after Tanner had

brought Jojo home. There were no functioning security cameras on the dock to provide evidence of her visit. I'd noticed no security cameras at her house when I'd gone by to speak to her and Tanner earlier in the week. Though it was possible any cameras could have been hidden, it would surprise me if they were. Most people wanted their cameras easily visible so they'd act as a deterrent to burglars or porch pirates who stole packages from people's stoops. So, presumably, there was no video evidence of her leaving the house after Tanner returned with Jojo, nor was there video showing that she and her SUV had remained at home after Tanner's dognapping escapade.

None of the roads between her house and the marina were toll roads, so there'd be no toll charge record to substantiate her alleged drive to the marina. Nor would the absence of a toll charge indicate that she had remained at home.

She claimed she'd filled the boat's life jacket bins with cold packs, doused them in camp fuel, and inserted a spark igniter. She said she'd bought the camp fuel and manual spark igniter for cash at an unknown hardware store somewhere in Nashville on an unknown date. Thus, that purchase was untraceable. However, she claimed that she'd pilfered many of the cold packs from the hospital.

That's it! The fact that could prove her innocence or substantiate her guilt. If the hospital audited its inventory of cold packs, compared the number currently in stock with the number ordered and the number used for patient care, maybe they could determine whether a large number of the cold packs had actually been pilfered. But the hospital wasn't likely to perform an audit at my request. After all, I had no standing in the case. But would they do it to help prove the innocence of an employee? They might, especially if her attorney made the request. As soon as Buck and I were done installing the generator, I'd determine who represented Deena.

I also considered the other suspects. It sounded like Sheila could be eliminated. Collin had said her story didn't jibe with the facts, that she claimed to have used dynamite on the boat and didn't once mention the ammonium nitrate. But could her story have been fabricated? A ploy to throw law enforcement off her scent? If so, why confess? Why not wait for law enforcement to round her up?

I also wondered about Jackie. She'd been divorced from Grant for several years now, long enough for him to meet and marry Deena. She could've just called him about the furniture, yet she'd come to the marina to speak with him. Her in-person visit said she was still hung up on him, didn't it? That she hadn't yet been able to fully let him go? If nothing more, her visit showed that she still harbored enough hatred for the man that she'd wanted to rake him over the coals one last time. But had she also created those proverbial coals by blowing up his boat? They say where there's smoke, there's fire. Jackie seemed to still be smoldering over the way Grant had treated her. I wasn't quite ready to rule her out. And I still wondered about that woman with the Audi and her sticky bottle of suntan oil. What had that been about?

A couple of scraped knuckles and a half hour later, the new generator was in place, fully tested, and found to be functioning as it should. Buck and I called it a day. He and Owen had fittings for their wedding tuxedos in a couple of hours, so it made no sense to get started on another task.

I knew that criminal court filings were a matter of public record, so I went inside the boat and logged into my laptop computer to run a search. Searching by Deena's name, I was able to see her pending charge of murder. When I clicked on the link for more information, her attorney's name appeared. Raphael Aguilera.

I then ran a search for Aguilera's legal practice. He was a junior partner with a mid-sized firm in the eastern part of Nashville, not far from where Deena and Tanner lived. Though I doubted the man would be at work on a Saturday afternoon, I nonetheless placed a call to his office. As expected, a recording told me that I'd reached the law firm outside of normal business hours. It invited me to use the employee directory to be routed to my party's extension to leave a message. I went through the rigamarole until a tone sounded, signaling me to speak. I hung up the phone, preferring to speak to the man in person. I'd call him first thing Monday morning.

Even though Grant's killer was likely behind bars, the explosion had left me unsettled and there was no way I'd leave Sawdust on the *Skinny Dipper* alone. I packed him into his carrier and dropped him back at home. Emmalee's calico kitten, Cleo, was overjoyed to have her housemate back. She pounced on Sawdust and held him down, licking his cheek over and over. He looked up at me helplessly, but I knew he was secretly enjoying the attention. Sawdust loved to be loved.

I returned to my SUV and typed Hugh Montaigne's address into my maps app. Off I went to Mt. Juliet. The voice told me where to turn, and a half hour later I was approaching Montaigne's house. The one problem was,

Hugh passed me in his gray sedan heading in the opposite direction.

"Wait!" I cried on reflex, slamming on my brakes. A futile effort if ever there was one. He couldn't hear me hollering inside my car. He wouldn't have even been able to read my lips because he hadn't been looking at me. His eyes had been on the woman in his passenger seat.

I turned into the nearest driveway and backed out, heading after him. Recalling how he'd seemed to be trying to avoid me at the marina for some reason, I held back far enough that he wouldn't notice me tailing him. I'd catch and corner him when he stopped.

He turned into the parking lot for a movie theater and parked. As he and the woman climbed out of the car, I parked and slid out of my vehicle as well. I hurried after them, hoping to catch Montaigne before he went inside. Unfortunately, a group of five excited and nearly identical redheaded children surged out of a minivan and stepped out in front of me, fanning out to effectively block my progress. "Stay close, kids!" their mother called in an attempt to corral the bunch. "I don't want to lose anyone!"

By the time I circled around the kids, Montaigne and the woman had already entered the theater. I scurried up to the ticket booth. "One ticket for the same movie they're going to." I pointed through the glass as the couple handed their tickets to the teenage girl at the entrance to the hallway that led to the theaters.

I whipped out my debit card, tapped it against the device, and took my ticket. "Thanks!" Hurrying inside, I stepped into the short line that had formed.

When I reached the girl, she took my ticket from me,

tore it in half, and handed the stub back to me. "Theater eight to your right. Enjoy the movie."

Enjoy it? I didn't even know what show I'd bought a ticket for. Nevertheless, I gave her a smile. "Thanks."

I strode down the hall and opened the door to theater eight. To my dismay, previews had already started and the theater was dark. I stepped inside and stood against the wall for a moment, waiting for my eyes to adjust. Once they did, I scanned the audience. *There he is.* Montaigne and the woman were seated five rows up in the center. The theater was sparsely populated, only a dozen or so people in the seats. Whatever movie was about to show must not be a new release.

I went up the steps and down the row, sliding into the seat next to Montaigne. He glanced over and gave me a look of equal parts surprise and irritation. He probably wondered why some strange woman had decided to make herself a third wheel on his date. He hadn't recognized me.

I leaned over to whisper to him. "Hi, Mr. Montaigne. My name is Whitney Whitaker. I've been working on a boat out at the marina. We spoke the other day about a missing dog?"

He frowned slightly. "I remember. Why are you accosting me here?"

The woman he was with leaned forward. I gave her a smile and raised my hand in greeting before returning my attention to Hugh. "I don't know if you heard, but there was an explosion at Old Hickory Lake."

He hesitated a moment, but said, "Yes. I heard about it."

"I saw you taking photos and recording videos in the area before the explosion."

"I was watching birds. There are ospreys at the lake as well as several other interesting species. It's a hobby of mine."

"I'd like to see those photos and videos."

"There are hundreds of photos and hours of video. I don't have time to show them all to you. I'm a busy man."

"You could e-mail the files to me."

"Sorry, I don't share my images or recordings."

"Why not?"

He hesitated a moment before snapping, "Because they're my intellectual property. I might want to sell them one day."

His defensiveness raised my suspicions. *Could he have been the person who killed Grant?* "I'm not sure I'm buying that explanation. It seemed to me that you were trying to hide your face from us when we questioned you about the missing dog."

He frowned. "It doesn't matter to me whether you buy my explanation or not. What matters is that you are harassing me in a theater when I'm trying to enjoy an evening out with my wife. Do I need to get a manager in here to remove you?"

Undeterred by his threat to have me ejected from the theater, I said, "It seemed to me that you took some photos and video of the *Sexy Sheila* and the guy who lived on it. He's dead now, and you haven't come back to bird-watch at the lake since. You have to admit the circumstances are suspicious."

He scoffed. "Are you implying that I might have killed Grant Hardisty?"

"So, you know his name." I arched my brows in accusation. "Interesting. I didn't mention it."

A woman in the row behind Montaigne sent both a scowl and a loud *shhh* my way. It was only the previews and people were still streaming into the theater, but she'd paid for a ticket and I supposed it was rude to be holding a conversation here, even if it was in a whisper. I leaned in closer to Montaigne. "Can we talk in the hallway?"

His frown deepened, but he agreed. "Make it quick. I don't want to miss the movie." He turned and handed his enormous cardboard tub of popcorn to his wife. "I'll be right back."

The two of us stepped out into the corridor. As people walked by bearing tubs and bags of popcorn, oversized drinks, and shareable-sized boxes of candy, I turned to the man. "Why should I believe you had nothing to do with Grant Hardisty's death?"

His eyes narrowed. Rather than answer my question, he posed one of his own. "Are you with law enforcement?"

"No," I said. "I've spoken to the fire investigator and the homicide detective who are working the case together, but I'm not in law enforcement myself."

"Why are you interrogating me instead of them?"

His tone told me he wasn't likely to cooperate with me. I didn't have a badge, a title, or any authority. Other than the wrench in my pocket, I didn't have a weapon, either. "You may have heard that a woman confessed to killing Grant."

"His wife. Yes, I heard. When someone is killed, it's often the spouse who did it."

"Well, her son doesn't think she's guilty. He says she confessed only because she thought *he* might end up getting arrested for the crime."

His mouth pursed in skepticism. "People don't generally confess to murders they haven't committed."

"True," I agreed, "but it's not totally unheard of. At any rate, law enforcement thinks they've got the guilty party. I'm not as convinced as they are. I want to ensure justice is done, that the truth prevails, so I'm chasing down loose ends."

"I'm a loose end, huh?" He chuckled and his shoulders relaxed a little. "I'm all about the truth." He huffed a breath and eyed me. "I suppose there's no harm in filling you in. With Mr. Hardisty dead and his wife in jail for his murder, it's all become moot."

"What's become moot?"

He reached into his back pocket, pulled out his wallet, and removed a business card. He handed it to me. His name was printed on the card, of course. Hugh Montaigne. But what was printed under it surprised me. *Private detective.*

I looked up at him. "I don't understand."

"You were right. I wasn't out at the lake to watch the birds. I was there to watch Grant."

"You were? Who hired you?"

"An insurance company. He'd filed a large personal injury claim for a slip and fall. His diagnosis was specious. Soft tissue damage, mostly. The doctor he went to has a reputation for questionable practices. There was also some speculation that it was a collusive claim."

"Collusive claim?" I repeated. "What does that mean?"

"It means Mr. Hardisty and the policyholder could have cooked things up together. Faked an injury to milk the insurance company with the intention of sharing the insurance proceeds."

"Like fraud?"

"Exactly."

My mind spun like the slushie machine in the theater's concessions stand. I wasn't sure what to make of this new information, how it fit into the bigger story. "Who was the policyholder?"

Montaigne shrugged. "Couldn't tell you. The insurance company hired me to gather evidence that Mr. Hardisty wasn't actually injured. The identity of the policyholder was irrelevant to my work, so they didn't provide it and I didn't ask."

His explanation was making sense. I felt a little ashamed for confronting him on his date. But how was I to know he was a private investigator? I suppose I should have googled his name once I learned it. There might have been a link informing me of this fact. *Live and learn.*

"I thought you might be on to me," he said. "That's why I snuck away from the marina earlier in the week. I hadn't heard yet that Grant had been killed and I was still working the investigation. The insurance company contacted me later and pulled me off the case."

"What insurance company were you working for?"

"I prefer to share that information with law enforcement only." He gestured to the business card I was still holding. "Feel free to pass my contact information on to the fire and police departments."

"I will. Now that we've come clean with each other, can I see the photos you took? And the video?" Collin and Landreth wouldn't have time to spend looking it all over, and couldn't justify taking the time with a confessor in jail. But I was self-employed. If I wasted my time, I only had myself to answer to.

"Sorry," Hugh said. "The photos and video belong

to my client. I can't release them without a subpoena, court order, or the client's agreement."

Ugh.

He jerked his head toward the door. "I better get back in there or my wife won't let me hear the end of it."

"Okay." I slid his business card into my purse. "Thanks for this information."

With a curt nod, he turned and walked back into the dark theater.

CHAPTER 22

HOME SWEET HOME

SAWDUST

As much as Sawdust loved to be with Whitney, he had to admit it felt good to be back home, napping on his usual bed. The cottage didn't bob up and down like the boat did, and no creature had ever come out from under the house to try to eat him. He shuddered in horror at the memory of that enormous fish coming at him, its mouth open so wide it looked like it could swallow Sawdust whole.

He'd missed Cleo, too. She was much younger than him, still kittenish, and could be annoying at times. She'd push him aside to eat out of his bowl, and sometimes he'd find her sleeping in his favorite spots. But she could also be a fun playmate when he was in the mood, and it was nice to curl up next to her sometimes. He could tell Cleo had missed him, too. She wouldn't stop following him around and giving him kisses. He supposed he should let her know he'd missed her, too. He turned his head and gave her a quick lick under the chin. She responded by butting her head up against his cheek. Silly kitten.

CHAPTER 23

APRIL SHOWERS

WHITNEY

The popcorn smelled so good I bought an extra-large bucket to go. The ticket seller gave me an odd look on my way out, probably wondering why in the world I'd spent a small fortune on a movie ticket and copious quantities of popcorn if I didn't plan to stay and watch the movie.

I ate the salty popcorn in my car on the drive home, wishing I'd sprung for a soda, too. As I munched and crunched my way to the bottom of the tub, I thought things over. Grant's insurance claim didn't seem to have any direct link to his murder that I could discern. I'd spent the afternoon chasing a false lead when I could have been doing something more productive. But that's what crime-solving was all about, right? Collecting clues and information, figuring out which pieces mattered and which were irrelevant. It wasn't an entirely efficient process, but the hope was that each step would lead closer to the truth.

Collin picked me up at my house that evening and took me out for dinner. Over veggie fajitas and salt-rimmed frozen margaritas at a Mexican restaurant, I told him about my conversation with Hugh Montaigne earlier in the day. "Remember the bird-watcher I told you about? The one who was hanging around the lake?"

"Yeah?"

"His name is Hugh Montaigne. I tracked him down today to see if he would let me take a look at his pictures and video footage. Turns out he's no bird-watcher at all. He's a private eye who's been investigating Grant's insurance claim. He said he couldn't give me access to the photos or videos because they belong to his client."

"That's standard," Collin said. "It's usually written into the contracts, in fact. Did he tell you who the client was?"

"Only that it was an insurance company. He said they thought Grant's injury claim might be fraudulent, that he could have been faking his injuries."

Collin grunted. "He wouldn't be the first."

"Montaigne also said he doesn't know who the policyholder is, but that the insurance company thought Grant's claim might be what he called a 'collusive claim.'"

"Really?" Collin had been about to take a bite, but stopped, holding his tortilla aloft. A chunk of tomato fell out and plopped onto his plate.

I nodded as I sucked frozen lime juice and tequila through my straw. "Mm-hmm." I set my drink back down. "Do you think it has anything to do with his murder?"

Collin took a bite and shook his head. Once he'd swallowed, he said, "If the claim was collusive, whoever

Grant had been colluding with would want him to remain alive to collect the settlement. With Grant dead, the claim becomes part of his estate."

I finished his thought. "Which means the claim now belongs to Deena."

"Yep."

I'd been hoping to find something to exonerate the woman, but it seemed like I'd only dug her in deeper.

Collin said, "I'm surprised you got that much information out of him. P.I.s are usually tight-lipped."

"He only told me because Grant is dead now. I don't think he'd have said much if Grant was still alive." *Or if I hadn't been such a persistent pain in the neck and he'd wanted to get me out of the way so he could enjoy the movie with his wife.*

Collin set his fork down and stared at me. "I have to tell you something. I suppose now is as good a time as any."

The intent look on his face set off alarm bells in my head. "What is it?"

"Deena's case was referred to the district attorney today."

"What does that mean?"

"It means you should expect a call from the prosecutor. If the case goes to trial, you'll be the star witness."

"What?" Panic welled up in me. I didn't want to be a star in any sort of show. I still harbored trauma from playing one of several rabbits in the second-grade class play, and I hadn't even had any lines. "Why?"

"You saw Deena deliver cold packs to Grant. You saw Tanner take Jojo from Grant's boat. You found the cold packs in your trash. That's all key evidence that points to Deena as the killer."

No. No, no, no! "I don't want to be the star witness. That's too much responsibility!"

"You won't have a choice, Whitney. You'll be subpoenaed. If you don't show up, you could end up in jail yourself."

Ugh! I felt hopelessly tangled and trapped, like a struggling fish caught in a drift net.

After dinner, Collin and I went back to my house, where we lounged on the couch and watched television. Emmalee was working a shift at the café, so we had the house to ourselves. Sawdust and Cleo climbed onto the sofa with us, situating themselves so that we could easily reach their favorite spots for scratching. Under the chin. On the chest. Behind the ears. I'd like to say I enjoyed whatever show we saw, but the truth was I had no idea what program had even been playing. I'd been too preoccupied by the thought that I could end up testifying in what was sure to be one of the biggest trials of the year.

At ten, I walked Collin to the door and we ended the night with a warm kiss. Seeming to sense my inner turmoil, he pulled me to him and held me for a long moment in a tight hug. "Try not to think about it," he said. "Chances are the case won't go to trial. The D.A. and Deena's attorney will probably work out a plea deal."

"I hope so."

Once he'd gone, I got ready for bed. I climbed in and pulled the covers up over me. It was nice to be back in my old bed, though a part of me missed the gentle rocking of the boat, the soft swells and the calming *shush-shush* of the water lapping up against the boat. I tried to force the worry from my mind. Emmalee and I would be hosting Colette's bridal shower tomorrow. I had a busy day ahead of me and needed to get a good night's sleep. I had little success until Sawdust curled up against my belly and began to purr, as if there was no need to worry. *Maybe he's right.* The sound and vibration lulled me to sleep.

I woke Sunday morning still feeling anxious, but with little time to dwell on the possibility of Deena Hardisty's case going to trial. There was too much to do.

Emmalee and I took quick showers and hit the ground running. We'd be hosting Colette's bridal shower here today, and we still had cleaning and decorating to do. Fortunately, Colette's mother and Buck's mom—my aunt Nancy—would be bringing the food. We'd debating hiring a caterer, but none could surpass Colette's cooking.

It was Colette's mother who'd suggested we leave the food up to her. "I'm the one who first taught that girl to cook," she said. "She loves everything I make. Besides, I never get to cook for her anymore. I miss it." She'd driven up from New Orleans a couple of days earlier, and had been staying with my aunt Nancy and uncle Roger. No doubt Colette's mom had enlisted my aunt as her willing kitchen assistant.

Emmalee and I were scurrying about, sweeping, mopping, and dusting, when Colette rolled out of bed. She'd closed the café the night before and hadn't arrived home until late.

She glanced around. "What can I do to help?"

"Nothing," Emmalee and I said in unison.

"This day is all about you," I added. "The only thing you need to do is get yourself dressed."

She grinned. "Can we do this every day, then?"

"No!" Emmalee and I said, again in unison, grinning right back.

Colette's mother and my aunt arrived at one o'clock. Emmalee and I went outside to help them carry the food into the house. Despite our earlier admonishment that she was not to lift a finger, Colette helped carry the bowls and casserole dishes in, too.

We arranged the food on the kitchen table. There was gumbo. Red beans and rice. Cajun pasta. Creole cornbread. Rather than a cake, Colette's mother had made the beignets New Orleans was famous for. My mouth watered and my stomach growled as we set the dishes out. I could hardly wait to dig in!

Colette squealed in delight when she saw everything her mother had made. "You did all of this for me?"

Her mother smiled. "I sure did. I made enough that you and your roommates will have leftovers for a month. I made some for Buck, too."

The guests began to arrive at two, coming alone or in groups of two or three, all wearing cute dresses and carrying gift bags or wrapped boxes. Some of the guests worked in Colette's café. Others had worked with her in other restaurants over the years. Some were friends from college, girls we'd met in the dorm or taken classes with years ago. Some were relatives of one degree or another. All were happy to be here to celebrate Colette's impending nuptials.

We kicked things off with mimosas and games, then dug into the food. The guests loved every bite. Once everyone had eaten their fill, I directed Colette to a chair we'd festooned with white tulle. "Sit here to open your gifts."

Over the next half hour, she proceeded to open the presents the group had brought. The vast majority were kitchen items from Colette's bridal registry. A fancy juicer. A food dehydrator. Specialized attachments for her standing mixer. I'd bought her an odd gift, but one I knew she'd appreciate—a rototiller she could use in her vegetable garden.

Colette laughed when she removed the paper from the tall, narrow box. "Leave it to Whitney to buy me heavy equipment."

The tiller was hardly heavy equipment. Heavy equipment was tractors and bulldozers and steamrollers. But I understood her sentiment.

She gave me a warm hug. "I love it. It'll come in handy when I dig a garden at Buck's place."

"It won't be Buck's place anymore," I corrected her. "It'll be *y'all's* place."

"Not until he gets rid of that garden gnome with his pants pulled down, it won't."

"Loonie Moonie?" I said. "He'll never get rid of that gnome. But you might be able to convince Buck to at least move him into the backyard."

My aunt and Colette's mother exchanged smiles and knowing looks. Colette's mom said, "That's what marriage is about, hon. Compromises."

In an odd, twisted thought, I realized that's what divorce was about, too. Compromises. Deena had been trying to get Grant to compromise on their property settlement but he'd refused. Jackie had probably compromised when she'd divorced Grant, too, giving him the man cave furniture he'd never paid for. Then again, he'd eventually paid with his life. I wasn't so sure that was a compromise at all.

By the time Emmalee and I finished cleaning up after the bridal shower, it was the middle of the evening. There was no point in driving out to the *Skinny Dipper* tonight. I'd sleep here and return to the marina in the morning.

My roommates and I donned our pajamas and reconvened in the living room. Emmalee curled up in her Papasan chair with Cleo on her lap, while Colette and I plunked ourselves down on the couch. Sawdust stretched out between me and my best friend. While she scratched his ears, I dug my nails in around the base of his tail, another of his favorite sweet spots.

Colette thanked us, once again, for throwing the bridal shower. "You two are so sweet. It was a wonderful day. I had a great time."

Emmalee grinned and wagged her brows. "Just wait for the bachelorette party."

Colette said, "If you're going to hire a guy to jump out of a cake, might I suggest Idris Elba?"

"I contacted his agent," I teased. "Unfortunately, he's tied up that day sitting shirtless in a dunking booth at a school carnival." Turning to other matters, I gave them an update on the explosion. "Collin said the police department has turned the case against Deena Hardisty over to the district attorney's office." I winced. "He also said I should expect to be the star witness if the case goes to trial."

"You'll have to testify in court?" Colette's gaze roamed my face, assessing. Noting my anxiety, she became worried in return. "But you didn't actually see anyone plant the explosives. All you saw was the boy with the dog."

I'd heard a *clang* afterward, too, though it might not have come from the *Sexy Sheila*. Even if it did, I wasn't sure exactly what I'd heard. "I'm hoping they'll work out a plea deal," I said. "Assuming, of course, that she's guilty."

Emmalee's head went cockeyed and her brow furrowed. "She confessed, right? Isn't her guilt a foregone conclusion? What are the odds she's innocent?"

"Very slim," I acknowledged, "but other people confessed too and she's recanted. Her son has asked for my help in exonerating her."

"That's not your job," Emmalee protested.

"You're right. It's not." But just because something wasn't my job hadn't stopped me from getting involved before. After all, it wasn't my job to investigate crimes, yet I'd become quite the armchair detective. "I would like to find out the truth, though."

"You'll get there," Colette said, reaching over to give me a supportive pat on the knee. "You always do."

I only wish I had as much faith in me as she did.

CHAPTER 24

SPLISH-SLASH

WHITNEY

On Monday morning before leaving the house, I did two things.

First, I phoned the office of Deena Hardisty's defense attorney. The receptionist put me on hold for several minutes, but finally patched me through.

"Hello, Mr. Aguilera," I said. "My name is Whitney Whitaker. I'm calling regarding Deena Hardisty. She might have mentioned my name to you?"

His tone was flat when he said, "She did. You're the one who claims to have seen her son take their dog Jojo from Grant's boat at Old Hickory Lake."

I didn't just *claim* to have seen Tanner take the dog. I had, in fact, seen Tanner take the dog. I'd even spoken with Tanner that night, promised him I wouldn't tell anyone I'd seen him there. I hadn't been able to keep that promise, of course. But there was no point in arguing with the guy.

Before I could even open my mouth again, the attorney said, "You're also the prosecution's star witness."

Ugh. My guts twisted. *I wish everyone would stop telling me that.* The thought that Deena's entire future depended on my testimony made me feel nauseated. And it wasn't just her future at stake. It was Tanner's, too. And Jojo's. I wanted to tell the man that I wasn't on anyone's side here, that all I was interested in was ensuring that the truth prevailed, but I decided saying so would sound melodramatic. Instead, I said, "Her son Tanner asked for my help in gathering evidence that might exonerate her. I have an idea, if you're interested in hearing it."

His tone was less flat now. "I'm listening."

"It's my understanding that Deena claimed to have pilfered a large number of ammonium nitrate cold packs from the hospital where she works." Collin had mentioned this fact to me, but I didn't tell the attorney where I'd learned it. I felt guilty using this bit of inside information to disprove Collin's case against the woman. In a way, I was working against him, maybe even undermining him. But I knew he wouldn't want an innocent woman to go to jail any more than I would. He, too, only sought justice. "An audit of the supplies might show whether she actually took the cold packs." I'd been a business major in college. What I'd learned often came in handy. If a crime involved money in any way, following the money trail could lead to clues.

The attorney was silent for a moment, probably mulling over the idea. "I appreciate the suggestion. I'll look into it."

I wondered whether Deena might have given her

attorney some information about her alleged victim. "While I've got you on the phone, can you tell me whether Deena ever mentioned to you that Grant had a pending insurance claim for his slip and fall?"

"No," he said. "She didn't mention an insurance claim. Why? Do you think it might have some relevance to the murder case?"

"I don't see how," I said. "I was just . . . curious, I guess." With that, I left him my phone number and e-mail address in case he needed to get in touch with me.

After I hung up with the attorney, it dawned on me that Tanner might know where Grant had suffered his accident. Of course, the kid would be in school right now, but I could call him later, once school released for the day, and find out what he knew.

The second thing I did that morning after calling Deena's lawyer was boot up my laptop so I could get on the internet to try to learn more about Jackie. At this point, I didn't even have a last name for her, but I figured I couldn't go wrong by searching for her under the name Jackie Hardisty. If she had ever used Grant's last name, something might pop up.

I typed the name into my browser. Some links popped up, but none appeared to be relevant. I then ran a search for Jacqueline Hardisty. Although there were several women with that name on social media, it took only a few seconds for me to find her particular Facebook page. It was interesting to note that she was still using Grant's last name although they had been married only a short time, had since divorced, and shared no children. *Is that a sign that she was trying to hang on to him?* If I'd gone through a messy divorce from a man who'd used me, I certainly would not want to keep his name.

I looked over her profile information. She was a legal assistant working in the commercial division of a large and prestigious downtown law firm. No doubt she earned a good salary, which was likely why the gold-digging Grant had pursued her. I wondered if her job involved drafting contracts. *Could she have helped Grant come up with the purchase contract for the* Sexy Sheila*? The one with the unenforceable buyback term?* Hmm. Maybe the two had still been involved somehow, even after they'd divorced. Maybe Jackie hadn't even been the one to file for divorce. Maybe Grant had submitted the petition. Maybe she had been hoping for a reconciliation.

I ran my eyes down her posts and found myself involuntarily murmuring, "Whoa." Jackie's Facebook page contained post after post after post in which she berated Grant for the way he'd treated her. She'd included photos in many of her posts, too. A recent one showed him lounging on his boat, a beer in hand, a bottle of suntan oil on the bench beside him, and Jojo at his feet, smiling as if he didn't have a care in the world. The date on that post was from a month earlier, just before Buck and I bought the *Skinny Dipper*. She'd written a scathing diatribe to go along with the photo, ending it with #WorstHusbandEver! But if she truly thought he was the worst husband ever, why hadn't she stayed away from him? Actions spoke louder than words. *Had she still been hung up on the guy?*

I scrolled down. While friends had commented on her older posts attacking Grant, they'd apparently tired of her constant criticism and had begun to ignore them. She'd received fewer reactions or comments on her more recent posts.

I scrolled way, way down, until I found posts of her with Grant while they were still married. There was pic after pic of them with their heads angled toward each other, both smiling. In many, one of them looked at the other adoringly. She'd gone overboard with those posts, too, garnering fewer and fewer reactions the more she posted. Back then, the hashtags she'd included were #BestHusbandEver and #SpoiledHusband, though she'd meant the latter in a good way. There were hundreds of them, posted daily. Some days she even posted multiple photos. In many, the two were showing off things she'd bought him. The latest iPhone. An enormous television and a sofa with built-in recliners and cup holders. A universal home gym system. The racy blue Camaro. She seemed proud of her status as a sugar mama with a slightly younger, very attractive boy toy.

The woman was obsessed.

Interspersed with the rants about Grant were the usual photos of her with her friends at wineries, restaurants, and various celebrations, drinks raised, showing the world what a great time they were having. I supposed I couldn't fault her much for those posts. My page contained many of those types of posts, too, and no doubt would contain several more after Colette's bachelorette party this weekend.

I wondered what Jackie's friends had thought of Grant. Did they think she'd been a sucker to fall for him? That he'd been a handsome face and little more? My eyes scanned the women in the photos. *Wait a minute.* A redhead in one of the pics looked very similar to the redheaded woman whose dating profile picture Grant had shown Buck and me on his phone, the one he'd gone to meet at the bar. He'd told us the woman who'd shown up had been dressed tacky, worn too much cloying cologne, and ordered expensive wine. I recalled thinking how she'd pulled a bait and switch of sorts. Of course, at the time, I hadn't assumed it had been intentional. I'd just thought that she'd put her best foot forward in her profile and, like many people on the dating apps, hadn't lived up to her own hype.

I was thinking maybe it was merely a coincidence that the two redheads resembled each other, until I noticed a dark-haired woman in the same photo with her hair pulled up in a sleek twist. Her brows were full and perfect. There was no doubt in my mind. She was the woman who'd come by the marina shortly after the explosion, the one who dropped the bottle of suntan oil in the parking lot. *Jackie and these women had to be in cahoots.* The only thing I wasn't sure about was what, exactly, they'd worked together to do. The dark-haired woman had seemed surprised that the boat had exploded, but it could have been an act. Maybe she'd been sent to the marina to gather intel, to verify whether Grant had been on the boat when it blew up.

Jackie had tagged the women in the photos, so I was able to get their names. The redhead was Wendy Kurtland. The dark-haired woman with the nice brows was Theresa Robbins. I found their Facebook pages, which fortunately were public. While Wendy listed her relationship status as divorced, Theresa hadn't listed one. Judging from her photos, she was likely divorced, too, as she had a couple of adult children.

I didn't know for certain whether these women had killed Grant Hardisty, but I knew they had been up to something. I figured the best way to get honest information out of all of them was to confront them face-to-face. To that end, I concocted a ruse and placed a call to Jackie. She had given me her phone number to relay to Grant, and I still had her listed in my contacts.

"Hi, Jackie," I said when she answered. "This is Whitney Whitaker. I'd forgotten that Grant had stored some boxes on our boat the morning his boat exploded. He wanted to get rid of the clutter because he had a date coming over later that day." *Your friend Theresa.* "I'd forgotten all about them until I opened the closet this morning and discovered the boxes sitting there. Since Deena is in jail for his murder, I thought maybe you'd want his things. There's a key in one of the boxes along with a contract for a storage unit. Maybe he stored that furniture you paid for there." It was a lie, of course, but it got her interest.

"I wouldn't mind taking a look."

"I'm part owner of the Joyful Noise Playhouse," I said. "It would be a much shorter drive for you than coming all the way to the lake. How about I meet you there tomorrow evening?"

"I know the place," she said. "I've been to a couple of shows there. It's a great venue."

We arranged to meet in the parking lot at seven o'clock, and ended the call. *Now for Wendy and Theresa.* It was probably wrong of me, and it surely violated Facebook's policies, but I created a fake profile and page using the same images Jackie had used. I then used this cloned identity to message the two women and invite them to meet me for dinner and drinks at the Collection Plate Café at the same time I'd be meeting Jackie at the playhouse. I'd bring Jackie to the restaurant, ambush the group there, and force them to admit their sins. Of course, I wouldn't do it alone. I'd bring Buck along for safety. Maybe he could even flirt with Theresa and Wendy to keep them occupied until I brought Jackie over from the playhouse.

I was about to log off when Sawdust jumped up onto the sofa, waltzed onto my keyboard, and moved his paws up and down in a tap-dance routine that would rival any Broadway star. My computer responded with unhappy noises. I gently pushed him off the keyboard and wagged a finger at him. "Naughty boy." He reached out to try to grab my finger. *So cute.* I ruffled his ears.

To my dismay, when I turned back to my computer, I noticed that, during his dance routine, he'd liked several of Jackie's posts. He'd hit the angry face on a couple of them, too. He'd even posted a comment on one of them. It read "xcvf4." I scrolled through, unliking the posts, undoing the angry faces, and removing the comments. The cat had inadvertently scrolled through several weeks' worth of posts. I hoped I'd undone all of the reactions. The last thing I needed was Jackie knowing I'd been checking her out. That woman seemed more than a little off-kilter.

My at-home tasks completed Monday morning, I left Sawdust at home under the temporary care of Emmalee. Buck and I were nearly done with the boat repairs and wouldn't be staying on the *Skinny Dipper* much longer. Besides, although Sawdust had initially enjoyed being on the houseboat, especially when he got to play with his new buddy, Jojo, before the dog was taken away, he'd become much less fond of life on the boat after taking the spill into the water.

I arrived at the marina shortly after ten o'clock. As I climbed aboard the boat, I spotted the rubber ducky float. He lay deflated on the dock, his eyes staring up at me as if pleading for me to perform CPR and bring him back to life. *What had happened to the ducky?* I bent down and picked up the flaccid vinyl.

Oh, my gosh! I gasped so deep I sucked a stray gnat down my throat. The duck's throat had been slit. A jagged hole appeared just under his bill. *It's a message, isn't it? A warning that Buck and I could be next.* I wondered if Jackie had done this. Maybe she'd become enraged after realizing I'd been snooping on her Facebook page and cut the duck's throat in retaliation.

"Buck!" I cried, banging on the door. "Buck! Get out here!"

Through the glass window on the door, I saw my cousin coming down the hall from his berth. His hair was mussed and he wore nothing but a pair of sleep shorts. He unlocked the door and pushed it open. "What're you out here hollering about so early?"

I scoffed. "For one, it's after ten o'clock. And secondly, someone did this!" I held up the duck and showed him the jagged slash across its throat.

He pulled his head back and grimaced. "This isn't good at all. This means someone came on the boat last night."

"The duck wasn't like this last night when you went to bed? You're certain?"

"One hundred percent. I went out to my van to get some wood glue around ten o'clock and the duck was still inflated." His forehead furrowed. "You think it could've been kids pulling a prank?"

"At a marina? On a school night?" There had been

only a few children around the marina at all, and those had been on the weekends with their families. "It's a message," I said. "A threat." The thought made my blood turn cold in my veins. A man had already died out here at the lake, in a gruesome and horrific manner. I didn't want to die. I didn't want parts of me washing up on the lakeshore or bobbing on the surface to be collected like so much flotsam. And I certainly didn't want my death to become a spectacle posted all over the internet, my body reduced to fish bait and my life reduced to clickbait.

"Call Collin," Buck said. "Or Landreth. Hell, call 'em both."

I decided to call Melanie Landreth first. After all, the case should have been hers all along. Collin got dragged into it only because Deena, Tanner, Mick, and Sheila had all confessed in error to the police, when they should have confessed to the fire department. I shifted the duck to my left hand and pulled out my phone. I'd input Landreth's number into my contacts and was able to use voice commands to place my call. *Flawed and frustrating as she might be, how had we ever lived without Siri?* When Landreth answered, I said, "Someone came onto our boat last night and slashed our rubber ducky's throat."

"You're sure?" she asked. "The duck couldn't have caught on something?"

"There's nothing out here that the duck could have caught on. Besides, it was lying right in the middle of our deck."

"I'll come out and take a look. In the meantime, you and your cousin should get off that boat, just in case. If someone came aboard to slash the duck's throat, there's no telling what else they might have done. They could've planted more explosives."

I shoved my phone back into my pocket, grabbed Buck's arm, and dragged him off the boat, bringing the ducky along with us.

"What are you doing?" he said. "I don't even have shoes on!"

"Landreth said we should get off the boat. Now!"

His face turned white, and an instant later it was him who was now dragging me away from the boat. We headed to the far side of the parking lot to wait for Landreth. Buck issued an "Ouch!" here and there along the way as he stepped on an occasional sharp pebble in his bare feet.

Fortunately, with it being a weekday and still only spring, very few people were about in the marina. Landreth arrived a half hour later in her fire department vehicle. A second fire department vehicle followed her into the parking lot. It held a female firefighter and a dog, a black Lab that resembled Jojo although this dog was pure bred and much better behaved.

Landreth pulled up next to where we stood. The other vehicle parked next to her, the driver leaving the windows halfway down to prevent the interior from overheating. Landreth and the dog handler climbed out of their vehicles and came over to talk to us. The handler looked to be in her mid-thirties, only slightly older than Buck and me. She discreetly checked out my cousin's bare biceps, pecs, and abs. Carpentry and other manual labor had definitely kept my cousin in shape.

While the dog handler ogled Buck, I showed Landreth the slashed throat on the duck and gave her the rundown. "I found the duck when I arrived a short time ago. I didn't stay on the *Skinny Dipper* last night, but Buck did."

After bagging the rubber ducky in an evidence bag, Landreth turned to my cousin. "Did you hear any suspicious noises last night? See any suspicious persons or activity?"

"No, no, and no," Buck said. "It gives me the willies to think that someone came onto the boat without me knowing." He shuddered and wrapped his arms around himself.

The handler looked less impressed now, though I was proud that my cousin didn't feel the need to act fearless and macho. Anyone in their right mind would be concerned and scared. After all, a man had been blown to smithereens out here just a few days ago.

Landreth swung her arm. "Send Dragon over there to check things out."

The handler gave Landreth a quick nod. She opened the back of her SUV, quickly donned a helmet and other protective gear, and released the dog—who I presumed to be Dragon—from the harness securing him to the seat. Dragon seemed an appropriate name for an animal trained to essentially breathe fire. Before stepping away, the handler asked, "Where's the gas cap? He's going to alert on that."

Buck told her where the gas cap was situated.

"Any propane or other fuel inside the boat?" she asked.

"No," Buck said. "Everything else is electric. It runs off the marina power at the dock and a generator on the water." Not that we'd yet had a chance to get the *Skinny Dipper* out on the water. At least we now had our boating licenses so we'd be ready once the boat was, too.

Though at the moment that seemed the least of our concerns.

The woman nodded, and she and her dog headed across the parking lot. I held my breath as the two approached the *Skinny Dipper.* I'd feel terrible if our boat blew up and either of them were injured. I closed my eyes and sent up a quick prayer for their safety.

The handler stopped approximately ten feet away from our boat and issued instructions to her dog. The dog sniffed its way around the outside of the boat, going up and down both sides at the handler's direction. The dog sniffed around the cap for the gas tank and sat down on its haunches, which I took to indicate he smelled the fuel. The handler gave him praise for detecting the scent, then directed him to sniff for additional flammable and explosive materials.

Luckily, Buck had left the back door open when he'd come out. The officer sent her dog inside to sniff around. He was gone for a minute or two before stepping out the back door. The woman then went inside with him. The two reappeared at the back door a few minutes later. She shook her head. "We didn't find anything!" she called. "It's clear!"

I closed my eyes again. *Thank goodness.*

The woman and the dog came back our way. I thanked her profusely. "I wish I could thank your dog, too."

"You can." She reached into her pocket and pulled out a bag of treats. She held them out to me. "Give him two of those."

I reached into the bag, removed two treats, and held them out to the dog. Wagging his tail, he took them from me. The handler reached down and patted him playfully. "Good boy, Dragon! Good boy!"

The handler took off her gear, packed it into her car along with the dog, and left. Meanwhile, I talked things over with Landreth.

"I don't understand why someone would threaten us," I said. "If Deena killed Grant, there's no reason for anyone else to try to scare us off."

"Maybe you've upset them for some other reason. Has something happened lately?"

I told her about my conversation with Hugh Montaigne, how he'd been spying on Grant because the insurance company suspected he might not actually be seriously injured. I also told her what I'd found on Facebook, how the posts evidenced Jackie's obsession with Grant. "My cat walked across my keyboard and accidentally liked or reacted to some of her posts. I immediately went in and tried to retract all of them. It's possible I missed something and that Jackie received a notification about my activity." If she had received a notification, she'd realize I was checking up on her. My head went light, thinking back on how she'd laughed on hearing that Grant had died in the explosion. *Yeesh.*

Landreth said, "I'll get in touch with Jackie. See what she says."

"Thanks."

After Landreth departed, I called Collin to give him an update. I didn't want him to feel left out of the loop professionally. And on a personal note, I needed to tell my boyfriend about the scary morning we'd had.

"Someone slit the duck's throat?" Collin said. "That's all kinds of creepy."

"I'm not overreacting, then?"

"No," Collin reassured me. "And, even if you were,

it's better to overreact than underreact. Not taking threats seriously is how people end up hurt . . . or worse."

I swallowed the fresh fear that clogged my throat. "What do you think this means? That Deena is innocent? That someone else killed Grant and that person is trying to scare us off? Maybe Jackie?"

"Hard to say. It seems to be a message, but it's not a clear one. I'm glad Landreth is planning to speak with Jackie. Maybe she'll learn something. In the meantime, you and Buck should get out of there, move the boat to a different marina."

I thought back to what Grant had told Mick and Sheila, that all of the marinas on the lake had extensive waiting lists. I supposed we could take the boat out of the water and work on it at a dry dock, but we'd have to find someone with a trailer large enough to move the houseboat. It was likely to be both expensive and a hassle.

"Moving the boat isn't an option." Neither was staying elsewhere at night. We'd be leaving the boat unattended, which would make it vulnerable. Lest we have Dragon return each morning to perform a sniff test, we wouldn't know whether someone had planted explosives overnight. "But we could put up cameras and motion-activated lights."

"Good idea," Collin said. "I'll also put in a request for regular patrols to roll by."

"Thanks, Collin." Maybe the cruisers would act as a deterrent.

"This could just be coincidence," he said, "but we released Mick last night. He withdrew his confession, too. Without it, there wasn't enough evidence to hold him. Everything else is circumstantial. Filling up Grant's gas tank, claiming he smelled gas in the boat, his possible attempt to steal the boat back. It's not enough."

"It's not enough to hold him," I said, "but it's still possible he's the one who killed Grant Hardisty, not Deena. Especially now that Buck and I have been threatened."

"You're right," Collin agreed. "It could have been him. If he shows up at the marina, call the police right away. Same goes for Sheila."

After Collin and I ended the call, I told Buck what I'd discovered when perusing Jackie's Facebook page that morning. "She and her friends were up to something. I just don't know what." I filled him in on my plans to lure her to the Collection Plate Café, where her friends would be waiting. I only hoped none of them texted one another beforehand or they might figure out I'd tricked them all into going there. "I saw Theresa ogling you when she came out to the marina for her date with Grant. You'd make a great distraction while they wait for me and Jackie to arrive."

"You mean you're expecting me to flirt with these ladies? Right in front of my bride-to-be and her staff?"

"Fill Colette in," I said. "She'll understand."

"I hope I remember how to flirt," Buck said. "After all these months of monogamy, I'm rusty."

I rolled my eyes. "It's simple. Just ask them about themselves and actually pay attention to what they say. Follow up with appropriate questions. Compliment them on something, and maintain eye contact."

"Shoot," he said. "I should've come to you for advice in my teen years. I could've been a player."

Moving on to pressing matters, Buck and I discussed various options for securing the boat and protecting ourselves. He made a list of items to buy, and headed out to a home improvement store. Meanwhile, I climbed to the upper deck where I could keep a watchful eye on the marina, the parking lot, and the lake all at once. The place no longer felt peaceful and calm, like it had when we'd first bought the boat. It now felt like hell, complete with a lake of fire.

CHAPTER 25
AN ALARMING DAY

WHITNEY

While Buck was at the home improvement store late that Monday morning, I sat atop the *Skinny Dipper*, pondering things. One of the things I pondered was the irony of pondering on what was essentially a large pond. Clearly, the warm spring sun was baking my brain.

My cell phone came alive with an incoming call. An unseen hand gripped my heart when I saw the caller ID. It read DAVIDSON COUNTY DA. I answered the call. "Hello. This is Whitney Whitaker."

"Hello, Ms. Whitaker," came a woman's voice. "This is Suzanne Lumley. I'm a prosecutor with the district attorney's office. I understand Detective Flynn told you I'd be calling?"

"Yes," I choked out. "He told me."

"I believe your testimony is going to be instrumental in getting a conviction against Deena Hardisty."

The ghost hand around my heart squeezed even harder.

Lumley continued, "I'm going to need you to come into my office so we can discuss the case. Any chance you're available this Friday at two o'clock?"

"Yes," I said. "I can meet then."

"Perfect." She asked for my e-mail address and said her administrative assistant would follow up with a reminder.

I still felt uneasy after we ended the call. Though Deena Hardisty had a motive and means for killing her husband, I still wasn't convinced she had the intent to do away with him. I remembered my first impression of her. It was of a woman who was tired, defeated, just wanting to move forward, but stuck in metaphorical cement her husband had poured. She hadn't seemed excessively angry or vindictive, though she certainly had a right to be. She'd just wanted it to be over. She just wanted out. And she had to know she'd be the first person law enforcement would suspect. *Would she really be so naïve and stupid as to think she could get away with killing him?*

On the contrary, I wondered if she was too intelligent for her own good. She'd come up with a compelling and credible story of how she'd killed her husband so that her son wouldn't go to prison. Then, it turned out her son hadn't been guilty, either. Her only fault in that case would be overestimating her son's anger and abilities—and a desire to protect him, no matter the cost.

A light breeze picked up a few strands of my hair, blowing them into my face as I gazed around the lake. I reached up and tucked the hair behind my ear. A few motorboats and sailboats glided about the surface at varying rates of speed and noise levels. Hawks circled overhead, slow-moving clouds drifting in the blue sky above them. A fish flopped nearby, creating a soft splash and leaving concentric ripples spreading across the water. Halyards on sailboats continued to clang against their masts. Boats bump-bump-bumped against the dock as the water swelled with the wake of a passing boat. It was a virtual paradise, but I couldn't relax and enjoy lake life today. Whoever had put an end to our rubber duck had put me on watch and on edge. I only wished I knew who that someone was.

Buck returned and we spent the greater part of the day installing security cameras and motion sensor lights on the boat. Buck had found some battery-operated motion sensor alarms, too. The devices would transmit an audible alarm signal to a receiver inside the boat, letting us know immediately if anyone approached. We installed one on each corner of the boat, as well as one over the back door. Nobody would get on this boat again without us knowing about it.

Once we finished with the security devices, I helped Buck install the new outboard motor on the deck. We had our backs to the dock when the alarm inside went off, alerting us to an intruder. *Beep-beep-beep-beep-beep!* We yanked our heads up and looked around. Nobody was approaching on the dock. My heart raced. *Is someone coming at us from the water?* My frantic mind immediately conjured up a vision of a torpedo headed our way.

I leapt off the deck and rushed around to the side of the boat. The intruders were indeed there on the water. The two ducks who'd set off the alarm turned my way and quacked. *Quack-quack!*

Ughhh. "False alarm!" I called to my cousin. "It's just a couple of ducks."

One of the ducks looked at me and quacked again, as if insulted to be called *just* a duck. *Quack!*

We got back to work. When we finished installing the motor, Buck stood up and wiped his hands. "This is it. The moment of truth. Let's take her out."

In case the *Skinny Dipper* ended up at the bottom of the lake along with parts of the *Sexy Sheila*, it was best Buck and I made sure we didn't go down with it. I rounded up two bright orange life jackets from the bin and we slid into them. I scrambled inside and returned with a captain's hat on my head. I'd ordered the hat online along with the pool floats for Colette's bachelorette party.

Buck eyed my hat and scowled. "Why should you get to be the captain?"

"Because I scored much higher than you on the boating license exam."

He formed a V with his fingers and pointed them at his eyes then mine, mimicking the Somali pirate from the *Captain Phillips* movie, and told me he was the captain now. "I'm the one who found this boat in the first place. I should get to take her out on her maiden voyage."

"She's decades old," I said. "Her maiden voyage took place when Jimmy Carter was president."

"Her refurbished maiden voyage, then."

He had a point. I rolled my eyes, but handed him the hat. "All right. Here you go, skipper."

Buck plunked the white hat on his head and pulled down on the blue and gold visor to shield his eyes. He took the helm as I cast off the moorings. He started the motor. It sputtered and puttered, starting slow and erratic before settling into a rhythmic cadence. *Putt-putt-putt-putt.* Excited and a little nervous, I climbed aboard.

Slowly and carefully, my cousin eased the big boat away from the dock. The houseboat was intended for calm waters only, and for slow cruising, not speed. We puttered past the other boats at a snail's pace, but eventually made our way out of the marina to reach the main part of the lake.

"We don't appear to be sinking," I said with equal parts delight and surprise. It looked like Buck's repair job on the pontoon was holding.

A speedboat went by, leaving a rollicking wake behind it. "Hang on!" Buck called as the waves headed our way. Though only a few inches high, they posed a virtual tsunami for the houseboat. I held tight to the rail as the *Skinny Dipper* rocked up and down, eventually settling back in the now-smooth water.

"We did it!" I cried, raising a palm.

Grinning, Buck slapped my hand with his in a celebratory high five. I pulled out my phone and snapped dozens of photos and video, publishing them to my social media with the hashtags #HouseboatsRock, #BoatLife, #LakeLife, and #BuyThisBoat.

Buck and I cruised around for a half hour before deciding to return to the dock. He pointed to the gas pump at the marina. "Should we stop and fill her up?"

"Are you crazy?" I said. "Until we know for certain the right person is behind bars for Grant Hardisty's murder, we should keep our gas tank as close to empty as possible."

"Good point."

After we pulled back into the dock, I eyed the time on my phone. 4:08. *Tanner should be out of school by now.* He'd given me his phone number when he'd come by, begging me to help his mother. I placed a call to the number now.

He answered his phone with a somber, "Hey."

"Hi, Tanner," I said. "I'm not sure if you'll know the answers, but I have a couple of questions for you. Do you know where Grant fell and hurt his knee?"

"Yeah," he said. "It was that old convenience store by the lake. The one that sells bait and stuff."

"The Get-N-Git?"

"I think that's what it's called."

Interesting. Captain Billy from the *Caudal Otta Fish* owned the store, along with his wife, and he and Grant fished together. Was the insurance company right? Had Billy and Grant cooked up Grant's injury in order to bilk the company out of thousands of dollars? In light of the fact that he'd essentially scammed a series of women into supporting him, I wouldn't put a fraudulent claim past Grant. But I hardly knew Billy. I had no idea whether he was the type to engage in such a rip-off. Ironically, if he were a con artist, it would mean he was less likely to have anything to do with Grant's death. With Grant gone, he'd no longer be in a position to benefit from a collusive claim.

I moved on to my second question, which was more open-ended. "What do you know about Jackie Hardisty?"

"Jackie?" Tanner said. "Grant's wife before my mom?"

"Right."

He snorted. "She's a total train wreck." He employed

multiple other slang words to describe her. *Basic. Thirsty. Salty.*

Seeking clarification, I said, "What did she do to make you feel so strongly?"

"She came by our house all the time to harass Grant. Sometimes she'd come to the door, but other times she'd just drive by like she wanted to see what was going on. She was hung up on him."

"Still in love with him, you mean?"

"Ehhh . . . I'm not sure it was love. Like, I don't think she wanted him back. She was just angry and wanted him to be as miserable as she was. I think he made Jackie feel stupid for falling for him. That's how my mom felt, too. Dumb. My mom is usually very smart and she said she should have known better."

"Jackie and your mom didn't like being duped." I could understand that. "Speaking of your mother, how's she holding up?"

When he squeaked, "Not good," I was sorry I'd asked. Of course, Deena wasn't doing well. She was in jail. Maybe rightfully, maybe wrongfully. But, either way, not a great place to be.

Tanner said, "You think Jackie might have killed Grant?"

"I don't know," I said. "It's a theory. She came by the marina twice looking for him."

"Did you tell the police? And that lady from the fire department?"

"I did."

His tone was angry when he spoke again. "She should be in jail then! Not my mom!"

Maybe so, I thought. But there was no clear evidence

against her and she hadn't confessed to anything. Maybe I'd get some evidence or a confession tomorrow night when I confronted her and her friends. Grant and Billy might or might not have colluded, but it was clear to me that Jackie had colluded with Wendy and Theresa. With nothing left to question Tanner about, I wrapped up the call. "Keep the faith, Tanner. The truth has a way of surfacing eventually." *Much like his former stepfather.*

With only a short list of minor items remaining, by Monday evening the boat was nearly done. I snapped a bunch of photos from different angles, both inside and out, along with photos of the sunset from the upper deck. I sent the pics to my computer, planning to design a flyer to post at places around the area to let everyone know the *Skinny Dipper* was up for sale and ready for offers. I'd be hosting Colette's bachelorette party on the boat this Friday night, and Buck's bachelor party would be held on Saturday. We could turn over the keys to a new owner as soon as their payment cleared our bank—which, if we were lucky, could be as early as next Monday.

Collin came out to the marina early that evening to see the progress on the boat. "Wow!" he said. "This looks like an entirely different boat than the one you bought."

"That's the idea," Buck said. "Let's hope potential buyers are as impressed as you are."

I caught Collin up on my phone call with Tanner. "He said Grant slipped and fell at the Get-N-Git. Doesn't it seem weird that Billy would be so friendly with Grant if the guy had filed a claim against him?"

As always, Collin didn't jump to any particular

conclusion, but mulled over several potential interpretations of the facts. "I could see how a claim could put people at odds," he said, "but these things happen all the time and people take it in stride. I saw it when I was a street cop. A person backs into their coworker's car. Someone gets hurt when their neighbor's kid beans them with a baseball. Someone's tree falls onto someone else's roof. Things get sorted out, the insurance company pays up, and it's no big deal. That said, I've seen things come to blows when the party who caused the problem doesn't take responsibility. I remember handling a call where a guy was driving way too fast and smashed into his neighbor's brick mailbox. His license was suspended for too many traffic tickets and he didn't have auto insurance. Things got ugly when he refused to replace the mailbox."

I chewed my lip. "I don't know. It just feels to me like this could be something. Could you talk to Hugh Montaigne tomorrow? Please? Find out which insurance company it was and see what they have to say?" I felt bad pressuring him, using our personal relationship to my advantage, but it was with good intentions. Getting to the truth.

Collin didn't hesitate. "All right. You've got good instincts, Whitney. It shouldn't take me long and I suppose it can't hurt. I'll have to clear it with Landreth first, though. She's been pretty patient about how mucked up things have become with everyone coming to Metro PD with their confessions, but I don't want to step on her toes unnecessarily."

"Understood. Thanks, Collin." I leaned over and gave him an appreciative peck on the cheek.

CHAPTER 26
LONELY KITTY

SAWDUST

Tuesday morning, Sawdust was beside himself. Whitney hadn't come home last night, and the poor cat had to sleep in the big bed all alone with only her pillow to curl up with. Where was she? Why had she left him here by himself?

Cleo had tried to console him. She'd given him kisses, and purred and rubbed up against him. When that hadn't worked, she'd tried to distract him with play. She'd batted her tinkle ball so that it rolled right in front of him. She carried her catnip mouse over and dropped it at his feet. She even ran at him and tackled him on the rug. He simply lay there, limp and lifeless. Cleo had finally given up on him and walked off to see what Emmalee was doing.

Please come home, Whitney! And soon!

CHAPTER 27
CASES AND CLAIMS

WHITNEY

Late Tuesday morning, Collin called me. "I spoke with the private investigator and the insurance company. Landreth, too. She and I are going to head over to the Get-N-Git to speak with the owners. We don't think it's going to amount to anything, but we need to gather information. Otherwise, Deena's attorney could use the pending insurance claim to confuse things and raise doubt at her trial. The prosecutor offered them a plea deal since she has no priors, but they didn't bite. If this case goes to trial, the D.A. wants it to be airtight."

When we ended the call, I told Buck I was heading to the Get-N-Git.

"We out of something?" he asked.

"Yeah," I said. "Answers."

He cocked his head, utterly confused. "Huh?"

"Collin and Landreth are going to question the owners about Grant's injury claim. I'm meeting them there." *They just don't know it yet.*

I went out to my car and drove to the store.

Billy's wife smiled from her place behind the counter as I walked in. Though her eyes were bloodshot and droopier than ever, they flickered with recognition. She offered a feeble smile. "Out of coffee again already?"

I chuckled. "Not quite yet. How's your mother doing?"

She paused for a beat or two, looking confused, then said, "Oh. Right. She's much better now. Got over that fall right away."

Hmm. Though she simply might have forgotten our earlier conversation about her mother tripping over her slippers and falling down, part of me wondered if the woman was shooting straight with me. I'd thought her worry over her mother was why she looked so weary. But could it be something else? "I'd like to take a look at your inflatables. Any chance you carry a rubber duck?"

"No ducks," she said, circling around the counter. "But we've got plenty of other options." She motioned for me to follow her to their water-toy section. "How about a unicorn? Or a turtle? There's plain air mattresses, too. We've got just about any color you might like."

"No, thanks," I said. "I've got my heart set on a duck. The one I had popped, and I want to replace him."

"Sorry we couldn't help you out."

The door opened and in walked Collin and Landreth. Though Landreth's brows drew inward on seeing me, Collin didn't look at all surprised. In fact, a grin tugged at his lips as he shook his head. I was lucky the guy was so understanding. He enjoyed solving crimes, so he understood my passion for the exercise—even if it wasn't officially my job the way it was his.

Landreth and Collin stepped up to the counter. After

Landreth introduced herself to Billy's wife, Collin also extended a hand over the counter. "I'm Detective Collin Flynn with Metro P.D."

"Christine Underhill." The woman's brows rose as she took his hand. "I don't think I've ever met a detective before, let alone have two investigators show up at the same time. Is there something I can help you with?"

I busied myself with the bug sprays, picking up the bottles, sniffing them, perusing their labels. *Mosquito spray is flammable, too? Who knew?* Though I'd stopped at the display as a ruse to eavesdrop on the conversation, I realized I should probably buy some of the bug spray. With the temperatures warming up, the mosquitos would begin to swarm soon. I'd been buzzed by two or three of them on the boat last night.

Collin glanced around. We were the only customers in the store. Billy was nowhere to be seen. "Is your husband around? I have a couple of quick questions for y'all."

"You do?" She angled her head. "About what?"

"Grant Hardisty."

"Oh." The woman inhaled a deep, long breath and shook her head. "That poor man." She turned her head toward a partially opened door behind the counter. It appeared to lead to a stockroom and office. "Hey, Billy!" she called. "Come on out here. There's two detectives who want to ask us some questions."

The door opened and Billy appeared in the doorway. "Hi, folks." He nodded to Landreth and Collin as he stepped up next to his wife. Spotting me loitering in the aisle, he raised a hand. "Good to see you again." He returned his attention to the investigators, looking calm and collected. "What can we do you for, detectives?"

Collin said, "We've learned that Grant Hardisty was injured here in your store."

"That's right," Billy said. He pointed to the display of suntan lotions and oils. "He fell right there. Someone spilled suntan oil on the floor and down he went. Messed up his knee something awful. He was in quite a bit of pain."

Was he? I wondered. *Or was he just pretending?* I still felt fairly confident I'd seen him waterskiing with the men from the bar that one day.

Collin continued, "I understand he filed a claim with your store's insurance carrier?"

"Well, sure," Billy said matter-of-factly. "That's how it's done when someone gets hurt at your place of business."

"Of course," Collin agreed. "You two were friends before the accident, correct?"

"I suppose you could say that," Billy said. "I didn't know him long and thought of him more as a fishing buddy than a friend, but that's just a matter of semantics. He started coming in here after he and his wife split, and he had to move onto his boat at the marina. He didn't know much about boats or lake living, and he hit me up with all kinds of questions. I could tell the guy was lonely and upset about his divorce, so I invited him out to fish a few times with me and another buddy."

Collin asked, "Were these fishing trips before or after he fell and filed the claim?"

"Both," Billy said.

Landreth chimed in. "His pending insurance claim didn't affect your relationship?"

"No," Billy said, shifting his focus to her. "Why

should it? Far as I was concerned, it was between him and the insurance company. Other than a small deductible, no money was coming out of my pocket."

Collin's head bobbed as he took in the information. "Were you aware that your insurance company knew you had a personal relationship with Mr. Hardisty, and that they suspected that you two might have colluded?"

Billy chuckled. "Of course, I was aware they knew of our relationship. Heck, I'm the one who told them that Grant and I went fishing together now and then. As far as the second part of your question, I'm gonna need some clarification. I'm not familiar with that term you used. You say they thought we *what* now?"

"Colluded," Collin said. "Your insurance company thought Grant's claim might be fraudulent, and that you were in on things with him so that you'd get a cut of his settlement."

"Are you kidding me?" Billy's dander seemed to be up now, though he remained professional. "That's just plain ridiculous. I've got no reason to engage in that kind of shady behavior. We make plenty of money. More than we can spend, in fact. I'd be happy to show you the store's books if you'd like. We've always made a good profit, and earnings are up even more the past few months. It could be our best year ever."

Collin said, "Would you be surprised if I told you the insurance company hired an investigator to keep an eye on Grant, and that the investigator has video of Grant water skiing only a few days before his boat exploded?"

Aha! So that's what Hugh Montaigne had been recording. Also, I had been right when I thought I'd seen Grant on skis.

"Well, I'll be damned." Billy scoffed and shook his

head. "So, it's true, then? Grant's knee injury was bogus?"

"Looks that way," Collin said.

Christine frowned. "Filing a false claim is an awful thing to do, especially against someone who's tried to help you out."

Billy cut a look her way. "I'll say."

Landreth chimed in. "Tell us more about the day Grant fell here in the store. What happened, exactly?"

Billy raised a shoulder. "Like I said, a customer spilled suntan oil on the floor. A woman told us about the spill, but we were busy, had a line all the way down the aisle to the back of the shop." He gestured to the refrigerated glass coolers at the rear of the space. "I set out an orange plastic cone to warn people away from the spot, but at some point the cone got kicked out of the way. Grant came up the aisle with a six-pack of beer and slipped. Went down on his knee, hard. Or at least I'd thought so at the time. Anyway, he keeled over, holding his leg and groaning. A couple of men helped me get him to his feet. He hobbled out to his car and drove himself to a doctor. A few days later, he came back in with his medical bills. I forwarded the paperwork over to my insurance company. It's been in their hands ever since." With that, he shrugged and raised his palms.

Seemingly tired of beating around the bush, Landreth cut to the chase, looking from one Underhill to the other. "Can you two account for your whereabouts the night before Grant's boat exploded?"

Billy barked a laugh and pointed first to himself, then his wife. "Do we really look like killers to you?"

Landreth shrugged. "You'd be surprised how normal a murderer can look."

Collin nodded in agreement.

Billy said, "We were together all night, at home." He hiked a thumb over his shoulder. "Our house is right behind the shop."

Although Christine nodded, I noticed she gripped the counter with one hand, as if feeling unsteady. I supposed being directly asked for your alibi in a murder case could be unsettling. *But could there be more to it?*

Collin and Landreth exchanged glances to ensure neither had any more questions. They both thanked Christine and Billy for their time and walked out to their cars.

I carried two bottles of bug spray up to the counter and set them down.

Christine rang them up for me. "You're smart to buy this stuff now. With the weather warming up, the skeeters are starting to bite. On the bright side, the fireflies will return soon, too."

The fluorescent green bugs lit up the Nashville area every June, thousands of tiny green Tinker Bells performing aerial acrobatics in the night skies. "I can't wait. I love fireflies."

Billy was still standing behind the counter, so he bagged the bug spray while I paid Christine for my purchase. When I went to take the bag from him, I noticed Christine watching her husband out of the corner of her eye. Though her mouth bore a practiced smile, her eyes were dark with some emotion that looked suspiciously like doubt and distrust. Or at least I'd thought so until she turned back to me and they gleamed with her usual mischief. "Thanks for stopping by. You got what you came for"—she pointed at the door—"now git!"

I drove back to the marina to find Collin and

Landreth waiting for me on the dock by the *Skinny Dipper.* I carried the paper sack containing my bug spray up to the boat, fully expecting one or both of them to chastise me for eavesdropping on their interrogation, but neither did, thank goodness.

"What do you think?" I asked. "Could Billy have something to do with what happened to Grant?"

Landreth said, "Grant's claim could have been a motive, even if Billy didn't know it was bogus. But he seemed pretty convincing when he said he felt it was between Grant and the insurance company."

Collin agreed. "Sounds like he's got an airtight alibi."

"What about Christine? Do you sense that she might have been involved?" I told them I'd seen Christine steady herself by grabbing the countertop, and that she'd given her husband what seemed to be a suspicious look. *Or maybe she'd been wondering whether he might suspect her . . .*

Landreth raised her palms. "We can't arrest people on strange looks alone. We'd need some evidence or testimony. Besides, people get nervous when law enforcement questions them. It's only natural. Sometimes it's difficult to tell what's natural nervousness and what's guilt."

So much for the Underhills, then, at least for now. Turning to another possible suspect, I asked, "What did Jackie say when you contacted her about the duck?"

"She said the last time she was at the marina was the day you informed her that Deena had confessed to killing Grant. She admitted she knew you'd been snooping around on her Facebook page, but she said she didn't think much about it. She said she'd snooped on yours, as well. She said it's just what people do."

Jackie had a point. If anyone was curious about another person these days, perusing their social media was step one. Still, something about the woman felt off to me. She was an odd duck, extremely open and blunt. Even so, that didn't necessarily make her a killer, did it?

I hesitated a moment, half expecting Landreth to say that Jackie had mentioned her plans to meet me tomorrow to purportedly collect some boxes of Grant's property. Landreth didn't bring it up, though. It appeared Jackie had said nothing about it. I looked from Collin to Landreth. "Thanks for indulging me, for following up with Jackie and the Underhills."

Landreth jerked her head to indicate Collin. "He says your input has been instrumental in solving other cases. Truth is, we need the public's help. We can't be everywhere and, without someone coming forward, there are clues we might overlook."

I looked from one to the other again. "What now?"

They exchanged a knowing look before Collin turned back to me. "You prepare to testify in a murder trial."

CHAPTER 28

APPS

WHITNEY

At seven on Tuesday evening, I waited anxiously in the parking lot of the Joyful Noise Playhouse. Luckily, I wasn't the only one there. Members of a band that would be performing at the hall that weekend had arrived for a rehearsal, and were unpacking their instruments and equipment from their vehicles. Jackie would be a fool to attack me in front of witnesses. Besides, until I led her over to the Collection Plate Café, she'd have no idea I'd lured her into an ambush.

My phone pinged and jiggled with an incoming text, and I pulled it from the back pocket of my jeans. Buck had sent a message. *The ospreys are circling.* In other words, Wendy and Theresa had arrived at the café. He'd keep a close eye on them until I could bring Jackie over.

A few minutes later, she pulled up in her silver Volvo, cut the engine, and climbed out. "Hello, Whitney. Sorry I'm late. Traffic was crazy." After I returned a greeting, she glanced around. "Where are the boxes?"

I pointed across the property to the restaurant. "They're at the café. One of the staff was unloading some kitchen supplies from my SUV earlier and took them inside. He didn't realize they weren't intended for the restaurant. Rather than carry them back out to my car, I figured you could just drive over and we can load them there."

"Okay." She gestured to her passenger seat. "Want to hop in and ride over with me?"

Tendrils of fear slithered up my spine. I hadn't expected the offer and had planned to walk down the path that led from the playhouse to the café. But it would seem strange if I refused. Then again, climbing into a vehicle with a potential killer wasn't exactly a smart thing to do. Stupid or not, I agreed to do it—but not until I surreptitiously unzipped my purse halfway so I'd have easy access to the large wrench inside if I needed to crack Jackie's skull.

After we climbed into her car, Jackie exited the parking lot for the playhouse and drove the short distance to the entrance to the café. The eatery was housed in the former parsonage, a single-story brick home we'd expertly converted. I worried she might recognize her friends' cars in the parking lot and become suspicious, so I did my best to distract her as we pulled in. "Sorry about that whole inflatable-duck fiasco this morning," I said, waving a hand dismissively. "Melanie Landreth told me she planned to call you about it." At the risk of discrediting a hardworking public servant, I rolled my eyes. "I knew it wasn't you."

"No worries," Jackie said. "She was probably just covering her bases. I told her she should talk to Tanner. Cutting up the duck sounds like something a teenage boy would do. He probably thinks you pointed the finger at his mother over the property settlement Grant refused to sign, and he lashed out. You could hardly blame him. The poor kid's caught up in a nightmare."

Her empathy surprised me. Was it genuine, or something she'd thought through and carefully planned to say to throw me off guard? I couldn't tell.

We climbed out of her car and walked to the door. I opened it and glanced inside to see Buck facing me as he spoke to the two women. They were seated side by side at the bar, their backs to the door. Although one of her bartenders was on duty, Colette worked behind the bar with him, filling a divided tray with cherries, olives, and lemon wedges to be used as drink garnishes. Though she appeared to be focused on her work, I had no doubt she was listening in on Buck's conversation with the two older women.

Buck had well-developed muscles, a handsome face, and a country charm many ladies found attractive. He'd donned a cowboy hat, along with khaki pants, boots, and a starched button-down shirt tonight, looking casual yet classy. He said something, and his mouth spread in a broad grin. While the two ladies laughed, Colette turned to the bottles behind her, but not before sliding Buck a little side-eyed glance of amusement.

I held the door for Jackie and followed her once she'd walked through. "This way," I said, putting a hand on her shoulder. I hoped she'd assume I was merely guiding her over to the bar, but the placement of my hand was also strategic. If she tried to run, I could grab her arm and hold her until police arrived.

As we walked up to the bar, Jackie spotted her friends. "Wendy? Theresa? What are y'all doing here?"

They gave her a confused look. Wendy said, "You messaged us on Facebook. You told us to meet you here for drinks."

Jackie froze in step. "No, I didn't."

I positioned myself the best I could to block in the women at the bar. "It wasn't Jackie. It was me."

As Buck shifted, similarly positioning himself to act as a barrier, a dark cloud crossed Jackie's face. She looked from me, to Buck, to her friends, and back to me again. "Someone want to tell me what's going on?"

"I know you and your friends were in cahoots," I said. "Wendy met Grant at a bar wearing cheap-looking clothing and too much cologne, and ordered expensive wine. Theresa came by the boat with a bottle of suntan oil filled with sticky stuff."

Colette blew her cover by leaning toward the women over the bar. "It was dark corn syrup, wasn't it?"

The three women glanced at one another, their expressions equal parts guilty and bewildered.

Jackie crossed her arms over her chest and stared me down. "There aren't any boxes, are there?"

"No," I said. "They were a ruse to get you out here so that we could confront the three of you together. We know you were up to something. Was it Grant's murder?"

Jackie eyed her friends, her face contrite. "Sorry, girls. I only meant for us to have some fun at Grant's expense. I didn't realize you'd be dragged into the Spanish Inquisition." Turning back to me, she said, "Look. Grant made a fool of me, and I wanted revenge. I'm human. My friends"—she gestured to Wendy and Theresa—"were kind enough to help me. They set up profiles on the same dating app where I had met Grant a few years back. I knew what kind of women he was looking for, and we made sure their profiles would interest him. They started conversations and he responded. We came up with the plan for Wendy to show up at the bar looking nothing like her profile and behaving badly. We thought it would be a hoot, you know? Like beating Grant at his own game. When he invited Theresa out to his boat, we thought it would be funny to swap out his bottle of suntan oil for one that was filled with something else, something sticky that he'd have trouble washing off."

Theresa actually beamed a little. "The dark corn syrup was my idea."

Colette raised a victorious fist in the air. "I *knew* it was corn syrup!"

I narrowed my eyes at Theresa. After all, when she'd learned Grant's boat exploded, she'd mumbled something about thinking Jackie might have done it. "You never believed, not even for one second, that Jackie might have killed her ex?" I arched my brows.

Theresa looked me directly in the eye, seeming to realize the moment I was referring to. "I was shocked when I first learned Grant's boat had exploded, and I might have muttered some nonsense, but no. Once I learned that the explosion was intentional and not an accident, I knew Jackie couldn't be behind it."

Jackie gave her friend a grateful smile before addressing me again. "Setting up Grant on bogus dates was an immature, vindictive thing to do. I admit that. But it was harmless. I never would have tried to kill Grant. I'm not a violent person and, frankly, it was more satisfying to see him living on that little boat and barely scraping by than it would have been to kill him."

Both Wendy and Theresa nodded. They seemed to thoroughly believe in their friend's innocence. Jackie had convinced me, too. She seemed sincere and I saw no holes in her story. I looked to Buck. He nodded. Colette did, too. The two of them seemed inclined to believe Jackie, as well.

My gaze moved among Jackie and her friends. "Well, then. I suppose I should apologize for luring all of you here under false pretenses. Dinner and drinks are on the house."

Wendy pumped her fists in the air. "Woot-woot!"

Jackie said, "Are appetizers included in that offer?"

"Sure," I said. "Get all the apps you'd like."

Buck, Colette, and I had dinner at the café Tuesday evening, as well. It was a few minutes past nine when I drove back to my house. I needed to design and print out the flyers about the *Skinny Dipper* going up for sale. I sat at the kitchen table with Sawdust on my lap. He purred loudly, his entire body vibrating. As I ran my hand down his back, he kneaded my thighs, his sharp claws digging into my flesh as if he never wanted to let me out of his grip again. I looked down at him. "I've missed you, too, boy. It won't be long until I move back home for good."

I planned on moving out of the boat on Saturday, after Colette's bachelorette party but before Buck's bachelor party got underway. Buck would leave on Sunday. After that, we'd count on our security system to keep the boat safe while we were away. We hoped that whoever had slashed our rubber duck wouldn't return.

I played with the angles of the photos and the wording of the flyer until I finally felt that it was the most enticing and eye-catching design I could come up with. The top read YOUR NEW VACATION HOME AWAITS! HOUSEBOAT FOR SALE. Directly underneath was a large photo of the *Skinny Dipper* from the side, flanked by smaller images of the interior. I made a list of points detailing its many features:

Completely restored!
Three berths!
New motor and generator!
Upper and lower decks!
Spiral staircase and slide!

Okay, maybe all the exclamation points were overkill, but I liked them. They added a bit of excitement.

I printed out two dozen copies of the flyer and slid them into a manila envelope for safekeeping. After searching various junk drawers, I found a cardboard rectangle impaled by colorful thumbtacks that I could use to post the flyers. I rounded up some painter's tape as well.

Sawdust saw me to the door, mewing pathetically. I knelt down and cradled him to my chest, giving him a big hug and a kiss on top of his head. "Nighty-night, boy."

The dress I'd wear as Colette's maid of honor had finally arrived. Just before noon on Wednesday, Colette and I were about to walk into the bridal shop for my fitting when Deena's attorney called me. Like the prosecutor, he, too, wanted to set up a time to interview me in person.

"Does next Monday work for you?" he asked. "Say, ten A.M.?"

"Sure." As my own boss, I could make myself available as needed. "Have you heard back from the hospital? Have they completed the audit of the cold packs?"

He hesitated a moment before responding. "Yes. They told me that, in theory, nurses are supposed to document the supplies they use in the patient charts, but that they're often too busy to put in that level of detail. A lot of the supplies go unaccounted for. Their orders for cold packs have been fairly standard and typical over the last few months, not unusually high, but they're a large operation and the disappearance of several cases could easily go unnoticed."

"So, they can't confirm whether or not cold packs have disappeared."

"No."

I sighed. *Could nothing in this case be certain?*

We ended the call, and Colette and I entered the shop and headed to the counter. I told the clerk why we were there and gave her my name. The clerk's gaze went up and down, taking in my work boots and coveralls, and she fought a smile. No doubt I looked nothing like bridesmaid material at the moment. I looked more like someone who'd come to repair a leaky pipe or install drywall. She rounded up my dress from the back and escorted me to a fitting room so I could try it on. She hung the garment on a hook inside the door. "Here you go. Can't wait to see how it looks."

Colette had already had her final fitting for her bridal gown and was all ready for her big day. She sat on an armchair in the oversized dressing room as I slid out of my boots and coveralls, and into the bridesmaid dress and a pair of ivory stilettos with bows around the ankle. The shoes felt entirely different on my feet than my steel-toed work boots, and although I'd tried on the dress in a different color and size before ordering it, this was the first time we'd seen the actual dress I'd be wearing in her and Buck's wedding in the correct size and color we'd chosen.

Colette's mouth fell open as she stood. "Wow!"

I turned to the mirror. *Wow, indeed.* The shimmery satin fabric was a perfect, lightweight choice for a summer wedding, and the pale blue shade brought out the blue in my eyes. The uneven handkerchief hemline was flouncy and romantic, and the spaghetti straps allowed me to show off my shoulders and arms, toned from all the heavy lifting I performed on the job and lightly tanned from my time working outside on the houseboat.

The clerk rapped on the door. *Knock-knock.* "How's it going in there, ladies?"

Colette opened the door. "You have to see this."

The clerk stepped inside, and our gazes met in the mirror. "Oh my!" She splayed her fingers, jazz-hand style. "You. Look. Stunning." She played with the fabric, looking for gaps or sags, but found none. "It's a perfect fit, too. No need for alterations." She whipped out a phone. "Can I get a photo for our website?"

I'd gone from blue-collar worker to cover girl in a matter of minutes. "Sure!"

She posed me against the wall, directing me to curve one hand in a clawlike manner over my hipbone, and to let the other hang loosely beside me. She snapped several shots from different angles and scrolled through her phone to review them. "The boss is going to love these."

Once she'd gone, I carefully slipped out of the dress and secured it in the zippered vinyl bag that came with it. I placed the shoes back into their box, and handed everything over to Colette so that she could take it back to our house. I put my coveralls and boots back on, metamorphosizing back into my everyday self, and we walked out to our vehicles.

"Sawdust misses you like crazy," she said. "He slept with me last night and followed me around the house all morning."

"I miss him, too. But now that we're putting the boat up for sale, it's best he stay home." The last thing I wanted was him escaping or getting locked in a closet or bathroom after a showing. Besides, some people were allergic to cats. We needed to keep the boat as fur-free as possible. I'd already spent a good deal of time vacuuming to make sure I'd sucked up all of the stray hairs Sawdust had left behind. "Give him a big kiss for me, though, okay? Tell him it's from his mommy?"

"I will."

CHAPTER 29

MAKING WAVES

WHITNEY

While Colette took off to go to our house, I returned to the *Skinny Dipper* for a quick bite to eat. When I finished my lunch, I found Buck putting fresh caulk around the shower stall in his bathroom. I held up the manila envelope that contained the flyers. "I'm going to put these flyers up around the area. I'll be back in a few hours."

He gave me a nod. "I bet we'll have this boat sold in a week. Maybe less."

With its shiny new coat of paint, the *Skinny Dipper* was definitely eye-catching. People had been constantly stopping on the dock to admire it, expressing surprise and delight at our marine makeover.

I walked out onto the dock with my purse and the flyers. A glance out at the water told me Billy and his fishing buddy were out on the lake today. An interesting coincidence. The first site on my list of places to take flyers was the Get-N-Git. When I'd gone to the store before, Billy had pointed out their bulletin board where the lake's locals could post boats and other items for sale. Of course, I'd also paid for a listing on a website for secondhand boats. Anyone from all over country could see the listing online. But the fact that the *Skinny Dipper* would come with an assumable slip lease should make it especially enticing to buyers in the immediate area who didn't have another place to keep it and wouldn't want to have to move the boat.

As I walked along the dock, I heard the usual clangs of the ropes on the masts. But I also heard another clang, a softer, higher-pitched one. I turned to see a man on the back of his ski boat. He'd just closed the top of the aluminum kettle grill attached to the back of his boat. My heart flopped in my chest, like a fish on a dock. *Could that be the sound I'd heard the night before Grant's boat exploded? Someone closing his grill?*

My gaze moved to the *Caudal Otta Fish*, which bobbed on the lake in the distance. My eyes narrowed in response to both the glare off the water and suspicion. *Hmm.*

I continued down the dock to my car, drove to the store, and went inside. With it being a weekday, business was slow. A young couple bought two sodas and a large bag of potato chips, but once they'd gone it was just me and Christine in the shop. She looked even more tired today than she had in the past. Dark circles underlined her eyes, as if she hadn't slept in days, and her shoulders slumped.

I stepped up to the counter and pulled one of the flyers from the envelope to show her. "We've finished our restoration work on the *Skinny Dipper*."

"You have? That was fast." She ran her gaze over the photos on the page, her head bobbing as she took them in.

Proud of the work Buck and I had done, I whipped out my phone and showed Christine the before pictures, too. "Quite a transformation, isn't it?"

She smiled as she looked up at me. "It hardly looks like the same boat! I wouldn't believe it if it didn't still say *Skinny Dipper* on the back."

Buck and I had debated renaming the boat, but finally decided it should retain its original name. It was amusing and, while we were happy to give the boat new life, we figured it should hang on to something from its past. Of course, if the new owners wanted to rename her, then so be it.

I lifted the flyer and held it up. "Mind if post this on your bulletin board?"

"Go right ahead," Christine said. "That's what it's for. I bet you'll have that boat sold in no time."

"I hope so." I walked over to the wall. In order to make space for the flyer, I had to rearrange some of the other posts so that there was no wasted space. I pulled four thumbtacks from my purse and inserted one in each corner of the flyer. When I was done, I stepped back to take a look. The flyer was right at eye level. It should grab a lot of attention. *Good.*

I turned around to leave. On my way to the door, an item on a shelf caught my eye once again. It was a jar of Gil's Fish Flavoring, complete with the smiling cartoon fish. The hook through its lip seemed especially ominous today. I stopped and stared at the jar, my mind processing a tsunami of thoughts that flooded my brain.

While I'd speculated about Christine before in light

of her increasingly haggard appearance, I now wondered about Billy. Though I'd never seen Billy board the *Sexy Sheila*, Grant had gone fishing with Billy and his friend shortly before his boat exploded. Surely, that outing had been planned at least a day or two in advance. That clang I'd heard shortly after Tanner had absconded into the dark night with Jojo could very well have been someone closing the grill on Grant's deck. Billy had to know that Grant would grill the fish he'd caught on their outing, if not immediately after returning to his boat, then within a short time thereafter. Grant had been about to fire up his grill when Buck asked him to take his boat out on the lake. Could Grant lighting the grill have been what caused the explosion? Had someone hidden ammonium nitrate not only in the life jacket bins and live well, but also under the charcoal, knowing it would set off an explosion when Grant doused it in lighter fluid and struck a match to light the grill? And could that someone have been Billy Underhill? If Christine knew that her husband was guilty, or at least suspected it, that could explain her appearance. She might have been unable to sleep, and the burden of carrying the emotional weight could have taken its toll.

I turned to Christine to find her eyes locked on me, almost as if she could read my mind. Her eyes were bright with anxiety and she held her lower lip tightly between her teeth as if attempting to hold in words on the verge of spilling out of her mouth.

Our gazes locked, I eased slowly up to the counter, as if approaching a stray dog who might bolt. "Christine," I said softly, "could Billy have planted explosives on Grant Hardisty's boat?"

Just as Jackie had surprised me by bursting into laughter on the dock after Grant's boat exploded, Christine surprised me bursting out in a cry. "I-I don't know!" She bit her lip again and her chest heaved with emotion.

I ran through the thoughts that had just formed in my mind. "Billy would know that Grant would grill the fish he'd caught. He could have put flammable chemicals in Grant's kettle grill. I heard a clang the night before the boat exploded. I'm fairly confident now that what I heard was Billy closing the lid on the grill. Shortly before that day, we saw Grant use up the last of his Gil's Fish Flavoring, but he had a new jar the day his boat went up. Did Billy take a jar to Grant that day?" Billy might have wanted to ensure that Grant had everything he needed to cook the fish so that he wouldn't delay. A delay could mean that Grant might discover the ammonium nitrate hidden on the boat.

Christine gulped. When she spoke again, her voice shook. "I-I don't know. He could have. I woke up the night before the explosion and saw that Billy wasn't in bed. I thought he'd got up to use the restroom, but the light wasn't on in there. I went through the house looking for him, but he wasn't inside. I saw a light on in the store, though. I figured he'd gone to stock shelves or check on something. He does that on occasion when he can't sleep. He takes steroids for his arthritis sometimes, and they tend to keep him awake. I went back to bed and, a few minutes later, he joined me again. I was half-asleep by then. I don't think he even realized I'd woken up."

"So, you don't know how long he'd been gone before you woke up?"

"No."

I mused aloud. "He was more upset about Grant's insurance claim than he let on yesterday, wasn't he? I saw you giving him a strange look."

She pressed her lips together, but gave me a quick nod. "He was madder than I've ever seen him. He said he felt used, like he'd been sucker punched."

"Christine, we have to tell Melanie Landreth and Detective Flynn."

Her hands fisted on the counter. "But he's my husband! I love him! I can't do this to him!"

I reached out and enclosed one of her fists in my hand. "I know this is hard, Christine. But can you let an innocent woman go to prison for something she didn't do? Can you let her son grow up without his mother?"

Her head shook as if on its own accord.

"I'll call them." I pulled out my phone, called Landreth, and told her what Christine had just told me. "Billy's out on his boat," I added. "I saw it on the lake before I left to come to the Get-N-Git."

"Bring Christine with you to your dock," she said. "We may need her help. Suspects are sometimes easier to deal with if a loved one is on the scene. I'll notify Detective Flynn."

Christine rounded up her purse, turned off the lights in the store, and turned the OPEN sign in the window to CLOSED. She hesitated for a beat before setting the alarm and locking the door, as if sensing things at the mom-and-pop shop would never be the same again.

A half hour later, Christine, Collin, and I climbed aboard a fire department vessel that had pulled up to the dock next to the *Skinny Dipper.* A captain and a second crew member were already aboard. Collin wore his police toolbelt, and his pepper spray, cuffs, and gun were all within easy reach. Landreth was similarly outfitted. I hoped Billy would surrender peacefully and that they wouldn't need to use their weapons. The captain handed each of us a life vest, and we slid into them. Ready now, we puttered out of the marina. Once we passed the buoy, the captain pulled back on the throttle. The engine roared to life and the boat picked up speed.

We scanned the main part of the lake. Unfortunately, the *Caudal Otta Fish* was nowhere to be seen now. Had Billy returned to his private dock at his house after Christine and I had left the Get-N-Git?

We cruised along, all of us looking left and right for the boat. The captain pulled into the various coves and we peered down the inlets to make sure we didn't inadvertently pass the boat by.

When we seemed to be making little progress, Collin turned to Christine. "Do you and Billy share locations on your cell phones?"

"We do."

She pulled out her phone, unlocked it, and accessed her husband's location. She handed her phone to Collin. He carried it over to the captain.

After consulting the map on the screen, the captain handed the phone back to Collin and called out, "Hold on, everyone!"

We all grabbed for handholds. The captain hooked a sharp turn, barreled across the lake, and turned down a long inlet, increasing speed as we went. The sound of the motor was deafening. My hair whipped in the wind, and I felt a cool, fine mist of lake water on my face and hands.

Landreth stood in the stern, her legs splayed awkwardly for leverage and support, holding binoculars to her eyes. After a minute or two, she pointed off to the left. "There he is!"

CHAPTER 30
WET PURSUIT

WHITNEY

The captain corrected his course, aiming for the distant boat bobbing in the water a quarter mile away. The sound of the engine increased to a roar as he sped toward Billy's boat. A moment later, we saw Billy stand up and look our way. He stood stock-still for a few beats, as if frozen by what he saw. Then he tossed his fishing rod over the side of the boat and ran for the wheel. His friend turned to him as he started the motor and took off so fast the boat seemed to pop a wheelie on the water. The other man dropped his rod and grabbed at the edge of the boat, desperate to stabilize himself.

The fire boat captain activated the siren and the flashing light atop the boat. *Woo-woo-woo!* We raced down the inlet, anglers on docks turning their heads as we sped past. It's not every day you see a high-speed chase on a lake. The *Caudal Otta Fish* continued to speed down the cove, though the fire department boat was gaining on it. The inlet shrunk, becoming narrower and narrower as we drew closer to the end, and the captain slowed the boat for safety.

Landreth raised a bullhorn to her mouth. “Billy Underhill! Stop your boat! Now!”

We watched as the *Caudal Otta Fish* decelerated ahead of us. It looked like Billy had decided to give up his attempt to flee and, instead, to surrender peacefully.

Christine put a hand to her heart. “Thank goodness!”

But if we’d thought her husband was giving up, we’d been wrong. He suddenly sped up again and whipped his boat around in a tight U-turn. His passenger was thrown clear, his arms pinwheeling in the air for a moment until he landed in the lake with a big splash. Christine cried out. “No!”

Luckily, the man surfaced a second or two later. The fire department’s boat was bigger than Billy’s, and less maneuverable in the narrow, shallow cove. The captain slowed even more to turn it around, but not before an officer tossed a life ring to Billy Underhill’s fishing buddy and hauled him into the boat.

Once he was seated, Billy’s friend looked around at the group. “What the hell is going on?”

Collin leaned over to fill him in, having to shout to be heard over the boat’s engine. “We’re trying to arrest Billy!”

“For what?” the guy hollered back. “A fishing violation?”

If only.

“No!” Collin yelled. “Murder!”

“Murder?” The guy’s eyes went round and his mouth hung open, like those of the fish he’d been after.

Billy had put some distance between us after we’d had to slow to rescue his friend, but we were gaining on him again now. We'd nearly reached him when he whipped his wheel again and sped down another inlet. *Ugh!*

He slowed as this cove, too, closed in on him, and we slowed behind him. The captain turned our boat sideways to form a blockade. Billy tried to pull the same maneuver he had last time, but he'd waited too long. When he yanked the wheel this time, the boat didn't turn around. Instead, it ran aground in shallow, swampy water.

Landreth held the bullhorn to her mouth again. "Stop right there and put your hands up!"

Billy leapt from the boat, going down on his knees in the muck along the shoreline. In an instant, he'd pushed himself back up to a stand.

Christine cupped her hands around her mouth. "Billy! Stop! There's no use in running!"

Billy didn't listen to his wife any more than he'd listened to Landreth.

Collin turned to our captain. "Get me close to shore. I'll chase him down!"

The captain eased the boat over parallel to the bank and Collin vaulted over the side. Though he sunk a little in the muck, too, he managed to stay on his feet. He took off running after Billy, who'd disappeared into the woods. Landreth whipped her gun from her holster and slid over the side, as well. She ran in the direction Collin had gone.

My heart pounded so hard I felt a throbbing in my ears. Billy had already proven that he was willing to kill. We didn't know whether he might have a weapon on him. What if he had one of those long fillet knives like Grant had used to gut his fish? Like Billy had probably used to slash the throat of our inflatable duck? He could stick a long, sharp knife like that all the way through Collin or Landreth. The thought made my head go light. Thank goodness I was wearing one of those life jackets with a head support or I might have keeled over.

The woods were too thick for us to see anything. We heard shouts and thrashing for several seconds, the snaps of branches breaking, then everything went suddenly quiet and still.

My chest heaved as I gulped air. "Collin!" I shrieked, shredding my vocal cords. "Are you okay?"

An eternity seemed to pass. Finally, his voice came back. "I'm fine! We've got him!"

Landreth's voice came through the trees a moment later. "I'm fine, too, if anyone's interested."

The captain and the crew member from the fire department chuckled.

Collin and Landreth emerged from the woods shortly thereafter with Billy between them, each of them holding one of his arms. Handcuffs secured Billy's wrists behind his back. His knees were muddy and his face was bloody, his nose having been injured in the melee and quite possibly broken. Though dirt and leaves marred their clothes, neither Collin nor Landreth appeared to be injured. *Thank goodness!* I closed my eyes and sent up a silent prayer of gratitude.

The two law enforcement officers wrangled Billy aboard and escorted him to the back of the boat, where they took seats on either side of him. He wouldn't be escaping again.

Christine cowered back against her seat and stared at her husband as if he were a stranger, her mouth agape. "Why, Billy? Why?"

Billy glanced around, seeming to realize his escape attempt would be his undoing and there was no point in holding back now. His confession was short and blunt. "I'd felt sorry for the guy, done him a favor by taking him fishing, and he repays me with a trumped-up claim that triples my insurance premiums? Nah. Nobody makes a fool of me like that."

I fought the urge to tell him he'll look even more foolish in a prison jumpsuit, but figured it best to keep that comment to myself.

We now knew the *why*, and Landreth took advantage of the fact that Billy was talking to find out the *how*. "How'd you do it?"

"I filled his grill with fertilizer and covered it with charcoal. Took out the life jackets he never used and filled the stowage, too."

I now knew for certain that the soft clang I'd heard after Tanner left with Jojo hadn't been a halyard banging against a mast. It had been Billy closing the lid on Grant's grill.

Collin's jaw flexed and his hands fisted on his thighs. "The explosion could've caused significant collateral damage. Other deaths." He cut his eyes to me before glaring at Billy again.

"I saw the kid take the dog from the boat, so I knew Jojo would be safe." Billy cast a remorseful look at me. "For what it's worth, I didn't expect the explosion to be quite so big. I didn't know Grant's gas tank was full. I also thought you and your cousin would be working inside your boat, where you'd be protected. I had no idea you'd be outside painting that day."

Thank goodness Buck had insisted Grant take the

boat out on the water before lighting his grill. Otherwise, the two of us could have been blown to bits, too.

I had to know. "Did you slash our duck's throat?"

The boat captain's and crew member's faces contorted in horror.

Billy cut them a look. "It was only an inflatable duck." He turned back to me. "And yes, I used my fillet knife to cut it. I wanted you to back off. I knew you were snooping around."

"How?" I thought I'd been fairly discreet. "The officers hadn't even come to the Get-N-Git to question you yet."

"Because I called my insurance company a few days back to ask about the status of the claim now that Grant was dead. I told them I'd thought his claim had been bogus all along, and that they should lower my rates back to what they'd been before he filed it. I'm almost certain Grant poured that suntan oil on the floor himself when Christine and I were busy with customers. Anyway, the woman from the insurance company told me they'd had an investigator look into that matter, and that he'd determined Grant's claim was invalid, that he wasn't injured. She read me the notes from their file. The investigator said you'd contacted him and asked about photos and video, and he'd told you they could only be provided to law enforcement."

Hugh Montaigne had informed the insurance company about our conversation. I supposed I shouldn't have been surprised, given that I'd forced him to come clean about who he really was. It was only natural that he'd inform his client about our interaction.

Christine stared zombie-like at Billy, and Billy stared

out at the lake, unable to meet his wife's gaze, as the captain piloted the boat back to the private dock at Billy and Christine's house. There, Landreth and Collin escorted Billy to a cruiser waiting in the parking lot of the Get-N-Git.

Still in shock, Christine watched the car carry her husband away. A tear escaped her eye, leaving a damp trail down her cheek. When Collin and Landreth walked back over, she heaved a shaky breath and asked, "Am I free to go now?"

"Of course," Landreth said. "Thank you for your help, Christine. It couldn't have been easy to implicate your own husband, but it was the right thing to do. I'll be in touch."

Christine aimed for her house, moving slow on shaky legs. I suspected she'd break down as soon as the front door closed behind her.

CHAPTER 31

FAMILY REUNION

WHITNEY

The fire department boat carried me, Landreth, and Collin back to the marina. We disembarked and raised our hands in goodbye as the captain and crew member set off to return to their station. Once they'd gone, the three of us made our way down the dock to the *Skinny Dipper*, where Buck joined us.

Before departing, Landreth turned to me and extended her hand. "We wouldn't have solved this case without your persistence. Thanks."

I gave her hand a shake and offered a humble smile.

Once she'd walked off, Buck turned to me and Collin. "Fill me in. What happened out there?"

The two of us gave him a quick rundown of the pursuit across the lake and into the woods.

"Boy," Buck said, shaking his head. "Billy Underhill didn't give up easy, huh?"

Collin said, "Once we got him in the fire department's boat, he confessed."

Buck snorted. "Billy makes what, the fifth person to claim they've killed Grant Hardisty?"

Collin couldn't help but chuckle. "True. But I'm hoping he's the last."

Now that the actual killer was in custody, Deena would be released. I wanted to be there when it happened. "Can I go with you now to get Deena out of jail?"

"Of course," Collin said. "It wouldn't be happening if not for you." He looked down at his muddy clothes. "Can I swing by my place and change first?"

"Don't you want her and the other cops to see how brave you were? I mean, you chased down a violent killer." I gestured to the mud and grass stains on his clothes. "There's the proof."

Collin eyed me. "You're playing me, aren't you?"

"Yes, but for a good cause. I don't want Deena waiting in jail a minute longer than necessary. It's my fault she's there." Like Christine, I'd been carrying a heavy guilt, and I'd love to unburden myself of it.

Collin acquiesced. "All right. I suppose a little dirt never hurt anybody."

I followed him to his unmarked car and we climbed in.

At the county jail an hour later, I paced back and forth in the lobby while Collin made the necessary phone calls and filled out the paperwork to have Deena released. *Why is it taking so long?* I knew there were a lot of boxes to check before a suspect could be freed, and that the wheels of justice moved slowly, but they seemed to have ground to a near halt.

Finally, everything was in place. We stood in the lobby, waiting, as a jailer went to round up Deena.

The door lock buzzed as she was released. *Bzzz.* She

walked into the lobby, dressed in the same scrubs she'd been wearing when she'd turned herself in. I thought she might be angry with me, and I was ready to issue profuse apologies for wrongly implicating her. But, to my surprise, she came my way, burst into happy tears, and wrapped me in a hug so tight I could hardly take a breath.

"Thank you!" she cried. "Thank you, thank you, thank you!" She released me from the hug and took a step back. "My attorney said you've been trying to find the real killer and get me out of here. I just never thought it would happen." She wiped a tear from her cheek.

"It's the least I could do," I said. "It's my fault you went to jail in the first place."

"No, it's not," she insisted. "I never should have confessed. I should have known Tanner didn't kill Grant, even if he did take Jojo from his boat. My son wouldn't do something so terrible. I just got caught up in the moment and I was so upset and worried that Tanner would be arrested that I couldn't think straight."

"It's understandable," I said. "You're a mother. A good one who would do anything for her child."

Deena gave me a shaky smile.

Collin said, "Your story was damn convincing, too."

"It was, wasn't it?" She chuckled mirthlessly. "The starter went out on our backyard fire pit last year, and I had to replace it. I'd asked Grant to fix it, but he never seemed to get around to any of the things I asked him to do. That's what gave me the idea for saying I'd used a spark igniter to set off the explosion." She looked from Collin to me. "Who actually did it? Who killed Grant?"

Collin held out a hand, deferring to me, letting me have the honors.

"Billy Underhill," I said, "the owner of the Get-N-Git. Grant's fishing buddy." I explained that Billy thought Grant wasn't truly injured, that he'd orchestrated the fall and only pretended to be hurt so that he could collect a settlement from the store's insurance carrier.

"I can't say I'm surprised." She inhaled a deep breath and slowly released it. "Faking a knee injury to try to make an easy buck is just the kind of thing Grant would do." Her gaze shifted, and she looked beyond us now, as if looking into the past. "Grant was a user, a taker. He manipulated me and a long line of women before me." She shook her head and looked down at the floor. "I can't believe I was so stupid. I'm a smart woman, but I was just coming out of my divorce from Tanner's father and I was in a bad place, vulnerable. Grant seized on that." She looked up again. "He had a knack for finding victims when they were at their weakest. He could be so charming. He made me feel loved and beautiful, and fed my ego. The honeymoon phase of our marriage was wonderful. But it didn't last long. Over time, he slowly drained me, financially and emotionally. He bought himself expensive things on my credit cards, all but wiped out our checking account. He used me, just like he used his other wives before me, just like he used Mick and Sheila, and Billy Underhill."

In no way did I condone murder, but Grant hadn't only taken advantage of people, he'd put himself at risk. Like Jackie had pointed out, if you keep doing people wrong, it might only be a matter of time before one of them sought revenge.

Deena shook her head, as if to shake off the bad

memories. "I can't wait to see Tanner! He's going to be so relieved."

Collin offered her a ride home.

She glanced at the clock on the wall. "Can you take me to his school instead? Tanner will be finished soon. I'd love to be there when he comes out."

"Of course."

We piled into Collin's car and, at Deena's direction, he drove to Tanner's high school. We'd been sitting at the curb out front for only a few minutes when the release bell rang. We climbed out to stand by the car as children began to stream out of the building, chatting and shouting, happy to be done with classes for the day.

"There he is!" Deena cried, pointing.

Tanner walked out of the door, his shoulders slumped and his face dull. He stared at the ground a few feet in front of him as he slowly shuffled along, the weight of the world weighing on him. But everything changed when he heard his mother's voice call, "Tanner! Tanner! Over here!"

He stopped in his tracks and raised his head. A couple of kids walking behind him bumped into his back before casting him confused looks and circling around him. Tanner glanced around to see his mother jumping up and down and waving her arms. His eyes popped wide, and his mouth fell open and spread in a broad smile. He bolted toward us, his backpack bouncing against his shoulders. As he ran into the crosswalk, a crossing guard stopped him with a raised hand in a white glove and an insistent blow on her whistle. *Tweet! Tweeeet-tweeet!*

Tanner threw up his hands before a big yellow school bus rolled past, temporarily blocking him from our view.

Once the bus had moved on, the crossing guard waved the waiting students forward. Tanner led the charge. He ran up to his mother and grabbed her in a hug, nearly knocking her over. He burst into tears. So did she.

She held him tight for a long moment, tears streaming down her face. Tears welled up in my eyes, too. Even Collin grew a little misty, blinking to clear the moisture from his eyes.

I slid him a glance. "I saw that."

"What?" he said. "It's just allergies. The pollen count is high today."

"Sure, it is." I knew better. Collin was a good guy. He hadn't joined the police department for the power and authority it gave him. He did it because he wanted to further the cause of justice, to help make the world a safer place. He had a clever mind and a good heart. I was lucky to have him in my life.

Finally, Deena and Tanner released each other. Grinning, Tanner said, "I never thought I'd be happy to have my mother show up at my school."

She barked a laugh. "And I never thought you'd let me hug you in front of your classmates."

Tanner turned to me. "You did this? You got her free?"

"I only came up with a theory." I gestured to Collin and his dirty clothing. "He's the one who chased the killer into the woods and tackled him."

"Dude!" Tanner turned to Collin and raised his hand for a high five. "Thanks, bruh!"

Collin slapped Tanner's hand.

Tanner said, "This means Jojo and I can come home now, right? Staying at dad's sucks. I never thought it was possible to get sick of frozen pizza, but it is."

Deena said, “How about we go out to eat to celebrate?”

Tanner’s face broke in a fresh smile. “Cool!”

We piled into Collin’s cruiser, and he drove Deena and Tanner to her house so she could get her SUV. The two thanked us again before heading off to round up Jojo and Tanner’s things from his father’s house.

Collin turned to me. “Maybe we should go out to eat to celebrate, too.”

“Let’s do it!”

CHAPTER 32

CAUSES FOR CELEBRATION

WHITNEY

The rest of the week was a whirlwind of activity.

Friday evening marked Colette's bachelorette party. Emmalee and I decorated the boat with the same white tulle with which we'd festooned the chair at our roommate's bridal shower. We added oodles of twinkle lights, too, for a festive atmosphere. We fixed a light pasta salad and an assortment of finger foods to snack on. Tiny sandwiches with a chickpea spread. Crudités and dip. Phyllo triangles filled with mushrooms and spinach. Emmalee carved a watermelon into the shape of a boat and filled the hull with a lovely fruit salad of watermelon, cantaloupe, honeydew, and assorted grapes. I filled the punch bowl with the ingredients for what we'd deemed Mermaid Paradise Punch.

Now that the food and drinks were ready, we used an automatic air pump to inflate the diamond-ring float, the mermaid tails, and the new yellow ducky Collin had bought for me.

Friends streamed onto the boat dressed in lake attire and carrying their overnight bags. We sent up a cheer when Colette arrived. We gathered around her like a Hollywood dressing-room crew, and she found herself wearing a fishnet wedding veil complete with colorful rubbery fishing lures, a lei made of silk flowers, and a white sash that read HERE COMES THE BRIDE.

Once everyone had arrived, we prepared to set sail. I'd practiced with Buck the day before to make sure I knew what I was doing. Emmalee and the other ladies cast off the ropes to free the *Skinny Dipper* from the dock.

I hit the horn, signaling our departure with one long blast of four seconds followed by three short blasts of one second each. Slowly and carefully, I eased away from the dock. We putted past the other boats in the marina, past the buoy that marked the no-wake zone, and out onto the lake. When we reached the center, I dropped the anchor and fed out the recommended seven times amount of line. Once the boat had stabilized and settled, the party began.

We donned our inflatable mermaid tails, leapt from the back deck, and raced one another around the boat. We took turns sliding down the spiral slide. The chute shot us out into the water, where we'd land with a big splash. We played beach-ball volleyball on the upper deck, not bothering to keep score. The rowdier among the crowd ran and jumped off the upper deck, performing cannonballs that sent plumes of water straight up into the air.

As the sun set, we motored back to the dock and tied the boat to its moorings. We spent the rest of the night drinking the punch, playing games, watching rom-coms, and giving ourselves seaweed facials.

Saturday morning, we slept in. We started the day late, with mimosas and the Life-Preserver Donuts around eleven o'clock. At noon, we wrapped up the party and sent Colette back to our house. Emmalee stayed behind and helped me clean up the boat so it would be ready for Buck's bachelor party that night.

Owen and Collin arrived around three in the afternoon to start setting up. First things first, they positioned a huge keg of beer on the upper deck. Emmalee and I helped them bring in the snacks they'd brought, most of which came pre-made or in bags, though Owen's wife had prepared a big batch of fresh, homemade salsa to go with their tortilla chips.

We left as Buck's friends began to arrive. As we went, I raised a hand to Collin and Owen, who stood at the rail on the upper deck. "You boys have fun!"

Buck pulled up in his van just as we were leaving. As we passed him, I said, "You're in for a really good time."

Early Sunday evening, I was back on the *Skinny Dipper* helping Buck get things back in place after the bachelor party, when Deena and Tanner came to the dock to pick up Grant's Camaro. They'd brought Jojo with them. The dog ran up and down the shore of the lake, chasing the tennis ball that Tanner threw for him. Tanner threw the ball out into the water, too, and Jojo swam out to get it. He returned to the dock, dropped the soggy ball at our feet, and proceeded to shake, sending up a spray of dog-scented water that doused us all.

"Jojo!" Deena cried, laughing as she threw up her arms to block the spray. "Stop!"

Jojo only shook that much harder.

Buck lifted his chin to indicate the Camaro. "What are you going to do with the car?"

Deena cut a sideways glance at her son. "Tanner's going to drive it. But if he gets a ticket, or even a warning, I'm taking the keys away."

Tanner rolled his eyes. "I'll be careful. I promise."

Deena smiled and gave her son a one-armed side hug. "I know. You're a good kid." She lay her head on his shoulder. "I'm the luckiest mom in the world."

"Ew!" He shrugged out from under her hug.

She laughed. "As you can see, things are mostly back to normal."

Relief washed through me. "I'm so glad, Deena."

As we stood there chatting, a boat pulled up on the water with Mick at the helm and Sheila beside him. It was another cabin cruiser, similar to the one they'd sold to Grant. The name across the back read SEXY SHEILA II.

After Mick backed it into the slip, Sheila hopped out of the boat and onto the dock. Buck and I helped her tie their new boat to the moorings.

When we finished, I stood to address the couple. "Nice boat."

Mick pointed to Deena. "It wouldn't have happened if not for her."

Buck and I turned to look at Deena.

She shrugged and said, "Grant ripped them off. I didn't want to benefit from the bad things he'd done. I turned the insurance proceeds over to them, less the ten grand he'd paid for the *Sexy Sheila*. It was the right thing to do."

Buck turned to Mick and Sheila. "Welcome back to the neighborhood."

"I can't even begin to tell you how much we've missed it." Sheila turned her face up to the sun and inhaled a deep breath of the fresh lake air.

Mick concurred. "It's like coming home."

"Will you be living on your boat?" I asked.

"Most weekends, yes," Mick said. "It's not practical for the two of us to stay on the boat full time, but we'll be out here as often as we can."

"By the way," Sheila added, "I've shared the information about the *Skinny Dipper* on my Facebook page. We've got some friends who want to take a look. They've sent you an e-mail."

"Wonderful!" Since posting the flyers and the listing online, I'd already received three e-mails and two phone calls inquiring about the boat. I had several showings scheduled for the upcoming week.

By Thursday, we had the boat sold and the money in the bank. We got every penny of the asking price, too.

"See?" Buck said, his chest swelling with pride. "I told you this boat would make a good flip project."

Fortunately for us, the couple who bought the boat had an extended European vacation planned and didn't want to take possession until late June. That gave us more time to enjoy the *Skinny Dipper* before we'd have to turn it over to its new owners.

* * *

Before we knew it, the day of Buck and Colette's wedding arrived. The weather was perfect, not too hot, the sky partly cloudy.

They'd scheduled the ceremony for five o'clock, which gave Emmalee, my aunt Nancy, Colette's mother, and my own mom plenty of time to decorate the Joyful Noise Playhouse and the Collection Plate Café with poofy bows, votive candles, and sweet-smelling flowers. Colette's staff scurried about the café, getting things ready for the dinner to be served after the ceremony, which all had been invited to attend. In fact, Colette had hired a temporary catering staff to take over serving and cleanup so that her employees would not have to lift another finger once the event kicked off. They'd be guests, too, and get to enjoy the party.

The playhouse had been our previous flip project, though after we'd transformed the church into a theater, we realized we could make more money by hiring a manager and renting the place out for performances and special events than we could by selling it outright. Besides, retaining ownership of the property meant Colette could fulfill her dream of owning her very own restaurant.

The exterior of the playhouse was a deep purple, akin to plum or grape jelly. The inside was painted a vibrant violet. Sunshine streamed through the stained-glass windows, creating a kaleidoscope of color inside the venue and giving the place a cheerful vibe. The double doors hung open behind us as I stood in the foyer with the ushers, greeting the wedding guests as they arrived. "Welcome!" "So glad you could make it!" "It's a beautiful day for a wedding, isn't it?"

Collin arrived, looking sharp in a light gray suit and teal tie that brought out the green in his eyes. "Hey, gorgeous." He gave me a peck on the cheek in greeting, and ran his gaze up and down me before leaning in to whisper, "I have the prettiest date at the wedding."

I reached out to give his tie a playful tug. "You're not so bad yourself—when you're not covered in mud, that is."

He glanced around. "Anything I can do to help?"

"Ring the bell?"

"I'd be happy to."

I handed him the keys to the bell tower and instructed him to ring the bell at 4:50, 4:55, and 5:00. "Five pulls on the rope ought to do it." Once the last *ding* had *donged*, the procession would begin.

"Five pulls," he repeated, pocketing the keys. "Got it."

Free from my duties, I went to check in on my cousin and best friend. Buck looked stylish and dapper in his classic tuxedo with tails. His blue cummerbund and bow tie matched the blue in my dress, the same blue on the ribbon that held Colette's bouquet together, the same blue in his eyes. He appeared much more excited than nervous as my aunt Nancy straightened his bow tie for the umpteenth time.

I gave my cousin a hug. "You're a lucky guy."

He grinned. "The luckiest."

"I'll deny it if you ever tell anyone I said this, but Colette is lucky, too. You're not so bad, Cuz."

He gave me a soft smile. "Don't go getting mushy on me, Nitwit." He reached out and gave my hand a squeeze that belied his words.

I gave his best man Owen a pat on the shoulder and

walked down to the bride's dressing room. Colette looked nothing short of gorgeous in her wedding gown. She seemed to glow. Like Buck, she seemed less anxious than enthusiastic. Clearly, neither of them had any doubts that they were marrying their soulmate.

Not wanting to risk mussing her hair or dress, I reached out to take Colette's hand. "I'm so happy for you two."

"We never would have met if not for you," she said. "I'm so glad you and I got paired up in the dorm all those years ago."

I gave her hand a squeeze. "Just remember this feeling when you're picking up his dirty socks for the millionth time."

Her laugh was drowned out by the bells ringing overhead. *Diiing-dooong. Diiing-dooong.*

Finally, it was time. I stepped out into the foyer. Collin rang the bells for the last time. He exited the bell tower and gave me a smile and finger wave as he headed into the theater to take his seat.

The organist launched into song, and the processional began. The first one down the aisle was the officiant, an uncle of Colette's from Baton Rouge who served as a deacon in his church. The grandparents went next, taking seats in the front row. Buck's parents—my aunt Nancy and uncle Roger—were the next to make the walk, both of them beaming. After Colette's mother gave her a final, gentle kiss on the cheek, an usher escorted the mother-of-the-bride to her seat in the front row, next to her own parents. Finally, Buck walked down the aisle and turned to face the door where his bride would soon appear.

Owen crooked his arm and I slid mine through it, keeping a firm hold on my bouquet with the other hand. We set off down the aisle. I smiled at folks along the way. Though there were some I hadn't met before, I knew the vast majority of them, and I was glad they were able to share this special day with Buck and Colette. At the end of the aisle, Owen and I separated. He went to stand by Buck, and I stood alone on the other side like a lady-in-waiting, ready to tend to the bride as needed.

The music changed to the "Wedding March," and everyone in attendance stood as Colette and her father stepped into the doorway. I turned to look at Buck. He sucked in air, overcome to see his beautiful bride in her fancy dress heading his way. But then his mouth spread in the biggest, happiest smile the world has ever seen as he welcomed his bride to join him at the altar.

Emotions, all positive, overwhelmed me, and I wriggled my face, trying to prevent the tears from carrying mascara down my cheeks. Luckily, I was facing the altar so nobody could see, and eventually I got my feelings under control and was able to face the couple with dry eyes.

The officiant spoke for a few minutes about love and marriage before Colette handed me her bouquet to hold. Our eyes met over the flowers. Colette and I had shared many rites of passage, but this was the biggest by far. Their marriage would change everything, but mostly for the better. I wasn't losing my best friend. I was gaining a cousin-in-law. We'd even share the same last name now.

Ve all clinked our glasses together and took a sip of champagne.

It was my turn now. I stood and held my glass in front me. "As y'all know, Colette is an incredibly talented hef. She knows exactly what ingredients work to-gether to make a perfect dish. She and Buck have all the ingredients for a successful marriage, too. Buck can sometimes be a little salty"—I turned and gave him a grin—"but that's tempered by Colette's sweetness. Together they've got just the right amount of spice to keep things interesting." I raised my glass. "May you two savor all life has to offer!"

Glasses clinked once more and everyone took another sip. Colette's father and Buck's dad made speeches next. More clinks and sips ensued, then it was on to the party part of the reception.

As part of the remodel, Buck and I had turned the two-car garage of the parsonage into a flexible space. We'd traded the old garage doors for glass models. In winter, the doors could be closed and the space could be heated, yet still provide an outdoorsy feel. Tonight, however, the garage doors were raised, the tables had been carried out onto the paved driveway, and the space would serve as a dance floor.

After the traditional father-daughter dance, the DJ got things underway with the Electric Slide. Nothing like a line dance to get people out of their seats and out on the dance floor.

After a half hour dancing to a mix of country, classic isco, and pop tunes, Collin and I drifted out to a table at e edge of the driveway to catch our breath. We pulled chairs close, and he draped an arm over the back of e.

Colette turned back to Buck. The two exchanged vows and rings. I handed Colette's bouquet back to her, and the officiant declared them husband and wife. He raised his arms. "May I present for the first time, Mr. and Mrs. Whitaker!"

CHAPTER 33

FRESH CATCH

WHITNEY

The audience stood and erupted in applause.

Wearing bright smiles, Buck and Colette made their return trip down the aisle. Owen offered me his elbow once again, and we followed the happy couple. Their parents joined them in a receiving line. Meanwhile, Owen and I stood at the end of the line, directing people to head down the path to the Collection Plate Café for dinner, drinks, and dancing.

Collin exited the church and came over to stand with me. Once everyone was on their way to the reception, the photographer spent a quarter hour arranging us in various groupings on the steps of the playhouse, snapping photos.

Finally, we were free to join in the fun at the reception. Collin and I walked down the path to the café, where he promptly removed his jacket and draped it over the back of his chair. Most of the other men had already done the same.

The café was decorated with adorab
tables and chairs we'd picked up at flea ma
hand stores, and garage sales. The dishes
random assortment of traditional china in a
colorful patterns. It gave the café an *Alice in*
land tea-party atmosphere. The only thing mis
a Cheshire cat.

Two bottles of white wine and two of red sto
each table. Collin poured us glasses of white to e
while the waitstaff brought out the first course, a d
cious roasted cauliflower and pine nut salad with lem
vinaigrette dressing, one of Colette's own recipes
Shortly thereafter, the entrées were served. The café filled with the aroma of delicious food and the happy chatter of the guests.

Once the guests had finished their meals, the waitstaff circled the room with flutes of champagne. The *clink-clink-clink* of Owen tapping a knife against his wine glass silenced the room. He stood to give his toast, raising his bubbling glass. "I knew Colette was the right woman for my brother when I realized he was more excited about her than he was about his new cordless drill." The guests chuckled. "As a married man and ca
penter myself, I've learned a little about what it ta
to build and maintain a solid marriage. It's much
building and maintaining a house. You need a s
foundation. You need to be careful about put
walls. It's best to keep things open. Once it's est
it takes a little maintenance and attention to
things don't fall apart." He raised his glass a l
"I know my cousin and his new wife hav
foundation, and I have no doubt the life
gether will be a happy one. To Buck and

I leaned back against him. "Colette's moved all of her stuff to Buck's place. I get to take over the master bedroom tomorrow."

"I'll come over and help you move your furniture."

I looked up at him. "That would be great. It shouldn't be too much work. The only thing I have to take apart is the bed. The rest we can put on sliders."

He eyed me closely. "You okay? Having some feels?"

"I am. I'm happy for Buck and Colette. I truly am. But I can't help but feel a little sad that she's moving out. She's been my go-to person for years. I know I'm not losing her, but it's only natural that her priorities will shift."

"You've got me."

"That's true. With her married, I'll come to you now for advice on haircuts and fingernail polish and boys."

"Boys." He grimaced. "Gross."

A grin tugged at my mouth. "You're not so disgusting."

"Oh, yeah? Prove it."

I stretched my neck to plant a kiss on his lips. "There. See? I didn't gag or anything."

The deejay announced that the bride and groom would be cutting the cake. We reconvened in the main room of the café where Buck and Colette posed together in front of a three-tiered traditional wedding cake. Italian cream. *Mmm. My favorite.* Of course, there was also a chocolate groom's cake. This one was in two pieces, designed and decorated to look like the Joyful Noise Playhouse and the Collection Plate Café. Colette's pastry chef had done an incredible job that would have won any bake-off.

After the cake, we danced some more. Before we

knew it, it was time to wrap things up with the tossing of the bouquet and garter.

Colette went first. She turned to face the wall while twenty or so single women, including me, gathered behind her. She called out, "One, two, three!" and let the bouquet fly. The flowers went up in the air and seemed to be headed straight for me. All I had to do was reach up, and the bouquet fell directly into my hands.

Colette spun around to see who had caught her bouquet. When she realized it was me, she bounced up and down and clapped her hands. "You're the next one down the aisle, Whitney!"

I carried the flowers over to stand next to Collin.

He looked down at the bouquet and said, "Uh-oh. I'm in trouble now." He faked a grimace and ran a finger inside the rim of his collar, as if it he were choking.

I swatted him with the bouquet. "You'd be lucky to have me."

Buck stepped into place now, and all of the single men gathered behind him. He raised the garter over his head. Like Colette, he provided a countdown. "One! Two! Three!" With that, he tossed the garter over his head.

Collin jumped for it, but there were too many guys in the way. It passed by the end of his fingers and was grabbed by a boy who looked to be all of eight years old. He held it up and danced around with his prize, smiling a gap-toothed grin.

A server came by with fresh flutes of champagne. "Would you like another glass?"

"Yes," I said. "Two please."

He placed two glasses on the table and took away our empties. I turned back around to find Collin strutting toward me, grinning and twirling the garter on his index finger.

"How'd you get that?" I asked.

He dropped into his chair. "Paid the kid twenty bucks. Can't have you catching a bouquet without me getting the garter. Otherwise, you'll dump me and go off and marry some contractor with his own bulldozer." He slid his hand through the garter and pushed it up over his white dress shirt until it hugged his bicep.

I chuckled and shook my head. "I wouldn't dump you for a guy with a bulldozer. If he had a skid steer loader, though? That would be a different story."

Shortly thereafter, the wedding guests lined up along the drive to send Buck and Colette off amid a shower of flower petals. Collin stuck around and helped me and Emmalee gather up the decorations and carry them to my SUV.

After he closed my cargo bay door, he gave me a quick peck. "See you tomorrow."

I drove home and slipped out of my bridesmaid dress before Sawdust could snag it with his claws. I pulled my hair out of its fancy updo and shook it loose. After washing my face and brushing my teeth, I climbed into bed. Sawdust curled up in my arms, purring. "Tomorrow, we move to the big room."

He turned his face to look up at me, as if he understood. He offered his approval. "Mew."

CHAPTER 34

MOVES AND MEWS

SAWDUST

The room where Colette used to live was empty. Though Sawdust missed her, it was fun for him and Cleo to run down the hall as fast as they could and slide across the wooden floor of the room. *Wheeeee!*

Sawdust heard a knock on the front door and ran to investigate. Cleo chased after him, curious, too. Whitney opened the door. Collin stood on the stoop. *Yay!* Sawdust liked it when Collin came over. He would pet Sawdust and play with him, roll his tinkle ball around or dangle a string with a stuffed spider attached to the end so that Sawdust could bat it around.

Collin played with the cat only a short time today, though. Then he went with Whitney into her bedroom and the two began moving things from her room into the one Colette had vacated. Sawdust traipsed back and forth between the rooms along with them. He mewed with all sorts of questions. *Why are you moving the furniture? Are we going to live in this room now? Could you put the bookcase under the window so I can sit on it and look outside?*

Although he didn't understand the meaning of the words, he heard Whitney say, "Put the bookcase under the window. That way, Sawdust can watch what's going on outdoors."

Collin pushed the bookcase over to the window, exactly where the cat had hoped they'd put it. He leapt up on top of it and looked out the glass, enjoying his new view of the backyard. There were birds fluttering in the trees and squirrels scampering across the grass, plenty of fun things to watch. *Hooray!*

CHAPTER 35

LIKE A DIAMOND IN THE SKY

WHITNEY

On the last night the boat still belonged to me and Buck, Collin and I took it out on the lake to stargaze. We stopped in the middle of the dark water and dropped anchor. No other boats were about. Other than the fish and turtles, we had the whole place to ourselves.

We turned off all of the lights except the emergency ones, and used the flashlights on our telephones to light our way up the spiral staircase. An occasional firefly lit up the night around us, like miniature shooting stars.

Collin set his telescope up on the upper deck, carefully locking the three legs in place. He gently manipulated the dials and peered through it, slowly turning it and adjusting the angle until he found what he'd been looking for. He backed up and held out a hand, inviting me to take a look.

I bent over to peer through the eyepiece. While I could see small stars in the background against the dark blue sky, there was a big, brilliant one in the foreground that took up nearly the entire view. "That's beautiful!" I said, still staring through the scope. "What am I looking at?"

"Twinkle, twinkle, little star. How I wonder what you are."

I stood. "What do you mean?"

He grinned and angled his head to indicate his right hand. It was then I noticed that he was holding a diamond ring in front of the telescope. That beautiful, brilliant light hadn't come from a star at all. I gasped in surprise and my hands reflexively covered my mouth.

He held the ring up while going down on one knee in front of me. He gazed up at me. "Will you marry me, Whitney, and make me the happiest man in the universe?"

"That's an awful lot of pressure," I said, grinning like mad. "Would you settle for being the happiest man in the galaxy?"

He stood and slid the ring onto my finger. "I'll take it."

RECIPES

MERMAID PARADISE PUNCH

Ingredients:
4 ounces coconut rum
8 ounces blue Curaçao
12 ounces chilled pineapple juice
24 ounces chilled lemon-lime soda
24 ounces chilled sweet-and-sour drink mix
twelve Swedish Fish
Ice
Small plastic or ceramic treasure chest (optional)

Directions:
Pour all liquid ingredients into a large clear glass punch bowl. Stir with a large spoon or ladle until completely mixed. Add Swedish Fish and stir once to distribute them evenly throughout the bowl. Carefully place treasure chest in center of bowl (optional). Serve in glasses over ice.

LIFE-PRESERVER DONUTS

Ingredients:

Box of white cake mix
2 cups applesauce
1 teaspoon ground ginger
2 tablespoons vanilla extract, separated (one for the cake mix and one for the icing)
16-ounce package of powdered sugar
Red food coloring
¼ cup water

Directions:

Preheat oven to 350 degrees. Stir together cake mix, applesauce, ginger, and one tablespoon vanilla extract in a bowl until well blended. Spoon mixture into a donut pan. Bake for 18 to 20 minutes, or until lightly brown on top and a toothpick inserted into the donuts comes out clean. Remove from the oven and allow donuts to cool.

Mix powdered sugar with one teaspoon vanilla extract and ¼ cup water. Stir until well blended. Move half of the frosting into a separate bowl and add red food coloring. Stir until the red frosting is of uniform color. Frost donuts in eight stripes of equal width, alternating white and red frosting.